Adam Glendon Sidwell

Other Books in the Evertaster Series

Other Books by Adam

EVERTASTER
The Delicious City

Future House Publishing

Text © 2016 Adam Glendon Sidwell
Cover illustration © 2016 Future House Publishing

This book is a work of fiction. Names, characters, places, and incidents are
either the product of the author's imagination or are used fictitiously. Any
resemblance to actual persons, living or dead, or to actual events or locales is
entirely coincidental.

ISBN: 978-0-9966193-5-6 (paperback)
ISBN: 978-1-944452-49-0 (epub)
ISBN: 978-1-944452-51-3 (mobipocket)
ISBN: 978-1-944452-50-6 (pdf)

Cover illustration by Goro Fujita
Developmental editing by Helena Steinacker
Substantive editing by Emma Hoggan
Copy editing by Alexa McKaig
Interior design by Samuel Millar

Acknowledgements

I don't think that the world would know about the Evertaster Series, or even me as an author, without the help of April Smith, Holly Baumbach, and Janae Rogers, all of whom were tireless in their efforts to arrange my book tours from state to state across the West. I also owe a big thanks to many enthusiastic booksellers, three of which are Amber Whitlow in Arizona, Laurie Aldern in California, whom I've shared adventures at many a school with, and Jennifer Zidon in Colorado.

Thanks to my editors at Future House Publishing: Helena Steinacker, who has a fantastic imagination, and Emma Hoggan, who is as precise as possible in very demanding circumstances (in other words, when I turn in my manuscript late).

And finally, thanks to my lovely wife Michelle, who I tricked into marrying me by saying the first Evertaster book was probably the last book I'd ever write. I'd thought that might be the case back then. Oh how things changed! She has since spent many nights alone, wrestling the kids to bed without my help while I was out on tour. She has incredible patience, and I'm grateful for her love.

To my dad, who is all the evidence the world needs
that good men are real.

THE FRUITFUL STREETS

PRINCESS
SUNDAY'S CASTLE

THE
CHOCOLATE
CRESCENT

THE MAYOR'S
MANSION

STRAWBERRY
FIELDS

THE DELICIOUS CITY

Chapter 1 — A Taste of Danger

Twelve-year-old Guster Johnsonville tasted a barely perceptible—but unmistakable—hint of danger in his tuna fish sandwich.

It lurked in silence between the relish and mayo, a blinking red blip on Guster's radar that told him something was horribly wrong.

He could not have known it were there if it weren't for the fact he was, like so few people are, an Evertaster—a remarkable boy with more taste buds on a single square inch of his tongue than there are cheese wheels in all of Wisconsin.

To Guster, bread was not sliced from a loaf; it was sliced from a world of experiences: the water the wheat drank, or the sun that shined on the field. Guster could taste history. He could taste time. He could count the wrinkles in a raisin with the tip of his tongue. The world was filled with wonderful delights and devastating disappointments, all waiting to reveal themselves.

But this tuna fish sandwich held so much more, and it worried him.

"This sandwich tastes . . ." said Guster before stopping himself.

Mom looked up from the kitchen counter where she had just pulled two loaves of her famous *Mabel's Bountiful Banana Bread* straight from the oven. Her fists balled up inside two quilted oven mitts which she placed firmly on her chubby hips and stared down at Guster, the bun atop her head bobbing forward like an apple. She raised one eyebrow. "Yes?" she asked, waiting.

"Delicious," Guster said, forcing a grin. He did not want her to misunderstand: it was not her sandwich-artistry, and especially not her cooking, that he questioned. Ever since making that unfathomable dessert called the Gastronomy of Peace one year ago, Mom had gained a new command of her kitchen. Whether it was her slow-simmered red ravioli sauce, or her fluffy-as-a-cloud eggs, she alone could make the foods that Guster craved.

It was as if the One Recipe had forged some kind of invisible link between them—one so strong that if dinner wasn't made by Mom, Guster didn't want it.

Even the neighbors had taken notice. Mom was no dunce when it came to the kitchen. They'd been buying up *Mabel's Bountiful Banana Bread* by the pound. Mom slapped a sticker on the loaves' plastic wrapping that said just that.

"Good." Mom smiled. "Tell your sister that I have some deliveries for her to make this afternoon."

Guster nodded and took his red plastic plate with the tuna fish sandwich on top out the screen door and onto the farmhouse's porch.

"This tastes funny," he whispered to Mariah who sat on the top step.

"You always say that," she shot back. "Whether it's too much clam in the clam sauce, or too much dough in the doughnuts. Guster, try to enjoy your lunch for once."

Guster winced. He'd hoped Mariah would understand. She knew he never complained about Mom's cooking. Not anymore

2

anyway. Not ever since he'd taken a bite of the legendary dessert called the Gastronomy of Peace when Mom had made it for him last summer. It was the most delicious thing he—or anyone—had ever tasted. He was certain of that.

I'm different now, he thought.

He hadn't been able to go without Mom's cooking since. It was the only food he craved. Restaurants held no appeal. Nor did frozen foods. They hardly had before anyway, but now it was much worse. It *had* to be home-cooked. Outside the borders of the farmhouse, there was nothing Guster wanted to eat. It had to be made by Mom.

With that bond came a price.

Guster knew Mom's cooking. He could tell which recipe she'd used, or which frying pan she'd cooked with, or even how long she'd stirred her sauce. That's what was odd. Mom had made him the tuna fish sandwich. She'd served it to him just minutes ago. Next to her signature mom-ness, slid between the tiny grains of relish and the squishy mayo, was something that she couldn't have put there. Something that had touched the tuna: danger.

Guster had never tasted anything like it before, and it baffled him. But he had also learned to trust his hunches.

"I saw a nature program once. It said wolves can smell fear in their prey," said Guster. "That's what this tastes like—like these tuna were afraid of something."

"Yeah," Mariah said. "Of becoming sandwiches."

Guster frowned. Now she was starting to sound like Zeke. That's not what he'd meant. He'd eaten plenty of tuna sandwiches that hadn't tasted like this.

"No. It's like . . . like something was hunting them," said Guster.

"Your tuna fish sandwich is coming after you?" asked Mariah quizzically.

Guster shook his head. "No, something was coming after

them."

Mariah peered at Guster. "You can tell all that from a sandwich?"

Guster shrugged. *I think so,* he thought. There were a lot of things he thought he noticed in his food ever since tasting the Gastronomy of Peace. Details that seemed to come to him in flashes. Details that came at a steadily increasing rate. He still wasn't sure what to make of it all, but he knew one thing for certain—there was something in that sandwich.

"Guster, you only think about how the taste of things affects you!" Mariah applied a fresh coat of lip gloss as she stared in a little handheld mirror. "Try thinking about others for once."

Guster was startled. *Try to think about others?* What did she mean by that? A year ago, Mariah had been more eager than anyone to help Guster solve the clues he'd found carved into the handle of an antique eggbeater. But now that Mariah was fourteen, she seemed far more concerned about makeup and boys than she did about listening to her brother.

Why didn't she understand? wondered Guster. But then again, there wasn't anyone who really could. Guster was the only person ever, in the history of the entire world, to taste the Gastronomy of Peace. He had held the fate of the world on the end of his spoon in that castle in France; sometimes the memory of it still haunted him. He tried to remember that single bite. It grew harder and harder to relive the memory as that day slipped further into the past. He longed to taste just one more bite of the great chef Archedentus' creation, to savor its flavor. But he couldn't. He'd made the right choice: the world was not yet ready for the Gastronomy of Peace.

"Guys, come quick!" A cry from the woods interrupted Guster's daydream. Zeke broke out of the trees on the edge of the Johnsonville property into the backyard. "There's something you've got to see!"

Mariah rolled her eyes. "What is it this time Zeke?

Mummies?"

Zeke smiled mischievously. "Nope. Even better. But you don't have to come if you don't want."

Guster still never knew when to believe Zeke's wild stories. Now that Zeke was sixteen, slim as a stallion, and licensed to drive, he didn't have much time for Guster anymore. Zeke was, according to Zeke, the shining star of the high school football team. Everything was about touchdowns and monster trucks. Zeke was at practice or Betsy's so much, sometimes it seemed like he'd already moved out of the house.

It was just one of the many things changing for the Johnsonvilles; Guster wasn't sure he liked it.

He wrapped his sandwich up in a napkin, set it down on the railing next to him, and followed Zeke to the edge of the property and into the woods. Mariah trailed behind them.

Guster wondered whether he should tell Zeke about the sandwich. He decided against it. Zeke wasn't likely to care what Guster had tasted, even if Guster could convince Zeke that the taste was real.

They hiked into the tangle of trees and past a small pond, little gnats buzzing around in the summer heat and landing on Guster's forehead. He and Zeke had spent many summer hours exploring the woods behind their house. Guster knew every path and tree within a mile.

He didn't mind exploring the woods. In fact, he preferred it. There was something liberating about venturing into the forest before dinner time.

The trail became spongier and wetter the further they went, and the trees changed until eventually Guster no longer recognized where they were. When they came to a fork, Zeke darted off the trail and whacked his way through a bush.

"Where are you taking us?" Mariah asked.

"You'll see," Zeke said, stomping down on a branch to make a path. "Betsy and I found this place this morning, when she was supposed to be doing chores."

"You and your girlfriend wanted a little alone time, Zeke?" Mariah teased.

"Bull's-eye, sister! When you've got a girl like Betsy, you take all the romantic alone time you can get!" Zeke said in a drippy, dreamy voice.

Guster almost laughed. Clearly Zeke wasn't ashamed of Betsy being his girlfriend anymore.

They followed him into the undergrowth. The leaves blocked out the sun so that the light splashed the forest floor in mottled polka dots. They weaved their way through old trunks and fallen logs until Zeke stopped in a clearing.

"Here," said Zeke.

Guster looked around. He didn't notice anything peculiar.

"What?" asked Mariah.

Zeke leaned up against the oak next to him and casually pointed straight up. Guster followed the trunk upward with his eyes. About three feet above Zeke's head there was a giant, crescent-shaped chunk of wood torn from the tree, like some enormous creature had taken a huge bite. Guster felt the air rush out of his lungs.

"You think it's a bear?" Mariah asked, her voice trembling.

Zeke looked smug. "Not a chance. Whatever took that bite was way bigger than a bear."

Guster knew Zeke was right. The missing chunk was at least a foot wide. Only a creature twice as tall as Zeke could have done something like that.

"You know what I think did it?" said Zeke. "A Sasquatch."

"That's ridiculous," said Mariah.

"Is it? I heard stories at Camp Cucamunga that Bigfoot roamed these parts before people ever got here. No doubt Bigfoot is angered by human settlements on his territory. It won't be long before he punishes us for our pride and carelessness!"

Mariah blinked at Zeke. "Right," she said. "No wonder

you're so excited to go to Camp Cucamunga this summer—so you can hear more tall tales. It was probably just a chainsaw. Right, Guster?"

Guster was barely listening. He approached the trunk, and, standing on the roots, he tried to get a closer look. The wood was shredded, like it had been torn away by an angry shark. A thin layer of spit oozed over the top of the splinters. This certainly was no chainsaw.

What sort of creature would eat a tree? Guster wondered. As far as he knew, there were no such things as giant beavers.

"Whatever it was, it was really big," said Guster.

Zeke's face went white. For the first time, he looked like he was actually taking his own discovery seriously. Had he thought it was some kind of joke?

"You . . . you think so?" Zeke stammered.

Guster nodded.

"We really should get back to the house," said Mariah. "You know, in case Mom's looking for us."

Guster doubted Mariah was worried about Mom, but he wasn't going to argue. He could hear the tension in her voice. They turned and bushwhacked back toward the path. Guster could almost feel Zeke's anxiety turn into smugness as they marched down the hill.

Whether he intended to or not, Zeke hadn't been fibbing this time, Guster thought as he brushed aside branches.

"With keen eyes like these, I'll be awarded a woodsman's badge for sure when we get to Camp Cucamunga next week," Zeke said, breaking their silence. "I'm going to get the highest score in archery. And row all the way across the lake. This is going to be a landmark year at camp—starring me." Zeke prattled on to no one in particular. It sounded like he was trying to take his mind off the splintered tree.

Guster sighed. He'd never been to camp. Last year had been the first year he'd been old enough to go, but the Chef in Red had attacked them in an abandoned patisserie in New Orleans, and Mom whisked them away to Aunt Priscilla's in Key West. By the time camp started, they were already halfway to Africa.

This year was going to be different. He was finally going to get his chance.

They crossed a small stream that ran back toward the farmhouse. Mariah bent down to get a drink. It was a hot, muggy Louisiana summer, and Guster was parched, so he knelt down too. The water tasted heavy, like it was thick with minerals, but it was fresh enough until something made the hairs on the back of his neck stand up. There had only been a trace, so he had almost missed it: it was the same taste of danger he'd found in his sandwich.

He shook his head. That was impossible. The tuna had come from the sea somewhere, probably caught in a net, and the stream was only a few miles away from the farmhouse. But the tastes were undeniably the same. Was the danger getting closer?

Guster tried to clear his head. *Am I sure that's what I tasted?* He filled his cupped hands with water again and brought it to his lips, then dropped it before he took a drink. *No, I'm being silly.* He stood up and turned down the path back toward the farmhouse. He couldn't tell Zeke. Zeke wouldn't listen any more than Mariah had.

So he took the lead. He tried to double his pace without looking hurried. Mariah and Zeke followed behind, matching his speed without complaint. The day was beginning to stretch into evening, and though there were a few more hours of daylight, the fireflies began to glow faintly, signaling that the night was not far off. Guster did not want to be caught out in the woods when darkness fell.

When they arrived in the backyard, a familiar silhouette was waiting for them on the back porch, its bun perched atop its head.

"Zeke! Mariah! Guster! " Mom shouted in the same sharp voice she always used to call them to action. If they didn't obey, there would be swift consequences. Guster knew that from experience. It also meant food.

The trio scrambled past Mom into the kitchen, fighting to be first. Henry Junior and their dad, Henry Senior, were already seated at the table. Mom's signature baby blue apron was stained with red sauce.

"Guster, you didn't tell Mariah about making the deliveries," said Mom. She sighed. The two loaves of banana bread were still on the counter.

Guster had completely forgotten. "I . . ." was all he could say. He was caught.

Mom shook her head. Disappointment crossed her face.

Without another word, she turned and removed a green casserole dish from the oven and set it on the center of the table, the smell of piping hot ravioli steaming up into their faces.

"Calories! Calories!" cried Zeke, pounding his fork and knife against the table.

One look from Mom silenced Zeke, forcing him to set down his silverware. He folded his hands like an angel.

"I mean, such a pleasure to dine with you lords and ladies this evening," Zeke said in the most sugary, polite voice he could muster.

Guster scrunched up his nose. The tomatoes in the sauce smelled fresh. Mom had clearly used the Felicity Casa special recipe, which meant that it would have plenty of spice and a robust, lingering flavor.

Dad blessed the food, and Guster served himself up a big helping of ravioli. The first bite was complex: meat and cheese, all wrapped in a pasta envelope. He sorted out the tastes in his mouth until he found familiar flavor that came with every dish Mom made.

He swallowed. He thought he saw Mom smile out of the

corner of his eye. She still did that every time he ate her meals.

"Mom, do they have power outlets at Camp Cucamunga for my blow dryer?" asked Mariah.

"In the bathrooms, dear," said Mom. "Which reminds me, you all need to get your backpacks packed by tomorrow night so that you'll be ready to go."

"Can't wait," said Guster.

Mom glanced at Dad.

"Mom, Guster said he tasted something funny in your tuna fish sandwich today," said Mariah. "He thought it was going to eat him."

Mom put her fork down.

Mariah had sold him out. Why would she do that? She seemed to be less and less on his side lately. Usually his older sister was someone he could talk to.

"It's not like that," said Guster. "It was like . . . like . . . something dangerous." And then he wished he hadn't said it that way.

It was frustrating. He couldn't explain what he tasted in that sandwich any more than he could explain the color blue. However he described it, he was bound to sound crazy.

Mom sighed and glanced at Dad again. Her round moon face tightened. "Guster, you're not going to Camp Cucamunga this year," she said.

The words fell like a stone on Guster's chest. "What!" Guster pushed himself back from the table. "Why?"

Mom spoke calmly, "We've been touch with Felicity Casa. She's coming here to help you with some special training."

He couldn't believe this. Did she know what she was doing to him? He'd been looking forward to going to camp for years. It was finally his chance to go, and now they were taking that away? He ran out the back door, slamming it behind him.

He stood on the porch, watching the sky turn twilight gray as the sun set. The screen door swung open behind him. Dad stepped out onto the porch.

Henry Senior was tall and slender, with a large nose that stuck out from his face like the bow of a battleship. His brown khaki pants were hitched up past his belly button, just like they always were. He wore the collared shirt of an insurance salesman.

"Son, your mother and I talked about this for a long time."

Guster stared at the barn. Its colors had faded in the dusk. He didn't know why they were making such a big deal about what went on inside his mouth.

"We know how much you wanted to go to camp, son," Dad said. He put a hand on Guster's shoulder. Guster didn't move. It had been almost a whole year since he'd seen Felicity Casa. Why did she have to come now? Guster didn't know if he could trust her completely. He didn't dislike her. That was far from the truth. In fact, Guster respected her skill. His taste buds tingled when he watched her cook on her weekly television show. But what special training did she have in mind for *him?*

"Why does she have to come here?" Guster asked.

"She suggested that she could help you, and we didn't want to pass up on the opportunity."

"Help me?" Guster asked. "With what?"

Dad sighed. "Guster, your mother and I are worried about the things you taste in your food."

Guster wondered what there was to worry about. Dad hadn't been there to see how Guster's taste buds had saved the family time and again last summer. Dad didn't know how useful Guster's taste buds were.

Plus, Guster wasn't a problem at home anymore. He ate everything Mom put in front of him. If his particular palette didn't bother him, why should it bother his parents?

"I'm eating all of Mom's dinners," he said.

"And a fine job you're doing, too. That's not what we're worried about. You still notice things. You talk about it all the time, and we don't want it to be a burden on you. You shouldn't have to worry about those kinds of things. We want you to be able to forget about it and go play baseball, or search for secret fishing holes with your brother."

"Zeke doesn't like fishing anymore," Guster grumbled. That was Zeke's fault, not Guster's.

"Felicity can help you," Dad said. "Think of her like a coach, or a tutor. She has some special training she'd like you to try. You should be flattered."

He didn't feel flattered. Instead, it sounded like being forced to take piano lessons—there were other things he'd rather do.

"Does it have to be this week?" asked Guster.

Dad shook his head. "Felicity is a very busy woman and we had to get her when we could," he said. "Your mom tells me that Felicity is very skilled, and that if anyone can help you, Felicity can." Dad knelt down to look Guster in the eye. "Guster, did you think about what you would eat while you were at camp?"

Guster had not thought about that. He had been so excited about archery and wood carving he had forgotten that he would have to go without Mom's cooking for a whole week. He didn't want to eat anything else.

"Mom could pack raviolis for me," he said.

Dad smiled and the wrinkles radiating from the edges of his eyes deepened. "Every mother should have a son as loyal as you," said Dad. He looked at Guster with a broad, gentle smile. Was that pride in his voice?

Guster had no idea how to respond. Dad was not making it easy to fight him, so Guster just leaned his elbows on the porch railing and stared at the night falling. He did not want to accept defeat, but there was nothing else he could say. Dad's mind was made up.

"No matter what, you're going to have to learn to do things without your mom hovering over you," Dad said. "Felicity will be here at noon tomorrow." He turned toward the door, his hand lingering on Guster's shoulder for one second more. Then he went inside and the screen door closed shut with a light clang behind him.

Guster grunted. That was like just Dad, extra cautious about everything, concerned about things he did not entirely understand. It was Dad's job to worry.

Guster should have kept his mouth shut and his opinions about food to himself. It would have kept him out of this mess. His parents were so confusing!

Guster pounded the porch railing with his fist. As he did so, he thought he saw a shadow move in the trees at the edge of the yard. It wasn't just a squirrel or a coyote, it was something big. Something very big. He peered into the darkness.

The screen door opened like a catapult, clanging into the side of the house as Zeke charged through it.

"Oh, you're out here," Zeke said, a bowl in hand. "How am I supposed to eat this ice cream in peace?"

In an instant, the shadow shifted and was gone.

"Did you see that?" Guster asked, pointing to the edge of the property.

"What?" asked Zeke. "Those trees have been there a long time, genius child. It's called nature."

"No, it was something else, like an animal," Guster said. He didn't care if Zeke taunted him. He knew what he saw. "I need a flashlight."

He ran into the house and grabbed a flashlight that was plugged into the kitchen wall for emergencies. He switched it on and leapt down the porch steps. Zeke set down his ice cream bowl and followed behind.

His heart thumping in his chest, and his nostrils sniffing the air, Guster shined the beam into the woods. He approached the line of trees slowly. He wasn't sure what he wanted to find—if there really was something out there, it might be better not to see it. His steps were slow and deliberate, with Zeke cautiously at his heels. When he came to the edge of the yard he stopped and shined his light down on the ground.

There, printed in the mud, was a footprint the size of a dinner plate.

Chapter 2 — Felicity's Experiments

Guster's sleep was fitful that night. Shadows raced across his dreams so that at first light, he woke instinctively.

"Monster toes!" Zeke had said, his voice barely above a whisper, when Guster had shown him the footprint the night before. "We could probably see it better in the morning."

Guster did not have to be persuaded. He had rushed inside, reaching the safety of the porch only a few steps behind Zeke's football-trained legs.

And now it was morning. Guster roused Zeke from sleep easily. Zeke was as eager to inspect the footprint in the safety of daylight as Guster was. Apparently this was, like football and pickup trucks, interesting enough to capture Zeke's attention.

"Hold on a second," said Zeke, rubbing sleep from his eyes. He reached under his pillow and pulled out a thick paperback book with a glossy white cover, then tucked it into the back of his sweatpants.

They made their way quietly through the hall, down the stairs, out the back door, and across the yard.

"Do you think it's safe?" Zeke whispered as they approached the footprint.

With a clenched face, Guster shrugged. He felt much better about being outside in the morning light, but there was still a chance that whatever had made that footprint was lurking nearby in the woods.

He moved toward the impression in the ground slowly, his back to the house so that he could keep one eye on the woods. He knelt in the dirt. He had to see the footprint up close. If there was some kind of clue that hinted at what kind of creature had left it, he wanted to know.

The footprint had eroded around the edges but was clear enough that Guster could make out the shape. He traced his fingertips over it. He could make out at least one padded toe with a single claw, like a dog's paw, only this toe was as big as the palm of his hand. The rest of the footprint was another two palm lengths across, and nearly as long as it was wide. Instinctively, Guster plucked up a bit of the mud to taste, but stopped himself. He didn't want Zeke to see him put it in his mouth.

"Aha!" Zeke started flipping frantically through the pages of his book. "I knew it!" He pointed to page 243, where there was a pencil drawing of a large footprint with five toes and huge claws. "It's Bigfoot, right here in our very own yard! Wait until I tell the team about this one!"

"Let me see that," Guster said, snatching the book away from Zeke. He held the drawing close to the dirt. Besides having too many toes, the claws and the heel in the drawing were much too long to be the same footprint. "What is this book?" Guster asked, flipping it over so he could read the cover: *Barrister's Certified Real Field Guide to Lesser Known Creatures.*

"Oh, that's a little something that Reggie on the team let me borrow," Zeke said. "There are chapters in there on the Loch Ness Monster, the Abominable Snowman, and these bloodsucking goat-eaters that live in the jungle. It's got the most scientific information I know of." He looked proud of himself. "Look, turn the page," he said, grabbing the book away from Guster and turning it for him. "This is what made that footprint." He pointed to a drawing of a hairy, gorilla-like man with heavy eyebrows and fists that dragged in the dirt.

"Impossible," Guster said. He tried to remember if the shadow he glimpsed the night before matched the drawing. The dark mass had disappeared too quickly to say for sure, but *something* had taken a bite out of that tree. And Guster *had* tasted danger in that stream.

"We don't have to worry about it right now," said Zeke. "Bigfoot is nocturnal, and he is rarely seen by humans." Zeke sounded like he was quoting the book. "But when we do meet up with him—grizzle me timbers!—he could tear our arms off at the elbows!" Zeke hung his head. "If only humankind had not built so many roads across the Bigfoot's territory and forced him into battle."

Guster coughed. There was no way Zeke was right, but for the moment it was the only theory they had. Whatever made that footprint, three things were certain: it was huge, it had claws, and it could take a bite the size of baby cow out of anything it wanted.

No matter how crazy Zeke sounded, Guster knew what he saw. It was dangerous. They were going to have to be careful at night. Maybe they would even have to tell Mom.

"Boys! Come in for breakfast," Mom called into the yard from the kitchen.

Guster's shoulders tensed at the sound of her voice. He hadn't realized how frustrated he still was after Dad had told him he couldn't go to camp last night. When Zeke and Mariah left tomorrow, he wouldn't be going with them. It wasn't fair.

"I've got some chores for you to do this morning," said Mom as the boys came into the kitchen. She served them each a plate of bacon and eggs. She tried to ruffle Guster's dirty brown hair, but he moved his head just in time. He didn't want that right now. He was still mad at her.

Zeke wolfed down half his eggs and bacon in two gulps; Guster pushed his plate away. The eggs smelled perfect. He just didn't feel like eating.

"I need you and Zeke to weed the tomato patch before Felicity Casa gets here," Mom said. "You don't have much time."

"Why can't Mariah do it?" Zeke asked.

"She's cleaning the barn," Mom said. "Do you want to trade her?"

Guster and Zeke both shook their heads. Cleaning out the barn was a far worse chore.

Zeke swallowed his last morsel, licked his plate, and sped from the room without clearing his dishes. He took one glance backward, like he was expecting a scolding from Mom. All he got was a sad look on Mom's face as she cleared his plate for him. The screen door banged, leaving Guster alone with Mom.

She put the frying pan in the sink. "Guster, Felicity is coming here to help," Mom said. "You should be grateful she's making such a long trip."

Guster grimaced. It still didn't make sense to him. She was coming all the way here to see him? What did she want from him anyway?

"But *why* is she coming here?"

Mom sighed. Guster had a feeling she was about to give him some pearl of wisdom that she'd claim would only make sense when he was older. "Because someday Guster, you'll have to learn to be independent, to live on your own without me there every step of the way."

Sure, of course he would. Wasn't that exactly the reason he should go to camp for a week? "I am independent right now," he said. Didn't Mom remember Felicity's Castle in France? Guster had saved them, all on his own.

Mom looked at him with sad, probing eyes, like she was

thinking something, but didn't say it.

He finished his eggs, cleared his plate, and went out the back door to the barn. Mom was still standing there, looking after him the whole time.

He found Zeke in the barn. "Just imagine, seeing a Bigfoot up close and face to face!" said Zeke as he and Guster grabbed a pair of hoes.

Guster tried to forget his conversation with Mom. Instead, it was much more fun to entertain Zeke's idea. "How will you defend yourself?" he asked.

"It is true. The power of the mighty Bigfoot is not matched in all the animal kingdom. However, by truly understanding this creature, we can gain its favor," Zeke said mechanically. Guster was almost sure Zeke was quoting the book again.

The tomato patch looked worse than Guster remembered. There were weeds as tall as Guster's waist, and clumps of weeds as thick as his arm.

He dug his hoe into the dirt. "What does Bigfoot eat?" asked Guster.

"Deer, grizzly bears, humans," said Zeke.

They hadn't even cleared a square foot of dirt before a dust cloud billowed out from behind a huge RV in the distance. Guster dropped his hoe and he and Zeke ran out front.

The massive RV pulled into the farmhouse's gravel driveway. The RV was twice as long as a school bus, tan with pink stripes, and had a huge satellite dish on top. There was a large 'FC' painted on the side in dark pink.

Felicity Casa. Guster almost expected her to fly in on a double-rotor helicopter, or land a rocket in the backyard. She was a billionaire, so she could afford fancy equipment.

The driver of the RV honked the horn and stuck his head out the window. It was an old man with gray hair, kind eyes, and a smart black cap. He winked at Guster.

"Braxton!" Guster said. He ran to greet the old man. Braxton killed the engine and hopped out of the driver's side door to the ground, spry as ever. He was wearing a slim black suit, with the same black cap he always wore. Guster hadn't seen him since last summer when he'd brought them a few very rare and special ingredients from their journey. It was good to see that some things never changed.

Braxton shook Guster's hand. "Well, howdy there young fella," said Braxton. "Looks like you've decided to get yourself knee-high to a skyscraper. What a pleasure to see your tongue's still tastin'."

Braxton always talked like that—in strange sayings that must've been from olden days. He was a brave and kind old man. Guster would never forget how he'd dared to fly them around the world last summer. Braxton even saved Guster's life once. Braxton started working for Felicity shortly after that.

Zeke stood, his mouth open and his knuckles dangling, almost drooling at the sight of the RV. "Is that a tank?" he asked.

"No," winked Braxton, "Just a duplex on wheels."

"You drove all the way here?" asked Guster.

"Nope, just from the airport in New Orleans. We brought it in on one of Ms. Casa's cargo jets. It's our mobile command center. Can't leave home without it. Been all across the countryside and halfway through Europe in this thing." He laughed and pointed to the satellite dish on top of the huge motor home. "It'll pick up any TV program you can think of!" he said. "Even ones that haven't been made yet!"

Mom came from the kitchen, Henry Junior on her hip, Mariah right behind her. Dad had left for work hours ago.

Mom licked her hand and smothered Guster's hair into place on one side of his head, just before the door slid open on the side of the motor home right where the 'FC' logo was painted.

Out stepped Felicity Casa herself. She was dressed as the most fashionable farmhand Guster had ever seen. Every hair was in place. She wore a set of blue denim overalls cut to fit perfectly around her slender waist, with a red checkered button up shirt underneath that. Two tiny pitchfork earrings dangled from either ear.

Felicity scanned the house and the land. "So, this is your home," she said. There was neither condescension nor compliment in her voice.

"Felicity, so good to see you," said Mom, drying her hands on a towel and stuffing it in her apron pocket. She embraced Felicity with her free arm.

"Likewise," Felicity said, smiling at Mom.

Guster was a bit surprised to see Felicity return the hug. He'd never been quite sure what to make of Felicity Casa, the Queen Bee of the American Household, the Czarina of Chocolate. She was very powerful and used to getting what she wanted. If that lined up with the Johnsonville's interests, good for them, but if it didn't, it wasn't wise to stand in her way.

Felicity turned to Guster. "Hello Guster. It is an honor to see you again." She shook his hand vigorously.

An honor? She was saying that to *him*?

Guster nodded. "Hi."

He didn't know what to think about her being here. They had been through a lot together, but she was the reason that he wasn't going to Camp Cucamunga and that bothered him.

Felicity grasped Guster by both shoulders and sniffed in a long, deep breath of air, almost as if she was smelling him. She closed her eyes and lingered there for a moment too long. It felt uncomfortable to be smelled like that.

"Now . . . that's unexpected," said Felicity in a low voice that only Guster could hear. She opened her eyes and studied him.

He squirmed. He did not like being the center of so much attention.

"Your mother tells me that you've been . . . tasting things," said Felicity.

So she's getting straight to the point, thought Guster. At least she wasn't hiding the reason for her visit.

"Nothing special," he said. He didn't want to tell her about the sandwich he had eaten the day before. He would ask her about that—and a hundred other questions—when everyone else had gone.

"We'll see," said Felicity. She nodded her head toward the giant vehicle. "I have so much to show you."

Guster looked back at Mom. "Now?" he asked.

Mom nodded and waved her hand toward the door of the RV like she was pushing him to it.

"I see no reason to delay," said Felicity. She turned and held her arm up toward the open door, inviting him in.

Guster had to admit, he was curious. There were things that Felicity would understand, things that he could ask her or explain to her that he would have a hard time explaining to anyone else.

He climbed the three steps into the RV. Felicity followed, and the door shut behind him. The latch clicked.

Inside, the RV was not like any other motorhome he'd ever seen. The countertops were sleek black granite, the sink and oven fixtures gleamed with silver polish. It was like a cross between a spaceship and a fancy furniture store.

To his right, there was a wall with a door that Guster guessed led to the driver's cabin, and on the other side of the kitchen was a hallway that must have led to the bedrooms and bathroom. If Guster hadn't just been outside, he wouldn't have known he was in an RV at all.

"Have a seat," said Felicity.

Guster turned toward the couch.

"Not there. Here," she said, pointing to a counter-height table in the kitchen next to the oven.

Guster took a seat on one of the chairs.

Felicity tied a white apron around her waist, and removed a small glass vial from one of its many pockets. The apron looked more like a lab coat than the cooking apron Guster usually saw Felicity wear on her show. She set the vial on the table in front of Guster.

Then she grabbed Guster by the wrist, and, without a word, swiftly pulled a needle from another pocket and stabbed Guster on the finger.

"Ow!" he cried, the pain shooting up his hand. The needle hadn't hurt him so much as it had surprised him. He hadn't expected Felicity to do *that*.

Felicity squeezed his finger until a few drops of blood oozed out into the vial.

"What was that for?" he asked.

She didn't answer. Instead she turned to the stove, setting the vial down next to a small saucepan. She turned on the burner, still not answering him, and began to add ingredients. First a cube of butter, then a handful of flour, then milk. She precisely measured everything in little cups before she stirred them into the pan. She worked so quickly that her hands blurred with motion. Guster could hardly keep up with his eyes.

"This is a mother sauce, Guster," Felicity said when she was finally done. A beautiful but indistinguishable smell rose into Guster's nostrils. It did not have any particular scent, not sweet, or savory, just mild and warm.

"The mother sauce is the base for a thousand different culinary masterpieces," Felicity said. "When cooking, a master chef begins here. It has infinite potential; it can become a savory pasta sauce or a gourmet fish pie. Its destiny stands at a crossroads and is determined only by the ingredients you add to it."

She tasted the sauce on the end of a wooden spoon. "Mmmmm." She sighed. "I want you to taste this now, so there won't be any doubt in your mind how different it is after I add the final ingredient."

She stuck a clean wooden spoon into the sauce then held a spoonful of thick, yellowish liquid out to Guster. He pressed it to his lips. The sauce was just as he'd smelled it—mild, and basic, with almost no significant flavor to it. Sure, he could taste the age of the butter, or when the wheat in the flour was harvested, but other than that it was, well . . .

"It's quite ordinary," Guster said.

Felicity smiled. "Good. Then you will notice the difference," she said, and she scooped up the vial, dripped Guster's blood into the sauce, and stirred.

Guster felt his stomach turn. "What are you doing?" he asked. It was too strange and sickening—adding a part of him to the sauce?

"We're going to taste Guster Johnsonville." said Felicity. "If my suspicions are correct—and I think they will be— we will learn something very important about you, Guster Johnsonville, Evertaster." She turned down the burner.

Guster did not like the sound of that. This was the same problem that had persisted for as long as he could remember: everyone was far too concerned with what was going on inside Guster's mouth. Hadn't he solved that?

"I eat my mom's cooking all the time now," he said defensively.

Felicity laughed. It was almost a cackle. "Oh, I don't care much whether or not you eat your mother's cooking. This is much bigger than that." She looked Guster square in the eye. "Guster, it is time for your training as an Evertaster to begin."

Guster looked down at his hands. That idea seemed strange to him. Zeke could train to get better at football, or you could practice to get better at the piano, but you couldn't just train to be an Evertaster. Could you?

She turned down the dial on the stovetop. "I've set this sauce to simmer. Three hours should do it."

"And now for something else," she said, turning to a cupboard. She removed two glass pie pans and a set of glass bowls of various sizes. In each of them was a different ingredient: ground beef, spices, a yellow sauce that Guster did not recognize, and a large lump of dough.

"Today we're going to make gourmet meat pies," Felicity said in a smooth, polished voice. "These are an Australian and New Zealand delicacy, rarely enjoyed here in America, and now I'm bringing it to you. You start with a mixture of the finest ground beef; you want to use a lean beef so that it will accentuate the flavor." She dumped the bowl of brown spice onto the meat and mixed it with a fork. Suddenly, Guster felt like he was watching her show.

She removed a rolling pin from a drawer, sprinkled flour across the tabletop, and rolled out the lump of dough. "You must make sure the crust is light as satin," she said.

It all smelled so wonderful, but why was she showing this to him? Was this how you trained to become an Evertaster? He didn't care so much about learning how to cook. What he wanted to do was taste.

"And in just a few easy minutes . . ." she said. She stopped, suddenly aware of herself. "I'm sorry. I was doing it again. It's hard to break showbiz habits."

And with that, Felicity suddenly pulled two fully cooked, steaming hot meat pies from the oven. Each one was complete. "You have the final product, delicious and ready to serve." She seemed to be in a trance, like she had floated away to an imaginary studio somewhere.

"Your guests won't stop talking about this taste experience." She smiled with her porcelain white teeth, shining in Guster's eyes. She smiled left, then right, as if to an imaginary audience.

"Ahem." Guster cleared his throat.

"Right," she said, straightening.

She set all three pies on the table in front of him, a fork

25

beside each of them. "Eat," she said. Suddenly the studio-poised Felicity Casa was gone. In her place was the Felicity Casa who meant business.

Guster did not have to be persuaded. The pies smelled so good, and he never passed up an opportunity to taste Felicity's cooking.

He pressed his fork into the first pie and scooped up a tender morsel of steaming brown meat and sauce wrapped in a flaky crust. He brought it to his lips and closed his mouth around it. It was delicious: savory, spicy, and succulent, a treat for a hungry palette. It melted onto his tongue, first with a bold and courageous meat flavor, then with a steady, confident soft crust, and then . . . Guster stopped chewing. There was something there, hidden between the flavors. It was hard to decipher at first, faint and elusive, but it was there nonetheless: sadness.

Felicity was staring at him, a tablet computer in one hand. She was tapping down notes. "Yes?" she said, expectantly.

Guster shook his head. "It's like there's a feeling inside this pie. This dish tastes . . . sad."

A slow smile spread across Felicity's lips. She tapped something onto the computer. "You can taste it." Her eyes glowed with excitement. "Guster, I did not make this particular meat pie. It was made by a man who'd just lost his brother to a heart attack."

Guster didn't know what to say. He felt sorry for the man, though he'd never met him. He wished he could reach out to him somehow and tell him that everything was going to be okay.

But how could Guster taste that from a pie? He'd tasted subtle flavors before, like an extra grain of sugar in a cookie. He could trace back the history of an ingredient, or tell you where it was grown, but feelings? Now that was new.

"Try this one," she said, pointing to the next pie.

He was curious, and a little afraid of what he would find.

He lifted his fork. The second pie tasted like the first, but this one had a layer of something bright inside it, like a springtime morning after the frost had melted away. It was a happy, thrilling taste that sent a tiny part of his head tumbling on a roller coaster of glee.

"What do you taste?" Felicity asked.

How could he describe it? "Happiness. Excitement," he said. They were the best words he could muster.

Felicity punched more notes into her tablet. "This one was made by a newlywed bride. I wouldn't expect you to understand romance at age twelve, but you've found it anyway."

If this were true, what else could he taste?

"Guster, your sensitivity as an Evertaster is growing," said Felicity. "You can taste emotion. You can taste experiences."

Guster shook his head. But how? And what did that mean?

"It's Taste Resonance Theory," said Felicity.

"Taste what?" asked Guster.

"The Theory that flavors resonate from creator to consumer, and with them they can carry information, or even emotion, to your subconscious. Have you ever seen someone stare at a painting and begin to smile? Have you ever read a book that made you laugh? Or seen the way music moves people at a concert? They begin to dance, or cry, or cheer, even when the artist who created the work isn't there. Each creator has a distinct level of power to convey emotion or experience through their work. Painters or sculptors are the first level. Authors have even more influence. Then musicians. The most powerful of them all, though, are chefs. They can communicate directly to your subconscious through taste."

That made sense. He'd felt it happen. He just wasn't sure he believed it.

"A chef can evoke his intent or emotion. Most of the time it's inadvertent. They don't even know they're doing it," said Felicity.

"Like this pie," said Guster.

"Exactly. But I think that Taste Resonance goes beyond just the creator," Felicity said. "Any object or flavor that comes in contact with a dish can affect it. It can transfer information about itself. It's like pouring strawberry sauce into a stream. Eventually it will spread to the ocean."

Guster pushed himself back from the table. She was right. Hadn't he even seen it in Mom's dishes? There were times when he was almost certain he'd been able to tell what mood Mom was in by eating her food. "Or like an echo in a canyon," he said quietly. "It can bounce away in many directions."

Felicity smiled knowingly. "I see I've made my point."

Guster looked up at her. There was something she wanted, but he still wasn't sure what. "But why come here to tell me this now?"

"Remember that dessert you tasted last year in my castle kitchen in France?" Felicity asked.

That was a silly question. Of course he did. It had changed the way he saw the world.

"The One Recipe," he said. "The Gastronomy of Peace."

"Yes," said Felicity. "Archedentus, the great chef, traveled far and wide to discover its ingredients and bring them together. He was an explorer."

She pushed the pies aside and unrolled a world map on the table. There were dotted lines in red and black zigzagging from one destination to another. He recognized some of them: Peru, Tanzania, Bear Island. He had been to them. The lines didn't stop there though. They circled the globe, some of them with question marks, others with notations in tiny, handwritten letters.

"Archedentus did not find those ingredients without searching. There were missteps along the way, backtracking and wandering. They were not his only discoveries. I am convinced there is more out there.

"Did you know that Italians didn't even have tomato sauce until after 1492? Imagine! Lasagna without marinara sauce! Spaghetti wasn't even born yet! Columbus brought tomatoes back from the new world. His journey changed the face of cuisine.

"That's what Archedentus did, but behind the scenes and with an even wider effect. His travels united flavors from across the world in a way that history does not even comprehend! He is the basis for modern cuisine as we know it, and we've only discovered a fraction of where he went and what he created. As near as we can tell, he created dozens of delicious things, all hidden out there, waiting for us to snatch them up and taste them!"

"We already found his One Recipe," Guster said. It was his ultimate creation. What more did they need?

Felicity nodded. "But he had so much more to give!" She pointed to a spot on the map in Northern Africa where the lines squiggled and spiraled. There were several dots and notations clumped together. "Archedentus may have left entire colonies of chefs behind, all trained at his hand!"

"Then what does this have to do with me?" he asked.

Felicity sat down across from him. "Guster, we need an Evertaster to find them," she said.

So that was it. Felicity wasn't here to help Guster overcome anything. She was here to use him, and it was all right under Mom's nose. He wasn't a bloodhound or a clever little detective. He was Guster.

"No," he said. He pushed the map away and stood up. "I'm doing just fine." It had been thrilling to see the things that he did last summer. Gorillas, giant chickens, Torbjorn and Storfjell. But it had also been dangerous. Part of Guster also wondered if going with Felicity would mean admitting that Mom and Dad were right—that there was something wrong with him.

But there wasn't. He was eating everything Mom made

him. And now Mom thought that was the problem. He couldn't win.

"Guster, imagine the tastes!" Felicity said. She sounded desperate.

He put his hand on the RV door and pushed it open. "No. I have everything I need right here," he said.

"Think of what you're turning your back on!" cried Felicity. He'd never seen her lose her cool like that. She was afraid of losing access to Archedentus's world.

Guster leapt off the steps of the RV without glancing back. He ran. He needed to be alone. He needed time to think. He circled the house until the RV was out of sight.

He knew the Johnsonville land like he knew his own face, which meant he knew the best hiding places. He passed the old well and reached the back of the barn where he swung aside a loose board and squeezed through a narrow gap in the wood. He ducked inside where it was musty and dim. The smell of dry hay filled the interior like a puffy pillow of air.

The barn was empty. Dad was at work, and Mom was in the house doing laundry. It was the perfect place to be alone.

Guster squeezed between two hay bales, slumped down, and sat with his back against the barn wall. He had to admit, he was curious about that map. Archedentus had practically spoken to him when Guster had taken that bite of his chocolate soufflé. It had been like a trance or a dream, and sometimes Guster still wondered whether or not it had actually been real. If he went with Felicity, they very well could find more treasures. Could he really let that go?

Something clattered in the loft above. Guster leapt to his feet. No one was supposed to be in there.

And there was the footprint. And Zeke was convinced Bigfoot was in the woods. What had he said though? That they didn't need to worry unless it was night? Maybe it was just Mariah doing her chores.

Guster peered up toward the loft. It was full of old junk, and Dad didn't like anyone playing up there. The wood was far too rickety and unstable.

"Mariah?" Guster whispered.

A metal can toppled out of the loft and clattered to the ground in the center of the barn.

"Zeke?" Guster whispered.

A large shadow dashed between the piles of junk up above. A rat or a raccoon couldn't make a shadow like that. It was something bigger.

Guster crept over to the old wooden ladder that led up to the loft. It was nailed into the wood above. He shook it. The entire loft trembled and groaned, old nails squeaking in their holes and wood rubbing against wood.

There was another clattering, louder this time, and a smash as something large dropped out of the loft and tumbled down the ladder. It smashed to the floor in a heap with a hollow clang.

Guster leapt backward, ready to run, when the fallen heap stumbled to its feet, arms and legs untangling themselves. It was a small man, no taller than Guster, with short, stubby limbs.

He was wearing a large rounded steel armor chest plate that made it look like his belly had swelled up into his chest. There was a steel helmet on his head that curved upward into a point, and his pants bulged out like two red and yellow striped balloons. He had a pointy mustache and a short, sharp beard that looked like a stubby stalactite hung from his chin.

Guster would've laughed had the little man not said what he said next. "Hello! My name is Gaucho del Pantaloon, and I am here to tell you that very soon you will be chewed into tiny pieces by a gluttonous beast."

Chapter 3 — The Most Delicious Thing

The little man held one finger up high, like he'd just finished declaring the world was round all over again.

"What?" asked Guster. He wasn't sure he'd heard what he'd heard.

"You are about to be devoured by a voracious monster!" said the little man once again. He smiled when he said it, his teeth shining.

Guster didn't know whether to believe him, or poke him with a pitchfork. He grabbed the pitchfork leaning against the wall nearest him just in case.

"You're going to eat me?" asked Guster.

"Oh no," the little man said, shaking his head. "I am no monster. I am Gaucho del Pantaloon, Shepherd of the Guardians of the Delicious City, and loyal to the crown."

Gaucho certainly didn't look like a monster. In fact, he was quite comical looking with his oversized chest armor and striped pants. Guster was certain he'd seen someone dressed like Gaucho in his history book, somewhere between the page with Genghis Kahn and the page with Winston Churchill. If only Mariah were here to see this. She would know where Gaucho came from.

"And might I add," said Gaucho, "that it is also quite an honor to finally meet you. I've been looking for you for a very long time. Please tell me your name."

Guster was puzzled. "It's an honor to meet me but you don't know my name?"

"I have traveled halfway across the world to make your acquaintance—sometimes by silver bird, other times by boats the size of islands. The strange things I have seen! Did you know there is a flat box that has moving pictures of people inside it that you can control?"

"You mean video games?" Guster said. This Gaucho del Pantaloon must have been living in a cave for the last 100 years.

"Yes! That's what someone called it," said Gaucho. "Now, if you please, what may I call you Señor?" Gaucho bowed low, like Guster was someone special.

"My name is Guster Stephen Johnsonville," Guster said.

Gaucho grabbed Guster's hand and sniffed it. "Ah, no wonder they are coming for you," said Gaucho.

Guster pulled his hand away. That was the second time today that someone had sniffed him. He'd just showered last night. It wasn't like he'd used Mariah's lilac candy cane conditioner. "Why do you say that?" Guster asked.

Gaucho stood, a look of ferocious importance burning in his eyes. "Guster Stephen Johnsonville, have you ever felt like you were being watched in the woods, or felt the hair of your neck standing on end?"

Guster nodded. He had felt that way just the night before when they'd seen the footprint.

"They have been hunting you, Señor Johnsonville. They left our great city almost one year ago. All of them at once, suddenly gone, as if something very important had called them away!" He looked concerned. "The city it is left unguarded, without Yummy circling its walls."

Gaucho made so little sense.

"What city? Where?" Guster asked.

Gaucho suddenly leapt backward, whipping a slender sword from his belt and waving it at Guster. "You'd like me to tell you that, wouldn't you? Scoundrel! I will never tell you the way to the blessed city, you robber! Never!"

Guster hefted his pitchfork. "Okay!" he shouted. "Just asking. Never mind." He hardly knew what Gaucho was talking about, but it had hit some kind of nerve.

Gaucho lowered his sword. "Forgive me. It is part of the code. I have sworn never to reveal the location of the majestic city, no matter the cost. It is not your fault."

Guster stepped back. Talking to Gaucho was like stabbing a hornet's nest.

"Let me start again," Gaucho said. "Something happened one year ago, and the Yummies left our city. Where they went . . . who knows? It is somewhere far and wide, farther than they ever wandered before, which is strange for Yummy. They did not return."

"And Yummy is the monster?" asked Guster.

Gaucho nodded. "The guardians of my blessed city went looking for something, as near as we can tell. This one that I followed, it has wandered, searching far and wide, tracking something down."

"Like what?" asked Guster.

Gaucho hesitated. "Yummy loves nothing more than the good things of the earth. Cookies. Pie. Sweet brownies smothered in chocolate sauce with whipped cream between its intricate layers!" Gaucho's eyes glazed over, like his heart had gone to a far off place. He swayed a little in the dim light of the barn, like he was moving to some magical music Guster could not hear.

"Yummy is looking for something very sweet, of that I am sure," Gaucho said. "I followed him from the city walls down over the cliffs for many weeks until he came to the place where lowlanders live. He stalked for days, always far from the buildings of stone and mirrors, and through the desert. He traveled at night, lurking in the shadows. I could not have kept up with him had he not wandered, sniffing and searching. Yummy has a keen sense of smell, so that he could sniff a speck of pollen on the breeze that had long since blown far away from its flower."

Guster could relate to that. He'd tasted all sorts of things that were impossibly far away.

Gaucho continued, "I could not follow all of them, so I chose to follow the one who is mine. He searched, and searched, and I kept my distance, watching from afar." Gaucho pointed to his eyes. "I have keen vision you know, and I can see their footprints. After so many years of tending to them I know them like they are my own little puppies. They cannot escape me.

"So we wandered, and came to a place of many towers where the land was green and the mountains were nothing but soft hills. There were so many delicious things there! Tiny puffs of sugar like a cloud! Sometimes Yummy sniffed a cupcake left in the garbage can, other times a shoe left on the road, or a stream where a tart had washed into the water. Always he was searching.

"Until we came to a castle with a big turkey bird for a fountain, and knives and forks crossed at its gate."

The Chateau de Dîner. It sounded like Felicity's castle in France. Could it be? Guster lowered his pitch fork. This story, if it were really true, had suddenly gotten closer to home.

"I may have been there," he said.

Gaucho clamped his hand down onto his curvy steel helmet. "Aha!" he shouted. "This must be why things changed then."

Guster was almost afraid to ask, but he did. "How?"

"He sniffed something in the broken remains of a kitchen there that we had found by the light of the moon. And then he howled a long song, and licked the walls all the while, moaning like he was a happy puppy! This is when Yummy began to run!"

It was the same kitchen that haunted Guster in his dreams. But this made so little sense.

"I followed him then, as fast as I could go! I was riding on great big yaks with wheels that were speeding through the cities."

"Cars?" asked Guster.

Gaucho brightened. "You know them?" he said. "They are very amazing animals."

Guster chuckled. "Know them? We have one."

Gaucho looked eager. "Can I drive it?"

"Not without asking Mom," he said. Even Zeke rarely got to drive the family suburban, and he had his license. But that might have had something to do with the way he liked to sneak up behind pedestrians and blast the horn in their ears.

"You have so many strange and wonderful things that we do not have in my city," Gaucho said.

The way he talked, Gaucho's city sounded so remote and old-fashioned. Maybe they were very poor, like some of the villages Guster had seen in Africa. But Gaucho's clothes, however much they looked like they belonged on a clown, were well-made and looked quite expensive. They weren't the clothes of a poor villager. Guster wanted to ask more about the city, but Gaucho's sword made Guster think better of it.

"I followed Yummy to the sea, where he climbed into a boat as big as the countryside. You should have seen it! A man would need to stop and rest before he could walk from end to end. Yummy hid in between the many boxes there, and we traveled for many days, rocking back and forth on the waves.

"Then, when we were far out to sea, and I could not see land anymore, and I thought we would fall off the end of the world, the boat dropped nets into the water and caught mountains of fish!"

Something about that caught Guster's attention. "Fish?" he asked. "What kind?"

Gaucho shook his head. "I don't know. They were delicious though. I overheard the sailors. They called them toona."

Guster's insides started to heat up. That wasn't what he wanted to hear. Tuna fish. Like his sandwich. Felicity had told him just minutes earlier that he was starting to taste things about the people that had made the food he ate. Guster was starting to feel what they felt. What if it were the same for the fish? What if they had been afraid of Yummy?

Guster had been right about the sandwich. It was a warning. He shuddered at the thought.

"Then where is Yummy now?" Guster asked.

Gaucho grinned a sheepish grin. He looked like he did not want to say. "Well, he has traveled very far, and that is why I am here . . ."

"Where is he?" asked Guster. He could not let this little man avoid the question.

The grin disappeared from Gaucho's face. "He is here, in the woods. He's been circling your house for days, waiting for his chance to gobble you up."

The barn was so quiet Guster could hear the wood creak. So maybe this creature was real. Zeke certainly thought so. Guster had seen the footprint for himself, and the tree with the bite taken out of it. Now Gaucho had explained everything. And of course there was the sandwich. There was too much evidence to think that Yummy wasn't real.

But one thing Guster couldn't believe was that Yummy was on a mission. Why, out of billions of people on the planet, would the monster come halfway across the world for *him?*

Zeke had been right: the footprint, the tree with the bite taken out of it. If those were clues, Yummy must be very, very big.

"What do you want me to do?" asked Guster.

"That is why I am here." Gaucho bowed low. "To warn you. You must run away."

"To where?" Guster asked. He couldn't just leave home. Where would he go?

"Somewhere far away, where Yummy can't find you," said Gaucho.

Guster couldn't leave home. If he did, what would he eat?

Guster shook his head. "I think you've got the wrong guy," he said. "Yummy doesn't want me. Give it a few days. Your monster will wander on, just like he's done for months. I'm staying."

Gaucho removed his hat and dropped to his knees. "Señor! I beg you, by all the Cookie Coins of the Princess of the Realm, do not ignore this warning!" He looked like he was going to cry.

It didn't matter. It was far too impossible, even with all that Guster had seen, to trust this little man's word and leave Mom's cooking behind without a second thought. No, Guster could not. He had to stick with what he knew.

Guster turned his back on Gaucho. His mind was made up. He wouldn't tell anyone about Gaucho del Pantaloon. Mom would overreact and lock Guster up until doomsday to protect him. Mariah would probably ignore him for the most part, telling him that they'd gotten too old for silly things like that before she stuffed her ear buds into her ears. Dad, of course, would just open and close his jaw like one end of a teeter-totter. Dad still had a hard time picturing these things in his head. Zeke—well, he'd of course believe everything that Gaucho said, telling Guster that Zeke's years of research and deep understanding of semi-supernatural creatures would aid Guster in evading the monster, blah blah blah. He'd probably pester him to read that monster book.

"I'm sorry," Guster said, and pushed open the front doors of the barn.

There wasn't much Guster could do. He could pay attention to his tastes. He could keep watch. He would stay close to home and stay safe. That was all. Except . . .

He came around the house and found himself staring at the gigantic RV. There they were, the letters FC emblazoned on the side of the door. Felicity.

Would she understand?

Guster shook his head at the thought. Felicity had treated him like he was some kind of experiment. He hated that.

He needed time to think about all this. He needed a place where he could concentrate.

The door of the RV burst open. Felicity leapt out, the saucepan in one hand, the wooden spoon in the other, the yellowish mother sauce spilling over the sides. Her eyes were electric, darting back and forth, her hair swooshing as she fixed her gaze on Guster.

"Guster Johnsonville! The mother sauce is ready. I've tasted it. YOU are the most delicious thing in the world!"

Chapter 4 — The Bus Station

Guster did not say a word. There was nothing to say. He'd never considered before how *he* tasted, and he didn't like being thought of that way. Suddenly, he was on the wrong end of the dinner spoon.

"It's incredibly sweet," said Felicity. She hadn't stopped talking since she'd burst from the trailer. "It was hard to believe at first, but in all my years of cooking, I've never seen a transformation in a dish like this. All with the final ingredient—a dash of Guster Johnsonville!"

She giggled, then seemed to notice how excited she'd become. She straightened and placed a strand of blonde hair back in place. "Guster, I have a theory."

Guster wasn't sure he wanted to hear it.

"What was the most delicious thing in the whole world?" she asked.

Guster muttered the answer she wanted to hear, though he wasn't sure he knew what she was getting at. "The One Recipe. That extraordinary chocolate soufflé. The Gastronomy of Peace."

Felicity's red-lipstick lips turned into a genuine smile. "Yes. Archedentus' greatest creation. And where is it now?"

she asked.

"Destroyed," said Guster. He was the one who had done it. He did not regret that.

"And who was the only one to taste it in the history of the world?" she asked.

The answer was obvious. Guster nodded his head. He was the only person to have ever tasted the Gastronomy of Peace. It had tasted like a dream.

Felicity grabbed Guster by the shoulders and looked him in the eye. "That recipe changed you. It must have done something to your blood. Its flavors were more concentrated than we could have guessed."

"I . . ." Guster stammered. He took a step back.

This was unexpected. The One Recipe had tasted amazing, but then it was gone. All he had was a memory, nothing permanent. Certainly, the Gastronomy of Peace had tasted better than anything in this world. Guster never expected to find its equal. But what Felicity was saying was insane. Was there suddenly a nutrition label tattooed on his tummy? He was not to be tasted. He was not food. Surely no one could think of him like *that*.

Yummy.

Guster staggered. Gaucho was right. Something had happened to him at the Chateau de Dîner.

"You want proof?" asked Felicity, holding up a spoonful of sauce. "Have a taste."

It might as well have been a spoonful of Guster.

"No," he said, holding up his hands to push it back. He wanted to throw up. He turned, spinning in the dirt and running back toward the house. He needed space.

He yanked open the screen door and dashed past Mom folding laundry in the living room. "How did the lessons go?" she asked.

He did not stop to answer. He leapt up the stairs, taking

them three at a time. First Gaucho, then Felicity. They both agreed. It was too unlikely a coincidence. If Felicity was right and Guster *was* incredibly delicious, and Gaucho was right that something with a sweet tooth was hunting him, then one irrefutable fact existed: Guster was like a tasty, flashing neon sign that said "Eat Here".

He hesitated at the top of the stairs. This news from Felicity was too much. He needed someone to help him. He needed allies.

Mariah's door was on his left. It was closed. Zeke and Guster's room was at the other end of the hall. Their door was open. Mariah would have good ideas. She always knew what to look up or where to go to solve their problems. He lifted his knuckles to knock.

But she'd been so distant lately. Low, sad, melodic lyrics snaked out from under her door—something about how the world's invisible heart doesn't know her name. She was listening to that music full of feelings again, just like she had been for months.

Guster paused. He turned toward his and Zeke's room. He found Zeke there, lying on the bed, his shirt off, sweating as he bench pressed a football.

"High reps. Low weight," said Zeke. He faked throwing it at Guster. "What do you want, P?"

Guster closed the door behind him. "Zeke, I'm running away from home."

***

It didn't take more than a few minutes to explain everything to Zeke about Felicity's mother sauce and Gaucho del Pantaloon. Guster was careful what details he used when he got to the part about Yummy—leaving out words like monster and hunting would keep Zeke from freaking out. It didn't matter.

"I told you!" said Zeke. He thrust *Barrister's Certified Real Field Guide to Lesser Known Creatures* in Guster's face. "I . . . told . . . you!" Zeke leapt up on the bed and started shaking his backside and flapping his arms like a chicken.

Guster frowned. Maybe telling Mariah would have been the better choice.

"Let's go see him!" said Zeke.

"Who?" asked Guster.

"Gaucho del Pants-bassoon!" said Zeke.

"That's not his name," said Guster. Zeke thought this was all so funny. He wasn't the one at the center of the mess. "Not now. We need a plan."

Zeke saluted. "Right. Let's pack our backpacks. Then we'll wait until dark. Then we'll steal the car and drive to California."

Guster sat down on the bed and curled his knees up to his chest. Asking Zeke to come up with a plan was likely to land them both in jail, or worse, get them grounded. The problem was, Zeke was kind of right. They had to get as far away as possible. Guster could see that now.

"What if we tell Mom?" asked Guster.

"Are you crazy?" said Zeke. "You'll be in so much trouble for endangering this family and bringing the horrible cousin of Bigfoot's wrath upon us! You've done this to us all!

"Besides, you tell her and she'll just call animal control. By then it will be too late. She's not going to leave this house again. Not after what happened last summer. Think of Henry Junior!"

"I didn't mean for this to happen!" Guster cried, just loud enough so his voice wouldn't carry. But he did think of Henry Junior. Henry Junior was big enough to toddle up and down the stairs by himself now, and loved nothing more than popping Guster's cheeks when Guster puffed them up like a blowfish. It was Henry Junior's favorite game. For all he'd grown, Henry

Junior was still just so innocent and tiny. He needed protecting.

If Guster stayed, there was no telling how many hours or minutes before Yummy chomped his way into the farmhouse, smashing it to splinters in search of a morsel of Guster. Time was running out.

"We'll wait until dark," said Guster, stuffing an extra shirt into his backpack.

Zeke leapt down off the bed, his eyes growing so wide with excitement they nearly popped the pimples right off his face.

"Now you're talkin'!" said Zeke, and started to pack his backpack as well. "We'll need this for reference," he said, stuffing *Barrister's Field Guide* into his pack. Guster hoped Zeke was wrong about that.

***

By the time the sun had finally disappeared, it was nearly nine o'clock. Felicity had chosen to cook her own dinner outside in the RV. Guster and Zeke had been very quiet during their dinner, which earned more than a few eyebrow raises from Mom.

Guster felt like he was eating his last meal. Mom made beef stroganoff, taken directly from season four, episode seven of Felicity Casa's show *Roofs*. It was pretty good too. Beneath all the noodles and sauce was her signature flavor, written in longhand across the flavors.

"How does it taste?" Mom asked Guster. She smiled an extra nice smile. Maybe she was trying to make it up to him after forcing him sit through Felicity's sessions all day.

"It's tangy," said Guster, his mouth full of noodles.

"I'm glad you like it." Mom smiled. "I'm making you a special dessert."

She wasn't making this easy. He nearly blurted out

everything right then, confessing all his plans. "I . . . I . . . Mom, there's . . ." said Guster.

Zeke stuffed a forkful of noodles into Guster's mouth. Guster almost choked, trying to force it down the right pipe. The morsel did its job; Guster settled back down in his chair and chewed quietly. He did not try to speak again.

After dinner, Mom sent everyone to bed early so they could get up in time for camp the next day.

But instead of sleeping, Guster and Zeke waited quietly behind their bedroom door. As soon as Mom and Dad's door closed and their light went out, Guster and Zeke tiptoed down the stairs to the garage.

"Wait," said Guster, stopping by the refrigerator. He couldn't leave just yet. The fridge was full of leftovers from Mom's dinners this week. It was his lifeline.

He found a small cooler in the pantry, got some ice from the freezer, and began stuffing it full of whatever meals he could find: lasagna from Tuesday, chicken pot pies from Wednesday, and the beef stroganoff from tonight.

It would last him for six or seven meals at least. After that, well, that's where his plan came to an abrupt end.

"Hurry," Zeke hissed, holding the door to the garage open for Guster. They snuck into the darkness of the garage where the family Suburban was parked. Zeke grabbed the keys from off the hook next to the doorframe and crept around the car to the driver's side. Guster opened the passenger door.

"Are you sure this is a good idea?" asked a voice in the darkness.

Zeke fell backward, stumbling into some cans.

Guster's throat tightened. They were caught. Mariah was sitting behind the steering wheel, her arms folded. What was she doing here?

"Quiet, Zeke. You wouldn't want Mom to wake up," said Mariah calmly.

"You were waiting for us," said Guster. "How did you know?"

"Henry Junior's old baby monitor has been in your room for weeks," said Mariah. "I could hear every word of your plans."

Zeke stood up and rushed to Mariah. "Extortion! Blackmail! You no-good eavesdropper! This is against my constitutional rights!" he said, pushing his face up to hers.

She'd betrayed them. Sure, Mariah had been so emotional lately, but Guster never expected *this*.

"Are you going to tell?" asked Guster. Maybe it would be better if she did.

"No," said Mariah. "I'm not here to rat you out, however much you may deserve it. Instead, I'm here to offer you a better plan."

Zeke craned his head backward, the disbelief almost shining off his face in the dark garage. "You're what?"

Mariah slid out of the driver's seat. "Zeke, if you start this car, Mom and Dad will be down here in 2 seconds flat. Besides, even if you do get as far as California, Mom and Dad are going to call the police, and you'll land yourself in jail for grand theft auto."

"They wouldn't!" cried Zeke.

Mariah shrugged. "Or, you could take the train with me to New York City."

"Wait, you want to go with us?" asked Zeke.

Mariah nodded. "There's more to Gaucho del Pantaloon and this mysterious creature than there appears. That much is clear."

Guster smiled a little. Underneath the layers of cherry lip gloss she was still Mariah, and Mariah could never resist a good mystery.

"So that's it? Take the train to New York?" said Zeke. "Some plan. At least California has movie stars."

"And New York has stock brokers," said Mariah. "But what

really matters are the smells. If this Yummy is tracking Guster because Guster smells like a fresh chocolate cream puff, we'll need to go to a place where we can hide. New York City has got a smorgasbord of smells. Think of all that food! There's no better place to mask your scent, little brother."

Little brother. She hadn't ever called Guster that before. He didn't like it. He was twelve—only two years younger than Mariah. And he was not a cream puff.

"Yes! Conventional wisdom states that rubbing your body in earthworms makes you invisible to Bigfoot, for example," said Zeke. He thought for a moment, scratching his belly, then a wide smile broke across his face. "Let's wrap Guster up in a pizza!"

"Shhh," said Guster. "Mom will hear." Zeke was ridiculous. Guster turned to Mariah. "So what now?"

"We get our bikes and ride to the bus station," said Mariah, holding up a few sheets of paper. "I've already printed out an itinerary for travel by train from New Orleans to the city. Once we're there, we'll drop in on Aunt Priscilla so we have a place to stay."

"She'll tell Mom for sure," said Guster. Aunt Priscilla had almost completely ignored them last time they needed her. They'd had to beg her for help.

"Not necessarily," said Mariah. "You know how little she seems to notice us. We're practically invisible. And even if she does tell Mom, we'll have a head start."

Mariah had a point. Having her be a part of the plan made Guster feel better about the whole thing. Mariah was always the obedient one. If she thought this was a good idea, it couldn't be *that* bad.

Besides, there was a part of Guster begging to go without Mom. He needed to be out there on his own to see if he could do it. Dad's words echoed in his brain: *You're going to have to learn to do things without your mom hovering over you.*

They steered their bikes out of the garage and into the backyard, where the shadows crisscrossed the grass. The crickets chirped and the moon was low as Guster hooked the cooler to his bike. He straddled his bike at the end of their gravel driveway and hesitated.

"Yummy's out there," he whispered. "And it's dark."

"Then pedal fast," said Mariah. She sped off without a backward glance.

Zeke took off after her. Guster took a deep breath and pedaled after them. It was better than getting left alone.

They pedaled as fast as they could, Guster looking over his shoulder into the trees the whole mile into town, until they finally reached the bus station.

Luckily a yellow light still shone inside the double glass doors. Mariah bought 3 tickets to New Orleans from the old conductor who sat behind the counter in a small booth.

He squinted over his glasses at the three of them. "You're Henry's kids, aren't you?" he asked. Almost everyone knew each other in their town.

"That's right," said Mariah. "Mom and Dad are sending us on a trip."

"That so?" said the conductor, taking the money and counting out the tickets. He slid them through the glass.

"Yep," said Mariah, and turned without further reply.

They crossed the small parking lot, locked up their bikes out of sight behind the station, then sat down on a bench under a dim lamp to wait. That conductor made him nervous. The sooner they got on the road the better.

A quarter of an hour later the bus arrived with a rumble and a hiss as the doors opened. The three of them climbed the stairs to the bus and found seats at the back. Guster set the cooler down on the seat beside him. There were only two other passengers aboard, both of which sat near the front.

Guster had just settled in next to the window on the long

48

bench when something clattered and clanged up the steps of the bus, tumbling over and nearly falling on the driver.

"Let me aboard!"

In the dim light of the bus Guster could make out a small man with stubby limbs and a pear-shaped metal chest piece. *Gaucho!* Guster charged up the aisle.

"Do you have a ticket?" asked the driver. His eyes darted back and forth, as if he was waiting for someone to explain who the strange little man was.

"He's with me," Guster said, stepping between Gaucho and the driver. Guster looked Gaucho in the eye. "Go have a seat. I'll take care of this." He jumped off the bus and purchased one more ticket from the conductor with a wad of dollars from his pocket.

When Guster returned, Gaucho was still at the front, bowing to the two passengers who sat there. "My compliments on such a marvelous metal machine," he said, smiling.

Guster sighed and ushered Gaucho to the back of the bus, past the passengers' bewildered stares.

Zeke's jaw fell open. "Are you a robot?" he asked, reaching out to rap Gaucho's metal chest plate. It clanged a hollow clang.

Mariah pulled Zeke's hand away. "Don't be rude," she said. "This man is a conquistador."

Zeke looked confused. Guster had heard that word before, but wasn't sure he remembered what it meant.

"Like Cortez or Pissarro," Mariah said. "They were Spanish conquerors who came to the New World after Christopher Columbus."

Gaucho del Pantaloon bowed low to Mariah, and then sat down next to her. "It is my pleasure to make the acquaintance of such a refined lady of taste," he said, removing his helmet.

Not exactly the words Guster would've called Mariah, but that didn't matter. "Gaucho, what are you doing here?" he demanded.

"Following you, Señor. I see you have heeded my advice to flee. I must make sure that you are safe from Yummy."

Guster could appreciate that. Gaucho seemed genuinely worried about him.

The bus engine rumbled and sputtered as the wheels began to roll toward New Orleans.

The whole way, Mariah explained how the conquistadors were Spanish explorers who sailed to America and built cities and fought wars. Guster remembered now where he'd read about them in his history book. "They sailed to Peru!" he said.

Mariah nodded. "And there are all sorts of legends about things they did, like finding the Fountain of Youth—it's somewhere in Florida, I think—or discovering a hidden city made of pure gold. They said that the City of El Dorado was the capital of a kingdom of gold. Its streets were paved with pure gold bars, the walls of its many pyramids were plated in gold, and its king bathed in gold dust."

"There were many who tried to find the lost City of Gold over the centuries, but whenever anyone set out to do so they never returned." Mariah looked over at Gaucho, her eyes curious. "Where is it that you said you came from?"

Gaucho's eyes darted to the floor nervously. "I did not say, exactly. I assure you, all of these things are just rumors and stories," he said. "I myself have never been to this land here until this year, when I followed Yummy here."

"Then where exactly is your city located?" said Mariah. Guster shot her a warning glance. Now was not the time or place for Gaucho to draw his sword.

"Doesn't matter," said Guster, trying to steer the conversation elsewhere. Mariah seemed to get the hint.

"How old are you?" Guster asked. If Gaucho was a conquistador, he should've died hundreds of years ago.

"I don't know. Perhaps thirty, or maybe fifty," he said. "It's not polite to ask a man his age. My grandfather's great-grandfather's father had sailed around the globe, exploring these places you talk about. But me? I prefer to stay put when I can and enjoy life's luxuries. When you've found a home as magnificent as mine, you like to settle down."

Mariah wrinkled her lips and squinted at him. She didn't look convinced. "Guster, I think he's talking about the lost city of El Dorado. The City of Gold."

"Gold?" said Zeke, his eyes glazing over. "Just think of the rims we could buy for Mom's suburban if we went there."

Guster jabbed Zeke in the ribs with his elbow.

"I've heard that no one has ever been able to find the city," said Guster.

"It's true," said Mariah. "Many people have gone into the jungles of South America looking for it, never to return."

Guster settled back into his seat and watched as the trees zipped by in a blur. El Dorado. The City of Gold. All protected by monsters.

At least he felt safe on the bus. The seat was soft, and the engine hummed as they sped along the highway. With each passing mile, his problems seemed to melt away.

He tried to sort out everything that had happened that day: Felicity, the mother sauce, Gaucho and the monster. There was so much happening all at once, and all of it was unexpected.

The bus slowed as they came to a four-way stop between an open field and a thicket of trees. Guster's head bobbed forward as the brakes hissed. Out of the corner of his eye, he thought he saw a shadow shift in the field.

He pressed his face up against the glass. There was nothing there but grass and weeds all the way to the woods.

Then, all at once, something enormous darted toward the road. It was massive—at least twice as tall as Guster, and three times as wide. It was bigger than a bear, with lurching arms and short hind legs.

It thundered across the road into the bus's headlight beams, turned, and then opened its jaws in a deafening roar.

Guster gasped. In the yellow light he could see the creature's true form. It was covered in shaggy white fur. There was no discernable head on top of its hulking shoulders. Instead, its tiny orange eyes were set in its round chest, nearly invisible behind its knotted, tangled brows. A large mouth spanned across the top of its torso, with teeth like rhino horns protruding from its gums.

Yummy.

Mariah screamed. Then the passengers up front screamed too, their bodies frozen in place, their eyes wide with horror.

"Bu . . . bu . . . bu . . . bu," said Zeke, his mouth popping open and shut like a trapdoor.

"It is him! It's Yummy! The Insatiable!" Gaucho cried.

"What the . . ." muttered the bus driver.

Yummy took two giant strides forward and swung his massive arms at the bus's grill, stabbing his claws into the metal.

"GO!" cried Mariah.

The bus driver hesitated, then unlatched his safety belt and shot like a bullet out of the driver's seat and down the aisle toward the back of the bus. "What is that thing?" he screamed. He dove into the tiny bathroom next to the last row of seats and bolted the door shut.

Metal scraped and groaned as the bus rocked back and forth.

"Zeke!" shouted Mariah, pushing Zeke out of his seat. He fell onto the floor with a thud. "Go! Drive!" she shouted. She picked him up off the floor with a surprising burst of strength, and shoved him toward the front.

Zeke hesitated. "But I don't . . ."

"You're the only one of us who can!" she shouted.

Yummy's claws raked across the front windshield. This was no time to think or make plans. Guster slid out of his chair, setting his shoulder onto Zeke's back next to Mariah and pushing him to the front. Zeke had gained a lot of muscle from so much football practice; he wasn't easy to push. His limbs were flailing and digging into whatever they could find: the floor, the seatbacks, the luggage shelves overhead.

"I don't know how to drive a bus!" he stammered, his face pale.

The bus rocked backward as the monster slammed into its front.

"You're the one with the license! It's just a big van!" hissed Mariah. She pounded his back with her fists.

The bus shook as Yummy smashed into it again.

"Alright! Alright!" said Zeke, breaking into a run and jumping into the driver's seat. He shoved the shifter on the column into gear and set his feet on the pedals. "Which one?" Zeke asked, staring bewildered out the front windshield. The shaggy white beast stepped back to get a running start before ramming the tops of its shoulders into the front grill again. Guster stumbled as the bus shook.

"Oh please, Zeke! This one," said Mariah, shoving Zeke's right leg down onto the gas pedal.

The bus lurched forward, throwing Guster back onto the nearest seat. There was a thump as the creature bounced off the front bumper and fell to the side, rolling into the brush and snapping branches as it tumbled away.

Gaucho rushed to the front of the bus, and, before they could stop him, yanked the lever to open the door as the bus picked up speed.

"Gaucho, no!" Guster grabbed the collar on Gaucho's armor and yanked him back.

Gaucho ignored him, struggling to get to the door of the bus as the asphalt sped past. Guster lost his grip on Gaucho, and the little man stuck his head out the door.

He raised his head to the night and, closing his eyes, hummed a long, low melody back toward the place where

Yummy had fallen.

A loud moan of anguish came from the woods. Gaucho hummed again, this time with a higher pitched tune that burst into spurts, then ended long and low like a whale's song.

Yummy moaned once more, and then was gone as Zeke drove the bus into the night.

Chapter 5 — Not Everyone's Your Friend in New York City

It took Zeke only one more hour to make it to the New Orleans Union Passenger Terminal in the middle of the city. By the time he pulled in to the station, he was sitting tall in the driver's seat. The grin across his pimply face was as wide as a frog's.

The driver didn't unlock the bathroom door until after the bus had come to a complete stop. He opened it a crack and peered out as the two passengers leapt from the bus, screaming as they ran into the terminal. Guster, Mariah, and Zeke did not wait for the driver to open the door all the way. Rather than get a scolding for stealing the driver's bus in the middle of the night, the three of them scrambled off the bus and disappeared into the terminal with their backpacks, cooler, and Gaucho in hand.

"Did you see that thing?" asked Zeke. "It was like . . . all white and shaggy. Just like the Abominable Snowman! You know, the Yeti? From way high up in the Himalayas. The first cousin of the Bigfoot, and just as ferocious." He flipped open the guidebook and pointed to a pencil drawing that looked nothing like the monster they'd seen on the road. "Exactly kind of like the one in my book! Yummy is Yeti!"

"The City of El Dorado is not in the Himalayas," said Mariah, rolling her eyes. "It has to be something else."

"And did you see how bad he wanted to eat Guster?" said Zeke. "He's not the Abominable Snowman. He's the *Insatiable Snowman!*"

Guster sighed. He did not like the way his day was turning out.

Mariah bought four train tickets to Penn Station in New York City. The train left at 7am, so they had to wait several hours for it to arrive. There were a few scraggly, rough-looking characters wandering through the train station, but no one gave them trouble. Perhaps because they had Gaucho with them. He did have a sword.

When the train arrived, the four of them were able to find two rows of seats that faced each other so they wouldn't be disturbed. The train was supposed to take a full day to get from New Orleans to New York City. That would give them time to rest. Guster was so tired, he leaned his head up against the window and fell asleep almost as soon as the train left the station, visions of golden streets and snarling beasts flitting across his dreams.

***

Guster woke to Zeke whispering intently to Gaucho.

"What does he eat?" Zeke asked. He was jotting down notes in a tiny spiral-bound notebook.

"Mostly sweet things. He likes vanilla and cinnamon too," said Gaucho. "They like the cold very much."

"Mmmhmm," said Zeke, chewing on the end of his pencil. He turned to his book, flipping furiously through the pages, and then folded the corners on a few to mark his place. "Very interesting," he muttered. Guster had never seen Zeke so studious in his life.

Guster's stomach told him that breakfast time had already passed. He opened his cooler and fished out a bit of cold omelet that Mom had stuck in the fridge. Mom put leftovers in the fridge, no matter what. She never let the smallest scrap of food go to waste. It was more than just saving money, she'd say in her most mom-wise moments. It was being thankful for what you have.

Right now, Guster was very thankful he had a mouthful of rubbery eggs for breakfast. It wouldn't have been his first choice, as cold and chewy as they were, but it was home cooking, and that's what he'd bonded with. It was filling at least.

"Oh good! Eggs!" said Zeke. He reached for the plastic bag.

Mariah batted his hand away and gave him a few dollars. "Go buy your own," she said. She seemed to understand what Guster needed. He was glad he didn't have to explain it to her.

It seemed like it was taking a whole decade to get to New York, the train rattling by endless miles of green countryside. Alabama, Georgia, North Carolina, and Virginia. The further they traveled from home, the safer Guster felt. At Mariah's suggestion, he jumped off the train at each stop and hugged a tree or rubbed his hands all over a bench or spit in a garbage can. "You have to leave your scent to draw Yummy away from home," she'd explained.

He didn't like leaving a trail for the creature to follow, but he had to get him away from the farmhouse somehow. He had to protect Mom, Dad, and Henry Junior. That was the whole point.

The train sped on through that day and into the night. Guster, Zeke, Mariah, and Gaucho all slept when it got dark.

Finally, after an entire day, a night, and a whole morning— thirty-two stops in all—when Guster could take no more of Zeke's air guitar or Gaucho's snoring, the humongous skyscrapers of New York City peeked out over the horizon.

The train rumbled over a few bridges, passed underground, then slowly rolled to a stop, its bells clanging and brakes hissing. It was completely full of passengers by now, and Guster, his siblings, and Gaucho had to press their way through the crowd of bodies. It felt good to stretch his legs.

They came out into an underground terminal with row after row of trains. It was a good thing they had Mariah with them, and that she'd planned ahead, because the platforms and maze of stairs would've sent Guster wandering in circles for hours.

"This way." Mariah led them up a set of stairs and out toward the open street. The city was all jammed together, with cars honking, dirty sidewalks, and very old brown brick buildings, the kind Guster had only seen in movies. There were billboards everywhere. One for shaving cream, another for a new car. There was even one with Felicity Casa on it, smiling down on them from above with a roast in her hands. There was a tagline below her picture:

Roofs
Season 7
This time, dinner gets serious.

Guster could even see the Empire State Building a few blocks away. It was enormous.

"I printed off directions to get to Aunt Priscilla's," said Mariah, pointing at her map. "If we walk a few blocks this way, we'll find her apartment."

She led the way, and they walked, crossing what seemed like two dozen crosswalks, passing under scaffolding and awnings and over metal grates that blasted air upward into Guster's nose.

Guster sniffed. Mariah was right. The city was full of smells. There were two doughnut shops across the street—both with a pretty tasty maple bar smell—a deli with salty corned beef, a diner serving a very strong and fishy clam chowder around the block, and a fresh and creamy slice of cheesecake hiding somewhere down the street.

It would have been heaven if all the smells had been so delicious. There was also rotting cabbage in the alley nearby, and a puddle of strange mixtures soaking into the sidewalk at their feet smelled so strongly of sewage Guster had to scramble to the next crosswalk to keep from throwing up.

And then there were the hot dogs—they were everywhere! Nearly every corner had a hot dog vendor with a red, yellow, and blue umbrella overhead, the smell of roasting weenies and vinegar-steeped mustard piercing Guster's nostrils.

The perfect camouflage, thought Guster.

A horn honked and a cab screeched to a halt inches away from his leg. Guster leapt back onto the sidewalk.

"Keep your eyes up," said Mariah.

They walked for another mile, absorbing the sounds and smells of the city, until finally they came to a clean street lined with trees poking out of the sidewalk at regular intervals and stone-carved buildings so grey they were almost white.

Mariah stopped at the steps of one of them and looked up. "This is it," she said.

"Now hold on a second," said Zeke. "Are we just going to stroll up there and ask Aunt Priscilla for a place to stay? It's not like Braxton works for her anymore. We haven't even seen her since we blew up her jet last year. I'm not so sure she'll be happy to see us. She's going to tell Mom we're here."

"And what if she does?" said Guster, a thought suddenly occurring to him. "At least she and Dad will come looking for us. That'll get them away from the house."

Mariah nodded. Zeke folded his arms. "Then we shoulda just brought Mom in the first place," he said.

That never would've worked. Guster knew Mom. She

always had layers upon layers of irrefutable reasons for things. "You try convincing her," he said. "You know it would take years."

Mariah nodded in agreement. "We're not turning back now. Don't you get it? We've run away from home. There is no going back. At least not until we've figured out what to do about Yummy."

She was right. This was still the best plan they had. There was nothing to do but knock. "Go ahead," said Guster. Maybe Aunt Priscilla would give them something to eat. She always had a nose for the finer things.

Mariah found a buzzer outside the glass entrance to the building. She pressed a black button next to Priscilla McStock, and the speaker crackled. "Yes?" said a gruff man's voice.

"Hello and good afternoon, we're here to see our Aunt, Mrs. Priscilla McStock," said Mariah calmly.

"I'm afraid she doesn't have any nieces," said the voice. "You'll have to come back later when she does."

Mariah looked confused. "This is Priscilla McStock's residence, is it not?" she asked.

A shrill, high-pitched voice came through the speaker, "Oh, Dermont! You silly man. Yes, I do have a niece. Certainly I must have told you about her. You've been working for me for almost a year now. Mary, is that you?" It was unmistakably Aunt Priscilla.

Mariah frowned. "Yes, it's me, Ma-ri-ah," she said, sounding it out carefully for Aunt Priscilla to hear. "Guster and Zeke are here too."

"Oh my, what an unexpected surprise."

"We've travelled all the way to New York to see you," said Guster.

There was a pause on the other side of the intercom.

"Can we come in?" Mariah asked.

Guster was positive Mom had already told her about her

jet getting blown up by the Gastronimatii. He was there for the phone conversation. But it should be water under the bridge by now. They had sent her some of the Arrivederci chocolate for Christmas that they'd gotten from Braxton. That alone was worth thousands of dollars. Besides, she was family. She'd even sent Guster a card on Zeke's birthday.

Maybe she hadn't heard them.

"May we come in?" Guster repeated.

"Oh my. Well, I have puppies, dears," Aunt Priscilla said. "They're a pair of new Chow Chows, just picked up from the breeder last month. Very fluffy. Very expensive. In fact, one of the most pricey breeds out there."

"We'd love to see them," Mariah said eagerly.

"No, I'm afraid you don't understand," said Aunt Priscilla. "Their psychologist said they are not to be disturbed for the first few weeks in their new environment. It takes time to settle in, you know."

Zeke shoved his face forward, his lips parted and his eyebrows rammed together in a look of disbelief. Psychologist? He mouthed at Guster.

Guster shrugged.

"We'll be out on the street. We've got nowhere else to go," said Mariah.

"Oh, and I'm very sorry about that, dears. So are the Chow Chows, believe me. You'll understand someday when you have dogs of your own. You ought to know, raising those chickens or possums or whatever it is your kind do out on the farm there. Goodbye." The intercom crackled, and then went silent.

Zeke and Mariah stared at each other in disbelief. They'd come so far. Aunt Priscilla was Mom's sister. She'd always been a little condescending, but she'd never turned them away.

Mariah rang the buzzer again. No one answered. She buzzed it over and over, finally pressing the button for a full minute until the intercom clicked and said, "No one is available to take your call."

She slumped down onto the step, dumbfounded. "But she's our aunt . . ." she said.

"What do we do now?" asked Zeke.

Mariah, for once, didn't have any answers to that question. She just stared into the street. Her brilliant plan had hit a deadend.

"She didn't even come down to see us," she said.

Gaucho sat down on the steps near the sidewalk, sighing as he did so, like he was setting down a heavy sack. "That is fine. Let us rest here on these marvelous flat stones you make here," he said, taking off his metal helmet and holding it upsidedown in his lap. He looked very odd there, with his striped balloon-pants and metal armor.

A man dropped some change into Gaucho's helmet as he passed. It clinked as it settled to the bottom.

Gaucho plucked a pair of quarters from his helmet and looked at them in confusion. "Can I eat them?" he asked.

Guster shook his head. He was getting hungry too. He plunked down next to Gaucho and opened his cooler. The ice was still cool. He popped the lid off a plastic container and stuck a plastic fork into the leftover beef stroganoff. It was cold, but it was familiar, and that was exactly what he needed right now in this faraway city with no place to stay.

"The least we can do is find some dinner," said Mariah, her eyebrows crossed. She stalked off, back up the street from where they'd come.

Zeke grabbed Guster and Gaucho by the shoulders. "Come on," he said.

Guster stuffed one last bite of stroganoff into his mouth. He didn't want to be left behind, especially since Mariah had all the maps. He jammed the Tupperware into the cooler and trailed after Zeke. Gaucho was right on his heels.

Mariah weaved her way back toward the busier streets.

"The arrogance!" she muttered.

"I think I'd need a psychologist too if I were stuck in that apartment with Aunt Priscilla all day," said Zeke. "I knew we should have gone to California." he whispered toward Guster in a low voice.

And now they were stuck in New York City, alone and with nowhere to stay.

Chapter 6 — Fatty Bubalatti's

They crossed two crosswalks, turned left, darted down a narrow one-way street, took a right, and rounded another corner until Mariah bumped right into a man in a black business suit with bright blue ankle-high socks.

"Excuse me," said Mariah, taking a few steps backward. She must have been so focused on putting distance between her and Aunt Priscilla she did not notice him standing there.

"You're excused," he said quickly. He did not take a second look at her. His eyes were focused on the back of the head of the twenty-something boy in front of him. In fact, there were about thirty or more people standing in front, and another thirty more waiting behind him.

Altogether it was a wall of middle-aged men in green fedoras, businessmen, moms with a kid strapped to their fronts, tattooed ladies with pink tank tops, stock brokers, elderly men with straw hats, and dudes dressed in checkered shorts—almost every type of person Guster could imagine, all waiting in one long line that blocked the entire sidewalk.

"What's the line for?" asked Mariah.

The man in the business suit turned to her again. "For Bubalatti's, of course!" he said, his face brightening in, if not a smile, at least a glow.

Guster stepped closer so he could hear. He knew that name. It was a faint memory from something a long time ago. "I think I've heard of that before," said Guster.

"Of course you have," said the man. "Everybody's heard about Bubalatti's. Franco Bubalatti is the finest pie maker in all of New York. I'd say even the East Coast." He pointed up to the store's front. It was dirty red brick, with a big window in front with the name "Bubalatti's" spelled out in gold lettering across the glass. There was a pie twice the size of a manhole cover turned up on its side. A glowing hour hand and a minute hand were fixed to its center, tick-tocking away the minutes on the tasty pie-face clock.

"The key lime is to kill for," said the man.

Of course. Last time they visited Aunt Priscilla, she'd served them a raisin-rhubarb Bubalatti pie. Guster had only gotten through one bite before he'd realized that it'd been laced with enough cinnamon to burn a hole in your cheeks. That had been the fault of one of the Gastronimatii though, not Bubalatti himself.

Aunt Priscilla had called Bubalatti the finest pie maker in all of New York City. Guster would love to try one for real.

"How much money do we have left?" Guster asked Mariah.

She stared him in the eyes. *Please,* thought Guster, *this is something I need.*

Mariah's face softened, just for a moment. "Enough," she said.

"And we have to eat some time," said Zeke, darting toward the back of the line. Guster, Gaucho, and Mariah followed him. It was so long, it bent around the corner. They found the end and lined up behind a young woman who was dressed in a trim black suit with a skirt.

They waited more than a half an hour, Gaucho humming a tune, and Zeke reading his field guide. Mariah studied the maps. Guster fumbled his thumbs in anticipation. He tried to keep his mind off the pies, but they smelled so good! When they finally got inside the door, it was well past dinner time.

Bubalatti's glowed with a soft yellow light as the last of the sun's rays bent through the glass. But instead of shining on fresh-baked pies behind the counter, it shone on several barrels of frozen ice cream.

Amid all the shouting and ordering and customers, there was not a single person eating pie. Instead, each one of them held a crispy brown waffle cone with a scoop of the most delicious-looking ice cream that Guster had ever seen.

Customers were ordering it by the second. There was cookies and cream with chunks of crumbly cookie dropped like black rocks onto a blanket of thick snow. There was a strawberry flavor so pink, Guster had to turn his eyes away before it blinded him. There was a rocky road with marshmallows and nuts and chocolate chunks arranged in a pattern so beautiful and complex, they could've been the jewels on a king's crown.

It was wonderful and beautiful and luscious all at the same time, and Guster wanted to eat every last flavor.

But one thing still didn't make sense. Bubalatti was known for his pies.

"Excuse me," said Guster to the woman in the black suit and skirt. "When did Bubalatti's start serving ice cream?"

The woman turned, surprise on her face. "You haven't heard? Bubalatti stopped making pies more than a month ago. So you haven't had the ice cream?" she exclaimed. "It's been the summer sensation across Manhattan since the middle of June. Sure he *was* known for pies, and they were remarkable at that, but no one can stop thinking about this ice cream—I mean no one. It's been written up in the New Yorker twice. And me, well, I can't help myself. I stop here at least twice a day: once on my lunch break, the other on my way home. Bubalatti won't say how he makes it. Just says it's made fresh every day, right here in the shop. He's very tight lipped about it, though every reporter in the city's tried to get it out of him. Says it's some kind of secret recipe or something. Me? Well, I think someone cast a spell on it, it's that good." And then suddenly she turned and zipped her lips, like she was embarrassed for talking so much.

Guster felt a thrill rise inside him, the same one that came right before Christmas, or before riding a waterslide. This was secretly one of the things he'd hoped for in New York: to find the tastes that people always talked about.

"I'm getting a double cone," he said.

Gaucho clasped and unclasped his hands, twiddling his fingers nervously as a bead of sweat dripped down his forehead.

"What's wrong?" Guster asked.

Gaucho shook his head. "Nothing, amigo. This place, it's just fine. Lovely in fact. Maybe too lovely." He turned to go. "I'll wait outside." And with that, he dashed out the door and hid behind a big blue mailbox.

"What got into him?" asked Zeke. Guster shrugged. He didn't know, but he would make sure to find out after all this was done.

When they got to the front of the line, Guster pressed his face up to the glass so he could see the flavors more clearly. There were several flavors, each one packed into its own wooden barrel with an open top. He could see the rough texture where the scoop had scraped along the cream. He could see the strawberries like little smiles peeking out of their pink burrows.

"Sample?" asked a fat man from behind the counter. His curling black mustache hairs were as thick as pasta noodles and sprouted out from under a large round nose that looked like a brown tomato stuck to his face. A gold chain hung down over his hairy chest, framed on either side by the V in his open-collared shirt. He smiled, revealing a set of tiny white teeth. He struck Guster as the exact kind of guy you'd see tossing dough on the front of a pizza box.

"There are samples?" Zeke said, his mouth open in awe. He was staring at the cookies and cream.

"Of course!" said the fat man. "You don't-a think Fatty Bubalatti's going to make you guess which one's da best! You have to know which one to put in your scoop!" His big round cheeks jiggled as he talked.

"   "This one," Guster said, pointing to the strawberry.

"Oh, Pink Shining Summertime on a Spoon?" said Bubalatti. "I think you'll be happy you made such a choice!" He pulled a small plastic red spoon from a bowl behind the counter and scooped up a morsel of ice cream the size of plump cherry. He handed it to Guster.

Guster could not stick the spoon in his mouth fast enough. The lump of strawberry ice cream softened as soon as it hit his lips, sliding through them and filling his mouth with succulent smooth flavor. It was cold and refreshing, like a dip in the pool on a boiling summer's day, and as the morsel melted in his mouth, the strawberries took the stage, whirling across his tongue and bouncing between his cheeks and teeth in a symphony. He smiled as it slid down his throat and soaked his brain with happiness.

And yet . . . it was odd. It was unlike any ice cream Guster had ever tasted. He could not tell this time where the cows that gave the milk had grazed, or where the strawberries were grown. Even the sugar inside seemed foreign, unlike any he had ever tasted. The sugarcane was not grown in the Pacific, nor did the vanilla come from Indonesia.

And there was something more: the ice cream was made with the pride of generations of confectioners honing their craft. It was made with the allegiance to an ideal, the taste of men and women and children all dedicated to a common, higher cause. Like a national anthem, or a pledge of allegiance.

Mariah shook Guster gently. "Guster, he's waiting for your

order," she said. Guster tried to clear his head, like waking from a daydream. He looked around. The line was starting to press in behind him, and there was even more commotion than before.

"Make your order!" someone shouted from behind him.

He clenched his eyes shut and opened them again. He had to know. "Where does this ice cream come from?" he asked Bubalatti.

Bubalatti looked down over the counter at him, raising his one big black bushy eyebrow that spanned his forehead. "I make it here of course," Bubalatti said.

"No, it comes from somewhere far away. A place that no one has ever been," said Guster. He knew he was speaking the truth. The ice cream was placeless.

Bubalatti's lips wrinkled, his eyebrow bending in the middle. He looked nervous, like he'd been caught stealing cookies from the cookie jar. "What? Everyone knows that I make-a my ice cream here myself! It's my secret recipe!"

Guster knew what he knew. "No," he said. "It has a history."

Two short men with stubby limbs came from the kitchen in the back of the shop. Each one carried a wooden barrel in his arms. They looked like brothers, each with a pointy black beard that made it look like they'd sharpened their chins, and a threadbare mustache that slanted out from under their noses. One was slightly taller than the other, and they both wore hairnets. Worst of all, they each wore a red apron tied around their waists.

Gastronimatii? thought Guster. It couldn't be. They had all been arrested and locked up. Or so he'd thought.

They set the wooden barrels of fresh ice cream down behind the counter.

Bubalatti took one look at them and a bead of sweat formed on his greasy forehead. "You can't say these things!" Bubalatti shouted at Guster. He looked back at the two short men. "This ice cream is my family recipe, homemade righta here! If you don't-a like it, you can get out of my shop!"

The line behind Guster was starting to bulge as people pressed closer, craning their necks to catch a glimpse of the commotion.

Mariah slapped some dollar bills down on the counter and grabbed Guster by the arm. "You're making him angry," she said. "Let's go."

She pulled Guster toward the front door. "But Guster didn't get his ice cream," said Zeke with a mouthful of rocky road, a waffle cone in one hand and his face smeared with chocolate.

"Later Zeke," said Mariah, nearly shoving Guster through the door.

"And don't come back!" shouted Bubalatti. Several customers stared at them as they left, clearly annoyed.

As he left, out of the corner of his eye, Guster noticed the two men with the sharp beards and red aprons whispering to each other and pointing in his direction.

Mariah hurried them along the sidewalk, rushing to get out of sight of the shop and the stares of the customers that had been forced to wait for them. "That was a mess," she said. "I have never been so embarrassed in my life." She shot a disapproving glance at Guster that looked exactly like one Mom would have used.

Guster barely noticed. Mariah wasn't Mom, and he had more important matters on his mind. He kept his eyes on the sidewalk, his head down, not really caring where they went, or noticing the streets as they passed by. There was something strange about those two men, and the shop, and Bubalatti's defensive nature. Most of all, there was something strange, but wonderful, about that ice cream.

"Where's Gaucho?" asked Zeke. They hadn't seen the little man since he'd hidden behind the mailbox. He hadn't been there when they came out.

Mariah turned the next corner. Someone came around the

corner from the opposite direction and bumped into Guster so hard he fell back onto the ground. He dropped the cooler onto the sidewalk. Standing above him was a man with a brown tattered trench coat buttoned all the way up to his chin, a wide-brimmed green felt hat bent down over his ears, and a pair of mirrored aviator sunglasses that hid most of his face.

"Excuse me," muttered Guster, shaking off his surprise. The man picked Guster up by the backpack with both hands and set him on his feet. He straightened Guster's backpack, then patted him on the shoulder and strode away without a word.

"Rude," said Mariah, glaring after the man.

They spent the next few hours on the edge of Central Park, Guster eating what was left of Mom's lasagna from the cooler, and Mariah and Zeke chewing on hot dogs. Their money was starting to run low. The train tickets had been very, very expensive, and, as best as Mariah could figure, they only had a few more meals before they were broke. Not to mention they had no place to stay, and sleeping on the streets of New York was a far cry from camping in the backyard of the farmhouse.

All in all, things were not turning out at all like Guster had hoped. He couldn't get his mind off that strawberry ice cream, and Zeke was complaining about his feet being sore. Mariah stuck her earbuds in her ears and turned on her music.

The sun was getting low, and the frequency of people walking through the park was getting less and less.

"We could go back to Aunt Priscilla's," said Zeke.

Mariah pulled her earbuds out. "You know that won't work," she said.

"This was such a stupid plan," Zeke muttered. "I told you California would be better. At least we could sleep on the beach there, and there would be movie stars to hang out with, and they have so much fruit there, you can just pick the grapes off the vine and smash them into your mouth until all the juice runs down your chin."

Mariah hit Zeke with her backpack. "Keep dreamin' bumpkin. We wouldn't even be there yet if we'd gone to California."

"What about Bubalatti's?" said Guster. He couldn't get his mind off that ice cream.

Zeke looked at Guster like he was crazy. "What about it?" asked Mariah. "We can't go back there."

Guster shook his head. "No. I know. I just . . . those two men who were re-stocking Bubalatti's ice cream, did you see their aprons?"

Mariah shook her head.

"They were red, like the Gastronimatii," Guster said.

Zeke's eyes widened. "Not possible," said Mariah. "Or, at least, not likely. You remember they were all locked up last summer."

"There could still be some out on the loose," said Guster. Interpol had said they'd rounded them all up, but how could they know for sure?

"Maybe," said Mariah. "But highly doubtful."

"There was just something about that ice cream that tasted—well, far away," said Guster.

Mariah rolled her eyes. "Did you taste danger too?" she said.

"That was real! You saw Yummy just as well as I did."

Mariah didn't have a reply for that. He knew what he had tasted, and his hunch turned out to be true. He was an Evertaster.

At least they were far away from New Orleans. From what little Gaucho had told them of Yummy, it would take at least a few days for Yummy to get to New York. They'd be safe until then . . . he hoped.

"I just don't understand why Bubalatti got so angry," said Guster. "Why would a world-famous pie maker suddenly switch to selling ice cream? I think he's hiding something."

"Could be," Mariah said. "Or maybe he just wanted to

expand his business. It makes sense. Pie goes with ice cream. But there's not much we can do about it now anyway. Our first priority is to find a place to sleep tonight." She stood.

"We could stay in the park," said Guster. It would be just like camping out. There were plenty of bushes they could hide in, and the summer night was warm.

Mariah turned, scanning the park. There were homeless people pushing shopping carts, and a few shady-looking men standing in the shadows of the trees. The sun was setting fast— it wouldn't be long before it was dark.

"Too dangerous," said Mariah. "We need to find someplace inside."

"We could walk the streets all night, and stick to the well-lit places," said Guster. It was possible, but even as Guster said it, he realized how tired he was. He needed sleep.

Mariah shook her head. "We need a place with seats or benches that won't be conspicuous."

"To the subway!" said Zeke, pumping his fist in the air.

Mariah pinched her chin. "Hmmmm," she said. "You may be on to something, Einstein." Her eyes narrowed, just like they always did when she was forming a plan. "If we ride it all night, we can sleep on the long trains, and switch between trains when we get to the end of the line. One of us can stay awake and keep watch. We'll take shifts." She shouldered her backpack.

"Oh," said Zeke, his shoulders drooping. "I meant that sandwich place across the street. It looks like they have meatball ones."

Mariah glared at him. Even if Zeke hadn't meant it, it did seem like a good idea.

The three of them walked back toward Penn Station. This time Guster took notice every time they passed an opening in the sidewalk with stairs that led down to the subway. It bothered him how each one looked like a wide-open mouth, like a snake in a hole waiting to swallow whoever was stupid enough to walk down into its belly.

After several blocks, Mariah stopped at one of the stairways. She took one last look at her maps then waved them downward. "Right here," she said. She tromped down the stairs two by two.

Guster hesitated. By now, it was getting just as dark outside as it was inside the subway tunnels. Zeke followed after her, and so Guster, not wanting to be left alone, went down the steps.

Mariah stopped at a large map on the wall with a confusing tangle of red, green, yellow, and blue lines spanning across the city. There were place and street names at regular intervals, all ones that Guster didn't recognize.

"If we take the blue line all the way to the end," said Mariah, tracing her finger along the map, "we'll have plenty of time to rest. It looks like it takes us all the way out to the airport."

Guster was hardly listening. There was dirt and grime pasted up against the corners where the floors met the walls, and the air felt thick and stale, which made it hard to breathe. The subway rattled and a wall of air pushed over them as the next train came to a stop.

Mariah bought three tickets from an automated teller. It took a few minutes to find the right buttons, and when she finally did the train had already gone.

They passed through the turnstiles and waited on the platform. There were a few dozen commuters on the opposite side of the track waiting to enter the other side of the car as well. It made the whole station feel too crowded for Guster. They were going to have to be fast if they wanted to get seats.

It made Guster wonder where Gaucho was. New York City was a big place. He hoped they hadn't lost him for good. At least Gaucho knew how to take care of himself, big shiny steel helmet and all. He'd probably collected enough loose change in the thing to buy himself airfare back to wherever it was he came from.

Two minutes later another subway car ground to a halt at the platform with a whine and a rattle.

"Not this one," said Mariah, peering up at the LED signs. "The next one."

The doors closed and the train pulled away, revealing a nearly empty platform on the opposite side. All of the passengers had cleared the platform except one: a man in a brown trench coat, aviator sunglasses, and a green felt hat.

As soon as he saw them, he bolted toward them.

Chapter 7 — Vanilla Midnight

"Run!" cried Guster. He didn't know who this man was, or why he was following them. He just knew they needed to get away fast.

They darted for the stairway that led back up to the street. The man in the green hat sprinted for the stairway across the tracks, matching their speed. He would come up on the opposite side of the street, which gave them only a few seconds head start.

All three of them were out of breath when they reached the top of the stairs. Night had fallen, and the yellow glow of street lamps cast a tangle of shadows in all directions.

Guster clutched his cooler to his chest and followed Zeke as he pivoted left and ran down the street.

Without warning, the man in the green hat burst out of the alley an arm's length in front of them. Guster didn't have time to change course and smashed right into him.

The man grabbed Guster's cooler, yanking Guster forward. Guster pulled hard on the handle, but the man was too strong, so Guster shoved the cooler into the man's chest and pushed off, boosting himself backwards.

He glanced over his shoulder as he dashed down a side

street. The man ran after them, his trench coat trailing behind him. Zeke and Mariah had followed Guster's lead, and were right behind Guster, barreling down the sidewalk as fast as they could.

Zeke was older and faster. In seconds he passed Guster, pumping his arms and legs like he was being chased by lions.

Zeke turned a corner up ahead under a dim street lamp. Guster was right behind him. He had no idea where they were. There were dark, red brick buildings, a dry cleaner's with a blue awning, and illegible letters scrawled in spray paint across the walls. There were few cars on the street, and almost no people.

They took a few more turns, trying their best to lose the sinister man in the green hat.

It was times like this that Guster wished Mom were here. Anyone would think twice about giving them trouble with Mom around. She was always so good about standing up to people, no matter how burly they seemed. She had a way of putting them in their place.

But Mom wasn't there. They were on their own.

"Hurry," said Mariah, leading them down another side street. There were no lights there, only shadows.

A single man walked down the side street on the opposite sidewalk. He paused when he saw them.

"Mariah," said Guster nervously, pointing ahead. The big man turned toward them, his massive round shadow crossing the street with him.

We should never have come here, thought Guster. He tugged on Zeke's sleeve.

Just then, the big man's cell phone lit up, showing his round cheeks, curling dark black mustache, and a tomato-shaped nose. He smiled, showing a grin full of tiny teeth. "Hey, it's you kids!" he said.

Guster recognized him right away. "Bubalatti!"

"I'm so glad I found you! This is-a no place for kids, these streets at night," said Bubalatti. He seemed eager to see them. So he wasn't mad?

"We're being followed," said Guster quickly. They'd only met Bubalatti a few hours before, but at least he was someone they knew.

"We don't want you to run into any unsavory characters." He smiled, the blue light from his cell phone shining upward. "I shouldn't have been so hard on you back at the shop. I've been looking for you ever since to apologize. Come back with me to my shop, and I'll give you a slice of pie," he said.

Mariah looked uncertain. Zeke's eyes widened at the mention of pie. Guster did not need convincing. The man with the green felt hat was probably just around the corner; they needed to hurry.

Besides, Guster had never gotten his ice cream cone.

"Yes, that sounds very good," he said, glancing back and forth behind him. "Let's go. Now."

"Follow me then!" said Bubalatti, waving his arm in the direction he'd come. They walked after him briskly, checking over their shoulders to see if they were still being followed.

Bubalatti led them across three streets, took two lefts, circled the block, and passed right by the glowing front window of the shop with the word Bubalatti written across it in golden letters. He turned the corner into a dark, narrow alleyway with dumpsters and trashcans lined up against the walls.

The place was a dead end, which made Guster nervous, but they had little choice. Bubalatti fished into his pocket for some keys and took them out, jingling them as he fumbled until he found the right one. He jammed the key into the lock.

He could not open the door soon enough, as far as Guster was concerned, and when the warm yellow light of Bubalatti's shop spilled out into the alleyway, Guster, Mariah and Zeke shoved their way inside without waiting for an invitation.

The back of the shop was a narrow entryway no bigger than a closet. It was crammed full of boxes and white buckets labeled with black permanent marker: sugar, flour, shortening. There was a large, silver metal fridge too, with a door that looked like it belonged on an army tank. Guster squeezed between boxes. Bubalatti had to slide in sideways behind Mariah and Zeke to fit.

He locked the door shut with a click. Guster heaved a sigh of relief.

"Welcome," said Bubalatti.

"Thanks, Mr. Bubalatti," said Mariah.

"No, no. You can call me Fatty, like my friends do," he said.

On the other side of the door was a small room with a single round table shoved into one corner and two chairs.

Bubalatti motioned for them to sit down. Guster slumped down into the chair with his back against the wall. He could see through an open door into the front of the shop where the glass case with the pies and ice cream was. It felt good to be indoors again, in a place closed off from so many strangers. It felt safe.

"I wanted to apologize for my behavior earlier," said Bubalatti, folding his hands over each other again and again. He looked nervous. "I didn't mean to be so rude. It's just that this ice cream— my ice cream—has been a great change for this shop, and I take-a my creations personally, like they were my own-a children, you know?"

Guster felt bad for him. He wasn't the first chef Guster had insulted, but he hadn't meant to hurt anyone's feelings. He liked the ice cream. That's why he was so interested.

"I tell you what!" said Bubalatti. "I'm-a gonna give you a special treat! A fourth flavor we don't have out on the counter. It's not served to everybody."

Zeke nodded eagerly. Guster liked the sound of that.

"Why not?" said Mariah.

Bubalatti wiped a bead of sweat from his forehead. "Because

it's-a so special! That's why. Heh heh." He chuckled nervously.

"No, I mean. Why not try it?" said Mariah. Her eyes narrowed. She was thinking something, but Guster didn't know what.

"Oh, yes," said Bubalatti. He tied a white apron around his bulging middle and waddled into the front, talking over his shoulder back toward the three of them as he did so. "It's called-a Vanilla Midnight, and I think you're a-gonna find it beautiful!

"When I was a boy, my momma taught me to make-a pies," said Bubalatti. "'Franco!' She says, 'you gotta make-a this pie just like I tell you, and it will turn out just fabulous.' They've been making the recipe in my family ever since, generations before we left Sicily to come to New York. It was my job to make it just a little bit better. That's-a what every generation does before they pass it on." Bubalatti took three plates, each with a slice of peach pie, and set them in front of Guster and his siblings.

The pie smelled even more delicious up close. Guster's slice was shining, the filling glistening like drops of morning dew over golden peach smiles.

Bubalatti set three forks onto the table. "And I think I did my part. Look at this shop," said Bubalatti, spreading his arms out as wide as he could in the cramped space. "It would make my Grandmamma proud, I think. Best pies in all of New York City, those Bubalatti's, they say. And I made the family name-a famous."

He sighed, like a balloon deflating, his shoulders and head sagging. "But sometimes you want to try something new, you know. Like maybe you don't want all those generations of grandmammas and grandpappas and Uncle Guido looking over your shoulder. You want something that they never would've thought of!" He turned and waddled into the front, reached down behind the counter where Guster couldn't see, and came back with a small wooden barrel under one arm and an empty ice cream scoop in his free hand.

"So one day these fellows come to me and says, 'Franco Bubalatti, we got an offer for you that you can't-a refuse.' So I says to them, 'call me Fatty.' They show me what they've got. And just like that, we start-a doing business together. I have to say the money's never been-a so green." He scooped out a gleaming white scoop of ice cream onto Guster's slice of peach pie.

Guster had never seen anything in all the world so white. It was like fresh snow; it was so pure and spotless it glowed and seemed to chase away the shadows in the tiny room. It smelled of deep vanilla, like a mist rising in the room.

Bubalatti finished scooping orbs of white ice cream onto Zeke and Mariah's pie then set three spoons on the table next to their forks.

Zeke did not wait for permission. He drove his spoon like a shovel down into his vanilla ice cream, shoving nearly half the scoop into his mouth.

Mariah was just as eager. She took a dainty bite, sliding the empty spoon out of her mouth as clean as if it had just been washed.

Guster lingered a moment longer, absorbing the fog of vanilla smells that was growing thicker in his lungs. Then he too spooned a large mouthful onto his tongue.

It was sweet and rich, and peaceful. The flavors sent a calm across his body that he could feel down into his toes. Suddenly he wasn't worried anymore about the man in the green hat, or Yummy following him, or even that he'd run away from home. His cares were melting and draining out of him, until there was nothing left but sweet serenity.

"It's called Vanilla Midnight," said Bubalatti. "It's a special flavor we reserve for only certain occasions." The smile left his face. He looked tired, the jagged wrinkles under his eyes deepening, like he'd finally finished with something he did not want to do.

Zeke was nearly finished now, shoveling the Vanilla Midnight into his mouth faster than he could breathe.

Mariah was sitting back in her chair, smiling. She'd eaten more than half her scoop. Suddenly she seemed to be her old self again, her face smooth and relaxed, like she'd grown a year younger.

Guster could feel the ice cream slide into his tummy. He was happy. He lifted each spoonful to his lips more slowly than the last, the moments lingering on as the world seemed to slow to a lull around him.

"Why's it called Vanilla Midnight?" Zeke asked when he'd finished. He hadn't even touched his pie.

"Because when you eat it," said Bubalatti, nodding his head to someone unseen in the front room, "it's like a lullaby. It makes you vanish into sleep."

Two short men with black spike beards and red aprons filled the doorframe. They held three large white canvas sacks in their fists.

That wasn't good. They looked like they wanted something. That wasn't good at all.

Guster tried to push himself up from the table, but it felt like his arms had disappeared. His legs and feet did not respond to his urgings to run. Panic rose inside him. He tried to call out. He had to warn Bubalatti.

Mariah was still, her eyes wide with fear. Zeke's head slumped to one side. Guster could feel his eyelids growing heavy . . . it was hard . . . to keep them . . . open . . .

There was a loud thump on the window in the front of the shop. The man in the green felt hat stood outside, pounding on the glass. Guster's vision began to narrow, but he managed to keep his eyes open long enough to see the man pull off his green hat and tear open his collar. He was thick necked, with hair cropped short like a soldier. Now that Guster could see his whole face those aviator sunglasses were unmistakable.

Felicity's Lieutenant.

He slammed himself against the glass, trying desperately to get inside. To save them.

As the canvas sack dropped over Guster's head, Guster's final thought before he fell into a deep sleep was that he'd made a very, very big mistake.

Chapter 8 — The Last Horizon

There was darkness.

A vibration grew across Guster's back to his head. It was faint at first, so faint that he almost hadn't noticed. His arms and legs were soft and limp until they too began to vibrate with the same mechanical rhythm as his head.

The vibration turned to pounding, and Guster's eyes flew open. He shook his head and rubbed his lids.

He was lying on his back in the cargo hold of what looked like a bus with tiny round windows. There were boxes and large tan canvas sacks piled everywhere. He was propped against one of them.

Zeke was draped across another sack, his mouth open wide. He was snoring.

Mariah was sitting next to Zeke, her back straight, knees drawn up to her chest. She was making notes on the back of one of her maps.

"Where am I?" Guster muttered. There was a low hum as the floor vibrated beneath him. He was so sore.

"In an airplane," Mariah said, pointing to the circle window. "I would've guessed we're flying over Canada, since those mountains are so high, but the sun is rising to our left, so we're headed south. Maybe the Andes? Whichever mountains those are, we've been kidnapped little brother."

Kidnapped? But why? By who?

Memories of the pie shop started coming back to him.

"Fatty Bubalatti," said Guster. It made him angry just to say it.

"Or his goons," said Mariah. "I saw one of them open the cockpit door an hour ago." She motioned toward a narrow door near the front center of the plane. It was lined with a steel frame. "I don't think Bubalatti's on this flight. He probably wouldn't even fit up there."

Guster licked his lips. A slight taste of Vanilla Midnight lingered on his tongue. "How long have we been out?" he asked.

"Not sure. A day? Maybe two," Mariah said. "I think Mr. Cortez Pissarro here can answer some of our questions when he wakes up." Mariah shifted to the side and reached over the sack behind her. She rapped her knuckles on something hollow and metal. *Bong.*

Guster pushed himself up onto his feet so he could see. Sure enough, Gaucho del Pantaloon was lying on his back, his metal chest plate rising up out of the ground like a mound, and his red and yellow striped pants ballooning out from underneath the armor. His eyes were shut. He was smiling.

"Gaucho?" said Guster. "How did he get here?"

Mariah shrugged. "I'm guessing that his cousins there had something to do with it."

"Cousins?" asked Guster.

"Sure," said Mariah. "Those pointy dark beards and mustaches aren't fooling anyone. I know a conquistador's cousin when I see one."

It kind of made sense. They did look like they could be related to Gaucho. Maybe that's why he got so nervous when they first spotted them in the pie shop. He knew them. That's when he'd gone outside to hide, and they hadn't seen Gaucho since. Until now.

"He sold us out," said Guster."

"No. I don't think they're on the same team. Considering this," Mariah said. She held up Gaucho's wrists. They were tied together with a length of rope. "He's as much of a prisoner as we are."

They'd been so stupid. They'd walked right into that trap, trusting Bubalatti based on what? The fact that his pies were so good? And his ice cream? Guster had to be more careful. He trusted his tongue too much, and this time it had gotten them into trouble. Just because something tasted good didn't mean that it was good. Trouble lurked in many forms, and sometimes it was mixed into Rocky Road.

"The Lieutenant—did you see him?" asked Guster. His memory was fuzzy.

Mariah nodded. "I did," she said. "But I wasn't sure if I dreamt it, or if he really was the man in the green hat."

"I think he was following us in case we needed help," Guster said. "Kind of like a bodyguard. He was trying to save us from Bubalatti."

Mariah looked down at the floor of the airplane. "And we were so stupid, we ran," she said.

Now they were kidnapped, flying to who-knows-where, with no idea why. It was times like this that Guster really wished Mom were there.

"But how did he know where we were?" Mariah asked. "New York City is a big place, and not even Felicity knew we were going to be there."

Guster shrugged. They'd gone to New York trying to disappear. Apparently it hadn't worked.

Nothing about their situation seemed to make much sense right now. There were a whole lot of questions that needed answering right away.

"Vanilla," Zeke groaned. His eyes were still closed. He was licking his lips. "So creamy." A big smile spread across his face. He must've been dreaming.

Mariah shook him. "The fun's over Zeke. Time to get up," she said.

"Just one more bowl," he said, turning over and curling up into a ball.

Mariah shook him harder. "Wake up! We've been kidnapped!" she shouted into his ear.

Zeke snapped upright into a sitting position. "Kidnapped?" he asked. He looked groggy. He smacked his lips together and rubbed his eyes. "What will we eat?"

Mariah shot him a disapproving glance. "Is that all you can think about?"

Zeke nodded, then looked around the cargo hold. "Cool. A submarine," he said. "Oh, hey Gaucho," he said, waving at the sleeping conquistador.

Mariah sighed.

Zeke pointed at Guster. "What's that?" he asked.

Guster looked down. His backpack was sitting on his lap. One of the pockets was glowing red.

Without thinking, Guster leapt backward, shoving the backpack away from him like it was full of rattlesnakes. It fell to the floor.

Mariah ducked behind a row of sacks. "What's in there?" she asked, peeking out like they were sandbags.

The glow from the pocket pulsed red, faded off, then glowed red again. When things did that they were usually lasers or explosives or something just as dangerous. This was not good.

"Lemme see," said Zeke.

"Careful. What if it's a bomb?" said Mariah. Guster backed away.

Zeke unzipped the pocket and pulled the glowing thing out. "Nah, it's just a jelly doughnut."

Guster let out a long whistle of air. He'd been holding his breath.

Zeke held the pastry up, admiring it. It was golden brown and covered in a crystal clear layer of glaze. There was no hole in the middle and a small drop of jelly filling peeked out one side where it had been injected into the dough. The jelly glowed bright red through the fried pastry dough.

Zeke shoved it toward his mouth.

"Stop," said Mariah, grabbing his arm just in time. Guster was sure he hadn't packed any doughnuts.

Zeke looked annoyed. "What did you do that for?"

"We've been kidnapped, we're riding who-knows-where in a plane piloted by some conquistadors, and you're going to eat some strange jelly doughnut that someone planted in Guster's backpack?"

Zeke shrugged. "I'm hungry."

She pried the doughnut from Zeke's fingers. "Let's approach this logically," she said. "Guster, did you put that doughnut into your backpack?"

Guster shook his head.

"Was it there yesterday?" Mariah asked.

Guster shrugged. "Not sure," he said. "Probably not." He hadn't checked the pockets very often. He'd mostly been concerned about what was in his cooler.

"Okay, so someone put this doughnut inside your backpack, and those two up there are the most likely suspects. Considering that they're probably not from the Red Cross, and probably not taking us to Happy-Snuggle-Land right now, my guess is that doughnut is bad news, just like the rest of the situation we're in."

Zeke raised his hand. "I told you we should've gone to California."

Mariah scowled. She looked like she was going to hiss at him.

"Fine," said Zeke. "I won't eat it. But I think Guster should." He held the jelly doughnut up to Guster. "You should taste it and do that mind-reading mega-taster thing you do with your food." Zeke pressed it carefully into Guster's hands.

Mariah shook her head.

"It'll give us some clues, and maybe help us figure out where we're going," Zeke said. He was serious. "But only if you want to P."

Guster took the doughnut. "I do."

Mariah threw up her hands, but she didn't object. If Guster had to guess, Mariah probably wanted to know what that doughnut could tell them just as bad as Zeke did.

So he held it up to his nose. It smelled good. The glaze flaked off and stuck to his hands. This was risky, but it was also one way to find out.

He touched his tongue to the squishy, glowing red strawberry jelly drop that had squeezed out the side.

It was cool to the touch, and vibrant and viscous, and, as is always the best part of all jelly in doughnuts, it did not resist—it came easily and willingly onto his lips when he squeezed the dough with both hands.

"Mmmmmmm," Guster sighed. He'd tasted just a drop, but it was delicious and wonderful and very, very familiar. Instantly he knew where it had come from. "Mom made this," he said.

He was startled as he said it and had to turn the doughnut around in his hands to get a better look. How would Mom's doughnut get here? He was absolutely sure now that he hadn't packed this. Its red glow pulsed on again. Mom had never made anything that glowed before.

"That doesn't make any sense," said Mariah.

Guster nodded in agreement. Mariah was right. It didn't make sense. "At least we know it's not dangerous," he said.

"Dibs!" cried Zeke. He lunged for the doughnut.

Guster drew it back under his arm, twisting aside as Zeke

brushed past. "No, we should keep this." He felt strangely protective of it now. Maybe because it came from Mom.

"He's right Zeke," said Mariah. "There's more to it than meets the eye."

There was a clang and rustle as Gaucho sat up and stretched. "Oh," he said, looking blearily back and forth at Mariah, Zeke, and Guster. "I see that I am not the only captive of the Extravío Vigilar." He tugged at his tied wrists.

"The who?" asked Guster. He assumed Gaucho was talking about the pilots.

"The men who have captured us and are taking us away. The Extravío Vigilar, of course," said Gaucho. "Everyone knows them. You know, Mayor Bollito's enforcers and thugs. He calls them guards, but they are really just bullies."

"So you're not one of them?" asked Zeke.

"Oh no!" said Gaucho, scowling. "I would never cast my lot with such scoundrels! They call themselves protectors! HA! El Extravío Vigilar will be the doom of the city!" He swung his arms like a sword as he spoke, his head shaking with anger. "I tell you, if I were in charge of the city, I would fire all such guards!"

Mariah pressed her face up against one of the small circular windows. "I've never seen mountains so impossibly high," she said.

Guster clambered over the piles of canvas sacks to the window nearest her. For the first time since waking up, he peered through the glass. They were flying next to an enormous mountain range. Not over it. Next to it. The ground was still far below them, and the mountains should have been too. Instead, the mountains towered over the landscape, brown and gray rock reaching up into space. Guster felt small, like a tiny gnat flying alongside the gigantic range.

"Gaucho, do you know then where they're taking us?" asked Mariah.

"Home," said Gaucho.

Mariah knelt down and looked him in the eye. Gaucho's sword was nowhere in sight. He couldn't have used it if he wanted to.

"And where exactly is your home?" she asked.

He closed his eyes and breathed a deep, long breath as if calming himself. When he opened them, his face was so serene and peaceful he could no more have lied to them than a baby could fake its first laugh.

"We are going beyond the last horizon, to where the highest mountain in all the earth has touched heaven and absorbed its goodness. In your language they call it the Himalayas. Really, they are the Mountains of Succulence, and they are the cradle of the jewel of the world, the Delicious City."

Just then, the plane took a sudden dive toward the earth.

Chapter 9 — The World's Most Dangerous Runway

Guster lurched backward, grabbing onto whatever sacks or boxes he could find for support. His stomach floated into his mouth, suddenly weightless as the plane fell.

"We're going to crash!" Mariah cried.

Guster clawed his way to the window, past tumbling cargo, and pressed his cheek up against the glass. It was hard to tell where the plane was going from that angle. What Guster *could* see was the valley they were flying through was a dead end, and they were diving deeper into it.

Zeke crawled to the steel framed door at the cockpit and began to pound against it. "Maniacs!" he shouted. "Pull up! Pull up!"

To Guster's surprise, the plane leveled off, the force of the maneuver pushing him to the floor. He pulled himself up to the window again, his heart thumping. The sheer rock wall rose in front of them like a giant that had stepped in their path. It was far too high to fly over now. They were headed straight for it.

Then he felt the plane tilt upward. The engines whined loudly in reverse.

At the foot of the massive rock wall was a smaller cliff,

and, below that, another sheer drop into the valley. The plane dropped quickly, the top of the cliff suddenly rushing up to meet them, then, with a thump and a squeal of rubber, the plane bounced once and finally set all 3 wheels on the ground.

The engines roared as the plane rolled uphill toward the sheer rock wall.

Guster wiped sweat from his eyes. The pilot had actually landed the airplane on top of a very short cliff going *uphill*. The plane braked abruptly to a stop.

"Everyone okay?" asked Mariah. She was shaking, her eyebrows quivering as she fought back tears.

"Yeah. Okay here." Zeke leaned over to Guster. "Are you in one piece?"

Guster nodded. He felt okay. Surprised that they were alive, but okay. He'd seen a lot of landings with Braxton, but never one like that.

Gaucho stood up and shuffled toward the side door that led out of the plane. "Ah, well, it will be nice to see the mountains again." Of the four of them, Gaucho seemed the least concerned about their landing.

"Have you done this before?" asked Mariah.

Gaucho shook his head. "Not landed here, no. But I flew away from this very place. I stowed myself away on an airplane here when I was coming to find you, Guster Johnsonville."

The plane turned off the main runway—which was not much bigger than the farmhouse's gravel driveway back home—the engines shut off, and the cockpit door rattled open.

The two men from Bubalatti's emerged, each with a short, sharp black beard that came to a point on their chins. They were wearing fur-lined boots and jackets. One of them was shorter than the other, with a much stronger build. "Hola, Gaucho," said the taller of the two.

Gaucho faced him and stared, his eyes slanted in anger, his face growing hot red. "Pancho de Pistachero," he said to the taller one. "And you, Camilo de Caramelo. Still immune to the laws of the City, even as you enforce them, I see. Will you always be nothing more than the Mayor's goons?"

The taller one, the one Gaucho had called Pancho de Pistachero, said something back to Gaucho in what sounded like Spanish. Guster didn't need to speak Spanish to know it was an insult.

Gaucho made a reply, and the shorter conquistador, Camilo de Caramelo, joined the argument. Their language was slow for Spanish, even for arguing. It had a steady, humming gait to it, plodding along much slower than any Spanish Guster had ever heard. It sounded like it could be very old.

Pancho de Pistachero made some reply to Gaucho in his strange language as well, which must have made Gaucho even angrier because Gaucho started shouting back at the man.

They shouted a few more angry, very quick words at each other, and then the shorter conquistador seized Gaucho by the arms, pulled a knife from his boot, and cut the ropes binding Gaucho's wrists. He swung the plane's outer door open and held his arm outward.

"Fine, do as you wish," Camilo said, sneering. "There is only one place for you to go."

The two conquistadors grabbed a pair of backpacks and stalked off the plane, shoving their way past Gaucho.

"What was that about?" asked Guster.

"I am a criminal and a fugitive from the Delicious City," said Gaucho. "When I came to warn you, I committed a horrible crime. They have brought me here to justice."

"But they're letting you go?" Guster asked. He had a hard time imagining eccentric but harmless Gaucho as a criminal.

"Well, in a sense. You, Guster, must go with them. They will make sure of that. They told me that I can do what I want, but now that I've found you, well, they know there is nowhere else for me to go but home."

Guster looked out the open door. There were a handful of simple, rectangular stone buildings with blue tin roofs surrounding the runway. A chain link fence separated the airport grounds from a small crowd that had gathered outside.

Next to a gate that led into the village was a polished stone statue of two men wearing old climbing gear. They had ropes coiled around their shoulders and ice axes in their hands. Their arms pointed skyward toward the peaks.

Zeke grabbed his backpack and clambered down the steps. Mariah and Gaucho went with him, so Guster carefully stuffed the glowing jelly doughnut into his backpack and followed.

A crowd had gathered on the other side of the fence, their faces pressed up against the links, staring at the strange new arrivals. They did not look like Gaucho or the conquistadors. Instead, their faces had fuller cheeks and no beards. They were pointing at Guster and his siblings and muttering back and forth to each other.

Zeke stopped at a blue sign hanging from the fence with yellow letters that said "Tenzing- Hillary Airport."

"Tenzing-Hillary?" said Zeke loudly. "What's a Tenzing-Hillary?"

A man next to Zeke in green puffy climbing jacket stopped immediately and stared at Zeke in shock, like he was trying to comprehend that anyone could ask such a stupid question.

"Tenzing Hillary? Tenzing Hillary?" he said in broken English. He shook his head disapprovingly. "Have you never heard of May 29, 1953?"

"I don't think I—" Zeke started.

Another man interrupted Zeke, repeating it louder. "May 29, 1953!"

The crowd around them began to chant, louder still, pumping their fists in the air, like they were at a football game. "May 29, 1953! May 29, 1953!"

Zeke looked just as confused as Guster felt. "Huh?"

The whole crowd erupted in cheers. "May 29, 1953!"

Mariah pointed to the statue. "That's Sir Edmund Hillary and the Sherpa Tenzing Norgay," she said. "They were the first people in history to reach the summit of Mount Everest. We're in the Himalayas, and they're kind of local celebrities around here."

Zeke nodded. "Got it. Kind of like when you go to Graceland to see Elvis." Zeke looked like he was thinking hard when his face slowly lit up. "Or when people show up in Louisiana just to see me play football," he said, pointing to himself with both thumbs.

"Kind-of-not-at-all," Mariah said. She pulled them through the crowd toward a plaque fixed to the base of the statue. "See, May 29th is the day Tenzing and Hillary first made it to the peak." She pointed to a date on the plaque: May 29, 1953.

So this was the Himalayas. Guster took in the peaks towering all around him so high they blocked out the sky. He, Zeke, and Mariah were standing at the feet of the highest mountains in the whole world. They were almost as far as they could possibly get from home.

Of all the places they'd traveled, this one made him feel the smallest and least significant. Like a mouse in a shopping mall.

The taller conquistador grabbed Guster by the arm. "Come," he said gruffly. "We must prepare for our journey. There are many miles ahead of us." He tugged Guster toward the narrow stone path that led between the rectangular buildings.

Guster looked back toward Mariah for approval, but where else would they go? They could try to escape into the village, but it was so small, they'd be found within the hour. The drop was so sheer below them, and the cliffs above so high, there was nowhere to go without climbing or falling. It was like trying to hide on the head of a pin.

And really, when it came down to it, Guster was not going to pass up on this chance of a lifetime—to see the Delicious

City for himself.

"We'd better go with them," he said.

Zeke nodded. "These guys made the ice cream right? I agree."

Mariah frowned. She clearly did not like the idea, but there was nothing she could do.

"This journey will not be for yellow-bellies," said Gaucho. "It will require much of your strength, and all of the courage you possess."

Guster nodded to Gaucho. He was ready. This was what he wanted.

Camilo de Caramelo tugged on Guster again. "We cannot wait," he said. "And it is not yours to decide. The Mayor and the City Council have already decreed that you must be brought to trial."

Guster allowed himself to be led up the stone path into the village. They passed through streets too narrow for cars. Guster doubted there were roads that led up to such a remote, isolated village anyway. The rest of the world was just too far away.

The air was thin up here, thinner than anything Guster had breathed, and as they climbed the short steep path into the village, Guster was surprised how light-headed he felt. No matter how deeply he breathed he just couldn't get his lungs full enough.

Pancho de Pistachero stopped in a small gray building built of cinderblock. The front of the shop was open, with racks of jackets, ropes, and packs hanging from hooks. Pistachero grabbed three coils of rope and a pair of tents, strapping them furiously to the backpacks, while Caramelo collected sleeping bags from the shelves. When Pistachero was done, Caramelo stuffed them into the packs one after another.

Caramelo paid the shopkeeper, his back to Guster, hunching over his payment so that no one could see. Guster thought he glimpsed a stack of golden brown chocolate chip cookies pass between them. The shopkeeper smiled a toothless grin.

The two conquistadors went around the back of the shop, and when they returned they were leading a line of four shaggy brown yaks around onto the stone pathway. The yaks looked a lot like the cows that grazed near the farmhouse back home, but their necks met their torsos in a high hump, their horns curved upward, and their fur hung so low, it dragged in the dirt around their knees.

Several men from the village arrived hauling cargo sacks from the plane on their heads. They harnessed them onto the yaks' backs with coils of coarse, braided rope.

Caramelo and Pistachero directed the work efficiently—they were obviously eager to begin their journey—and in just a few minutes their caravan was ready to leave.

Two women from the shop brought out steaming plates of rice slathered in a bland lentil sauce. Zeke wolfed it down, but it was too plain for Guster's liking, so he only picked at it.

Mariah didn't eat at all. She just leaned back on a bench and covered her eyes from the sun. Her face looked pale.

Caramelo handed Guster a puffy red parka and a large backpack from the shop. "You will need these. The journey is a cold one." He gave parkas and packs to Mariah and Zeke as well.

They stuffed their parkas into their packs—the sun was still too warm for such a big jacket—and shouldered their backpacks.

"We go," said Caramelo. He led the yaks under the strings of brightly colored red, blue, and yellow flags that crisscrossed over the stone path. Guster, Zeke, Mariah, and Gaucho followed, and as they walked the stone gave way to a muddy path, the buildings thinned, and the people were less frequent. It wasn't long before they passed a gate on the edge of the village and stepped foot into the rugged Himalayan wilderness.

Chapter 10 — The Mountaineers

Everything in the vast Himalayan mountain range was, by nature, far away. However colossal the mountains seemed looming overhead, they remained forever out of reach no matter how many hours upon hours Guster, Mariah, Zeke, Gaucho, and their strange conquistador captors hiked toward them.

Whenever they seemed to get close to one mountain range, another would grow up out of the ground, blocking their path and hiding the first from view. It was a twisted maze of ice and cliffs, and of all the places they'd been since last summer, Guster began to see it for what it was: the most impossible and forbidding place on Earth.

On the second day of their trek they crossed yet another swinging suspension bridge that spanned a wide, deep ravine. Guster tried not to look down through the metal grating that was the bridge's narrow floor. Far below was a churning, roiling river of ice-blue water that tumbled over the rocks, charging its way downhill.

The first two nights they slept on foam mattresses in wooden houses that were little more than shacks built on the side of the trail. They ate more lentils, beans, and rice. Some were spiced; some were bland. They were served a sugary, orange, powdered drink with every meal. Guster mostly picked at his food, forcing a spoonful to his lips before spitting it back out again. Zeke and Mariah didn't seem to mind it. He, on the other hand, was going to have to get to the Delicious City soon or he might starve.

He could only imagine the things that the people ate there. If it was anything like what he'd tasted in Bubalatti's it would be more than worth their journey.

The trails were always uphill, and the higher they hiked the harder and harder it got for Guster to breathe. It was like the air wasn't there, no matter how far his lungs reached for it—he just wasn't getting enough. For the first time in his life his lungs started to understand how his stomach felt.

Mariah was even worse off. She needed more rest than Zeke or Guster, and would often stop on the side of the trail, leaning her head forward with her hands on her knees, gasping for breath. At night she complained quietly that her headache pounded against the back of her eyes. Other than the occasional groan, she rarely spoke. Her appetite was very thin, and she seemed to get worse with every mile they climbed.

At one point, they saw a faded map tacked to the wall of one of the wooden shacks. It showed that they were nearly 20,000 feet above sea level. "That's almost as high as airplanes fly," Mariah managed to mutter between breaths.

Caramelo and Pistachero did not make much effort to guard them. They would sleep in shifts, so one was always awake and watching, but they didn't chain Guster and his siblings to anything. It was apparent that escape was even less likely now than it had been in the village. What could Guster do? Try to climb over one of the mountain ranges? That was impossible.

Each night, when everyone but Caramelo or Pistachero was asleep, Guster would hold his backpack close and sneak a peek into the pocket that held the jelly doughnut. Some nights it blinked rapidly. Others, it was a slow, faint pulse.

It made no sense. Was it thinking for itself? He couldn't throw it away, but it made him nervous, like he was carrying a ticking time bomb on his back.

On the fourth day there were no more bridges, just ice and snow with mountains bigger than the world itself towering over them, so enormous they bent over in the sky. The trail had only been a faint impression in the snow for miles now, and Guster couldn't remember the last time they'd seen another human being. Was it yesterday? Or maybe it had been the day before that.

It was getting harder and harder for Guster to drag his legs with each step. It was like invisible stones had been tied to his ankles.

Mariah was struggling too. Caramelo and Pistachero had transferred her pack to the yaks to make things easier for her, but her headaches were getting worse.

Only Zeke seemed unaffected by the altitude. He was slower, that was certain, and probably couldn't run at a full sprint like he could back home, but he didn't complain or show any signs of lethargy or pain.

Guster kept his head down, staring at the backs of Mariah's feet as they crunched along the trail. He wanted to keep an eye on her so he could make sure she didn't stumble or fall behind.

"Here," said Pancho de Pistachero, swerving off the trail. "There is a storm tonight. We wait until the snow comes to cover our tracks."

"Please," said Gaucho, hoisting his pack. "You do not think that we have been followed." The yak in front of him stopped and stomped his foot in the snow.

"We cannot take the risk," said Camilo de Caramelo. "You know the rules of the Sacred City. Just because you have turned your back on it, it does not mean that we will."

Gaucho frowned. These men were from such a strange place with so many different customs, that Guster could not begin to understand why they did what they did.

They pitched tents in the snow right next to the fading trail as a thick, gray cloud rolled over the mountains and swirled around them. They were so high they were actually inside the cloud, and it left Guster with the sick feeling that something very bad was coming soon.

Guster huddled down in his sleeping bag and Zeke buttoned the old canvas tent shut just as snowflakes began to flurry across the snow-covered plains.

"What are we doing up here?" Guster asked in a whisper.

"Whatever they want us to," Zeke said glumly. "We are in the realm of Bigfoot's distant cousin, the Abominable Snowman, who likes nothing better than to crunch the bones of tender boys and their feeble sister!"

Guster found himself wishing Mom were there. She always knew what to do. Or Dad, with his wise sayings. Or even Felicity. She would have her small army of mercenaries. Pistachero and Caramelo would be no match for them.

"I wish we had a heater," said Mariah, her teeth chattering. She looked pale. She was getting sicker all the time.

The wind began to howl, blowing the left side of the tent inward like a sail. Gaucho had helped them anchor the ropes deep into the snow. Guster hoped they held. He huddled down into his sleeping bag.

He awoke to something shaking his shoulder. It was Zeke.

"Get up," Caramelo said. "We go. Now!" His pointed face was peering into the tent door. It was dark outside. The snow was still blowing furiously outside.

How much time had passed? Guster hadn't slept particularly well; it was too cold out for that.

He forced himself out of the sleeping bag, reluctantly crawling out like a snake shedding its skin. "What time is it?" he asked. He tried to wipe the sleep from his eyes.

Zeke shrugged. "I don't know, but it's too early for even

football practice." He was sitting up, his legs still inside his sleeping bag. Mariah was still huddled in her bag, asleep, her face hidden.

"Give her a minute," said Guster, zipping up his puffy parka. He stood and dressed, packing his things as best as he could into brown canvas bags.

"Now!" Caramelo barked. He pulled on Mariah's sleeping bag until she tumbled out in a heap onto the cold canvas they used as a ground covering. Guster helped her get to her feet.

They dressed as quickly as they could. Caramelo and Pistachero packed the yaks with their tents and most of the gear then swatted the yaks from behind. They ran off into the snow the way they'd come from the night before.

"Those are our tents!" cried Zeke.

Gaucho was already dressed and waiting. "We will not need them any longer. From here it is too treacherous, and tents will be of no help to us," he said.

The yaks bellowed and disappeared into the snowstorm. With them went a piece of security.

"This way," said Pistachero. He shouldered a very large pack that was higher than his head. It was so tall it looked like it would topple him over as it swayed with each step. A black cauldron hung from it, swinging in the wind.

Caramelo's pack looked just as heavy and was at least as tall. A few coils of rope hung from it. Next to it were two axes, each one with a narrow, pointed head, the same kind Guster had seen mountain climbers use in pictures.

Guster steadied Mariah and they set out, doing their best to keep pace with Pistachero and Caramelo. Zeke took up the rear, carrying what little they still had with them.

The snow was not deep, not yet anyway, but the wind was biting, and flurries of cold, icy flakes pelted the exposed skin on Guster's face. They hiked on for what seemed like hours, the cloud and blustering snow swirling around them, blocking their view of the mountains.

It was hard to tell if they were ascending or descending. All Guster could do was concentrate on a single step at a time, picking his way along carefully in the storm.

Suddenly, Pistachero stopped short. "Not a step further," he said, "if you ever want to taste sweetness again."

Guster, Mariah, and Zeke halted in their tracks.

Between waves of blustering snow, Guster could make out an icy chasm at their feet, too wide to jump, and so deep that he could not see the bottom. He stepped back from the edge.

Caramelo took one of the ice axes from the backpack and pounded it into the ground. He dug a small ring in the snow, and looped the middle of the rope around the knob of snow left in the center. He packed it down, anchoring the rope, then threw both ends into the chasm where they uncoiled, disappearing from view. Guster did not hear them hit bottom.

"You first," he said, pointing to Guster.

"First what?" said Guster. He was afraid he knew the answer.

"You must go into the crevasse," said Caramelo. Before Guster could object, Caramelo looped an old tattered length of rope around Guster's waist and between his legs, cinching it off in a knot at Guster's waist, so it formed a makeshift harness. Caramelo hooked the harness to a metal carabiner. He grabbed the rope he had dropped into the chasm and clipped the carabiner to both lengths, wrapping them twice around the metal ring, then pushed Guster toward the edge.

"I've never done this," said Guster, digging his feet into the snow.

"You will learn," growled Caramelo. He gave Guster one last shove, sending him backward into the chasm.

Guster felt his stomach lurch and his arms flail as he fell.

The rope caught him.

He was dangling from the edge, the soles of his boots

pressed up against the vertical ice wall in front of him. His head was only a few inches below the lip. Zeke's white face was staring down at him.

"You okay, P?" he said, sounding exasperated.

Guster patted himself with his gloves. He wasn't sure why. Was he checking for damage? He couldn't feel any broken bits. "Yeah, I'm okay," he said, out of breath.

Gaucho knelt down and leaned his face toward the edge. "Pull the back of the rope upward, and you will go down easy," he said.

He was glad Gaucho was there to help. Guster pulled the loose end of the rope upwards with his right hand like Gaucho said. The rope slipped through the carabiner. Guster began to drop, so he let go of the rope and the carabiner caught him, stopping his fall. His stomach lurched.

He shuffled his feet along the cliff face, careful to maintain what footing he could.

The truth was, when he thought about it, he had done this before. In the well at Chateau de Dîner in France. The Lieutenant had hooked him to a cable and dropped him into the well so he could escape. Only this time there was no one to lower Guster, which frightened him.

Guster breathed. Maybe if he only swung the rope halfway, he could slide slowly, and keep himself under control.

He tried it, swinging the rope up just a little. It worked, and he slid foot by foot down the rope until he could not see the top of the cliff any longer.

"Do you see the bottom?" cried Zeke, his voice echoing between the cliff walls and ringing in Guster's ears. Somewhere behind him, the ice creaked and groaned like an old house waiting to collapse on itself.

"Quiet, fool!" hissed Caramelo. "Do you want to bring an avalanche crashing down on him?"

"Sorry!" Zeke squeaked.

Guster felt his heart squeeze in his chest. The ice wall bulged outward just below him, the rope dangling over the edge so that he couldn't see the bottom.

He carefully lowered himself past the ice bulge, which left him dangling in midair. There was nowhere to plant his feet and they kicked wildly into empty space. Luckily, he could now see the bottom of the chasm below him.

He was eager to settle onto solid ground once more, so he slid down the rope the rest of the way without braking at all. His feet hit the snow with a wump, and his knees buckled under him. Luckily, the snow was soft enough to cushion his fall.

He almost shouted to the top, but then decided against it. He did not trust Caramelo, but he didn't want to risk an avalanche either. He tugged on the rope instead.

Gaucho came next, sliding easily down the rope. Clearly he had done this before. How many times had he been here? It had been so difficult to get this far into the mountains. Surely it was a once in a lifetime journey.

They sent Mariah next. Mariah was shivering when she hit the bottom, her face huddled into her hood. Zeke slid down so fast, he nearly knocked her over. The grin on his face made him look like he was actually enjoying himself.

Something tugged on the rope from above. Caramelo or Pistachero were on their way next.

"Listen to me, Señors." Gaucho reached over to grab Guster and Zeke by the shoulders. "You are about to do a very hard thing. One that will take all of your courage to do." His eyes were serious and his mustache curved down with the frown on his lips.

"We are about to enter the Delicious City," he said. "Whatever you do, you must not panic. You must trust me, yes?"

A very hard thing? What could possibly be harder than what they'd already done? Whether they trusted Gaucho

Del Pantaloon or not wouldn't make much of a difference. Pistachero and Caramelo were in charge now. Even if they were to escape, where would Guster and his siblings go?

That set Guster on edge. He was helpless, and he didn't like being helpless. He also hated not knowing what was to come.

Pistachero and Caramelo hit the chasm bottom one after the other. Pistachero yanked one end of the rope toward the ground. The other end flew upward. Pistachero pulled several more times, until he'd pulled the end up and over the ice knob above and the entire rope came tumbling down in a tangled heap. He coiled the rope and hooked it onto his pack.

"This way," said Caramelo pointing toward a crooked, narrow end of the crevasse. The walls on either side were icy blue, bending jaggedly around corners so you couldn't see what was ahead.

They followed Caramelo, hiking carefully over blocks of fallen ice and snow. The cold blue walls formed a shelter from the storm, making the crevasse eerily silent.

They scrambled around one final corner and came to a flat spot where the snow was piled up in soft, white drifts between the walls.

Caramelo held up his hands. "Stop," he whispered. "Here is where we make something delicious to the city. If it accepts our offering, we will enter. If you are brave of heart and worthy, it will accept you. If you are not . . . well, then . . ."

He set the black cauldron down on the snow. He took a bundle of kindling from his backpack and lit a small fire on a flat rock near the side of the crevasse. He set the cauldron on the fire, then opened his backpack and removed what looked like a brick wrapped in a white cheesecloth.

"Now, we cook." He unwrapped the brick. It was a rich, golden-brown color. He tossed the brick into the cauldron, then took several more from his pack and unwrapped them too before dumping them in all at once. In just a few minutes, the contents began to bubble and a rich, caramel smell floated up out of the cauldron and wafted its way over to Guster. He breathed in deeply.

It was good. Too good for something in such a frozen, forbidding place.

"Caramel!" Zeke shouted, his voice booming and echoing through the crevasse.

The walls creaked and the drifts of snow above them groaned as if waiting to shift and come crashing down upon them. Lumps of cold white snow dropped like sandbags and landed heavily at their feet, dusting Mariah and Gaucho's shoulders with a layer of white powder.

"Silence!" Caramelo whispered. "You will bring the snows down on us before their time!"

Caramelo shooed them back with his hands, then prodded the snow around him with the toe of his boot as if testing it.

"Here," he said, nodding to Pistachero. They each shoved their hands into a pair of thick oven mitts, then lifted the bubbling cauldron and poured it out onto the snow in six distinct parallel holes, each two to three feet wide.

The snow sizzled audibly, and a wall of white steam rose up where the caramel melted the snow. The sweet, warm, buttery smell grew stronger and rose softly to the sky like a mist.

Guster took a step forward, transfixed by the golden mixture. The caramel sunk as it melted its way downward, inch by inch. It was carving—no, burrowing—its way deeper into the snow. In less than half a minute, the caramel had melted a hole into the snow. He stepped up to the edge of the hole and peered down into it. It was already several feet deep.

"Cover your face with both hands," Gaucho said. "And whatever you do, do not struggle. You must let the city accept you."

"What?" said Zeke. It sounded like nonsense.

"You will see," said Gaucho.

"I don't understand," said Guster.

Caramelo and Pistachero did not answer. Instead they began to sing a low, sad song in some language that Guster could not understand. It was more moaning than words, and it began to echo through the crevasse, shaking the air and ice. Gaucho joined them, adding his voice to the deep melody.

The cliffs began to creak, and the snow shifted again, dropping lumps onto their heads. Guster pulled Mariah away from the cliff face. Zeke huddled close to them, his face pointed upward.

The avalanche began all at once, snow sliding in sheets off the top of the cliff, breaking into chunks the size of cars as they tumbled down toward Guster and his siblings.

Suddenly, Caramelo was behind Guster, hands on both of his arms. He shoved Guster face first into the hole. Guster fell, tumbling down into the hole as the snow above came crashing down on top of him like a soft, cold boulder.

"Cover your face!" cried Gaucho. Guster put his hands up to his face just as there was a rush of air and a soft wump as the avalanche buried him alive.

Chapter 11 — The Delicious City

Guster fell, sliding and tumbling head first down the long, narrow tunnel that the steaming caramel had bored through the ice.

The avalanche followed him, the snow pushing him with incredible force, like water from a fire hose.

He hit his shoulder, then his back, on the rough-hewn walls as he shot downward.

And then it was over. He hit a soft, sizzling snow bank with so much force it knocked the air from his lungs. The avalanche behind him smashed him into the snow beneath him, as if it were pinning him between two mattresses.

Everything was dark. It was hard to breathe. He was still conscious, his hands covering his face, the cold snow pressing against his chest.

It was crushing him. He tried to kick his legs, but they were pinned beneath the snow. He was trapped.

He opened his eyes, but it was so dark it made no difference, so he shut them again and tried to concentrate on breathing. What was it that Gaucho said? Don't panic. Cover your face. Easy enough for him to say, when all Guster wanted to do was thrash his limbs about and try to climb his way to the top.

He wondered how long until he ran out of air.

No, I have to keep calm. They'll come for me, he thought. They had to have seen what happened. But Caramelo had *pushed* him. Caramelo wanted him buried in the avalanche. Why carry them all this way just to get rid of them now?

Then he started to feel the snow warming at his back. It gave way, just a little. It was shifting, now sinking, downward.

Suddenly, the snow beneath him collapsed, and he fell, tumbling down into open air and dim sunlight, landing hard on something cold and smooth below him.

He gasped, panting and struggling on his hands and knees to find his breath again.

He was in a shallow snow cave, the ceiling no taller than his head if he stood. The floor sloped upward, so he could not see outside, but soft, blue light filtered in through the opening and lit up the ice at his feet. His pulse was racing and his veins were full of adrenaline. The air tasted so good.

"What . . . was that?" Guster asked aloud.

There was a scraping noise above him. Something huge burst out of the snow and fell onto Guster's back, knocking him to the icy floor.

He rolled, shoving the thing off him.

"Oh, sorry, P," said Zeke, getting to his feet. "Didn't see you there."

Guster winced. "Ouch." He'd borne the brunt of Zeke's fall.

A brittle caramel slab clattered away from Guster as he got to his feet. The caramel had frozen as it lost heat melting the tunnel.

"Where's Mariah?" asked Guster.

Zeke shrugged. "I don't know. They shoved me down a hole right after you."

They heard a soft thump above them and a faint whimper.

"I think that's her," said Guster. "Help me dig."

He and Zeke jammed their mittens into the snowpack above

their head, scooping away chunks of hardened snow as best they could. In seconds, the snow broke, and another hardened caramel chunk clattered to the ice floor. Mariah fell into Zeke's arms.

"You okay, sis?" asked Zeke.

She whimpered in reply, her hair caked with tiny ice crystals. Guster brushed the snow from her shoulders. She was shivering. "Cold . . ." she chattered.

They gave Mariah a moment to rest, then, exhausted, they picked their way up the sloped cave floor toward the light.

The shallow cave opened onto a beautiful valley below, where the sun shone with glimmering winks across a vast, green meadow.

Above the meadow on a raised pillar of snow and ice was a golden city, with towers that reached heavenward and arches that spanned across the empty sky, with ivory buttresses and silver parapets, all encircled by two emerald walls that joined at the center in a golden gate.

It was like an enormous castle, an entire kingdom contained within those emerald walls, with so many golden towers and polished ruby spheres that glinted atop the highest golden domes.

The city seemed to glow like it was made of pure gold.

Just looking at it warmed Guster's shaking, shivering body, and, somehow, it made him happy. In all of their travels across the globe, to deep jungle and high mountaintop, Guster had never known that Mother Nature and humankind could collaborate in something so magnificent as what he saw before him in that moment.

Mariah raised her head. Her eyes widened as she peered out onto the shining city. "The Lost City of Gold," she whispered.

"We made it," said Guster. Just the sight of it melted his worries away.

"I'm so . . . glad," said Zeke. He sighed.

Gaucho climbed out of the cave and stood next to them. He smiled. "You like it?" he asked, sweeping his hand out toward the city before them as if pulling back a curtain.

"I . . . I've never seen anything so majestic," said Guster. It wasn't easy to find the words.

"The Lost City of El Dorado, the City of Gold," said Mariah. "Gaucho, I was right all along . . . only, El Dorado was supposed to be hidden in the jungles of South America." She chuckled weakly. "Only it's here. In the Himalayas."

"I told you so," Zeke mouthed behind Mariah's back, but he didn't say it out loud.

Then the breeze shifted, and a cloud passed over the sun for just a moment, transforming the city from glowing gold to gleaming white. The entire city shifted, no longer shining, but appeared as something else entirely.

At the same moment, something sweet on the air touched Guster's tongue, and he caught a fleeting glimpse of the city for what it truly was, as if a fog had been wiped from his mind. Instead of shining ruby orbs, there were glistening red cherries. Instead of emerald walls, there was deep green mint. And when the sun no longer shone on the towers, they no longer glinted gold, but gleamed as white as pure vanilla.

The city was alive with stories and scents of chocolate, strawberry, mint, butterscotch, and marshmallow.

Gaucho chuckled a little and placed a hand on Guster's shoulder. "Not El Dorado, my friends," he said. "The City of Gold is but a myth."

"This is El Elado, the Delicious City. *It* is made of the thing that is most precious in all the world. It is the City of Ice Cream."

Chapter 12 — Mayor Bollito

The cloud passed and the sun shone on El Elado once again, turning it to gold. "I'm going to eat that whole tower," Zeke whispered, his finger pointing to the center of the city.

Guster pressed Zeke's pointer finger down. As soon as Guster had sniffed the city on the breeze, he'd known that's what he wanted too. Despite how cold and wet he was, there was nothing more important in all the world than for him to taste it.

But eating up prime real estate didn't quite seem polite. El Elado was so majestic, so perfect, Guster felt as if they were gazing upon sacred grounds. He could not defile them. He wanted to taste El Elado properly. They would have to go about it in just the right way.

"But this is impossible," Mariah muttered weakly.

"You must believe your eyes," said Gaucho.

"And the storm . . ." she said. "It's gone."

Guster had been so fixated on the city, he had not realized that the storm had passed without a hint that it had ever been. It must not have been able to penetrate the wall of mountains that surrounded the valley. Either way, the sun shone bright and the skies were clear.

"Such sits El Elado," said Gaucho, "in the Valley of Golden Light."

It did look like gold. Down below them in the lush green meadow a dark brown river ran in winding arcs toward the city and shimmering strawberries glinted in the sun like polished red rubies. They covered the plain so that it shone and twinkled as the sunlight reflected off the strawberries' red skin.

Caramelo and Pistachero climbed up out of the cave behind them. They had gathered their cauldron and equipment and stowed it in their packs.

"Look, they are coming to greet us," said Caramelo, shoving past Guster.

Out on the strawberry plains a small procession hurried along. There was a half dozen or so men dressed in shiny armor just like Gaucho's. On their shoulders they carried a small platform. A man in a black suit was seated on top. Behind them were another half dozen men, all dressed in red robes.

They scurried along the plains, darting this way and that down a path that ran more or less parallel to the brown river.

"Come," said Pistachero. "We are received by his Honor. We must meet them." He and Caramelo herded Guster, Mariah, and Zeke down the slope and out the mouth of the cave until they were in open sunlight.

They picked their way down a steep, rocky path that led down to the green meadow. Guster chose his footsteps carefully, keeping his eyes on the ground. Here and there the ruby red strawberries peeked out of the brilliant green grass. The further they went, the thicker the strawberries grew, until soon enough they were standing in a field that was more red than green.

Caramelo halted there and waited as the procession met them on the flat plain. As the procession drew close, Guster could see that the man seated on top of the litter not only wore a black suit, but a black top hat and a shiny glass monocle over one eye. On his left lapel he wore an enormous bright blue and white ribbon that opened like a blooming blue sunflower. In the center was a button that read 'Mayor.' A shiny silver spoon peeked out of his right breast pocket.

He was short, with a protruding round paunch that rose all the way up to his chin. His face was scrunched like a bulldog's, and Guster wondered if at any moment the man might bark out loud.

"His Majesty, the Mayor of El Elado, Mayor Bollito," announced one of the men carrying the litter, breathless. They all set the litter gently on the ground.

Caramelo and Pistachero both bowed deeply. When Gaucho did not, Caramelo pulled Gaucho down into a bow by Gaucho's shirt collar.

The Mayor strutted forward, stepping down off the litter onto the green field. He adjusted his monocle, setting it firmly between chubby cheek and lumpy brow. He stared at Guster carefully for several moments, his eye magnified to double the size by the glass, so that Guster began to feel uneasy under the weight of his glare.

A line of men in red flowing robes encircled the Mayor from behind the litter.

Were they? No, this was too far away for Gastronimatii. They were all gone, weren't they?

These men's red robes were actually woven with parallel strips of red and brown that hung down to their ankles, with sleeves that opened wide at the wrists. On top of their heads they wore a strange flat square, like a thin book balanced on their scalps. The strangest of all was a long, wavy strip that hung from the center of their square caps that looked like a strip of bacon.

Guster sniffed. Salt. Their clothes were made of cloth to look like bacon, but that tassel on their hats was actually real bacon.

They were of all different heights. Most of them were older

than Dad, but some of them were just a few years older than Zeke. All of them were at least a head taller than Gaucho or Mayor Bollito.

Caramelo looked up from his bow. "Your Majesty," Caramelo said. "We apprehended the traitor Gaucho del Pantaloon and brought him back to your custody! We leave him in your hands for punishment."

The Mayor peered down his nose at Gaucho, his eyes narrowing.

Gaucho grinned sheepishly, turning his helmet in his hands.

The Mayor's monocle eye settled on Guster, Mariah, and Zeke once again. "And the Flatlanders?" he asked in a voice so deep and low it sounded like it came straight from his chest.

The men carrying the litter began to mutter one to another. "I've never seen a Flatlander before," one of them whispered.

"Your Majesty," Caramelo said. "We think he's the one Yummy has been looking for. We have not failed you. He knows things from a single spoonful that others cannot ever tell. This one has vision of tongue like we have not seen."

Guster felt his insides turn hot. He'd been too obvious. Is that why they were in this mess? Because he'd given himself away at Bubalatti's?

The Mayor removed the monocle from his face, breathed on it, then rubbed it on a handkerchief. He placed it back on his eye—the right one this time—and leaned forward, examining Guster closely.

Guster could feel the Mayor's breath on his cheek. He stared into the Mayor's scrunched face, trying his best not to look away. He wouldn't let this man intimidate him.

The Mayor reached out a white gloved hand, took hold of a single hair from Guster's head, and plucked it free.

"Ouch!" Guster cried. He covered his mouth. He hadn't meant to let that slip. He was trying to sound brave.

The Mayor held the hair up to his eye, and sniffed. He seemed to be considering it. The men in the red robes surrounded the Mayor, whispering and muttering back and forth over their shoulders to each other and to him. Some of them were even scribbling down notes with feather quill pens on scrolls.

"The Exquisite Morsel," said one.

"Could it be?" said another.

"Evertaster . . ." a third whispered.

How could they know about Evertasters way out here? Guster hadn't heard anyone use that word since last summer, aside, that is, from Felicity a few days ago.

Guster dared not ask. They were so intimidating, standing there, towering over him with their shiny red robes, all standing in a ring like a herd of old goats.

One of them whispered in the Mayor's ear, loud enough that Guster could hear. "Trial by Taste," he said.

The Mayor seemed to consider Guster for a moment, his bottom lip protruding outward like a wrinkled worm. His eyes widened as an expression of realization spread across his scrunched face. He nodded. Then he took the silver spoon from his pocket and pointed it at Guster.

"You shall undergo the Trial by Taste!" he barked in a voice that seemed to reach the mountain tops.

Gaucho stomped his foot. "You can't!" he cried. "It's too much! He's just a boy."

If Gaucho was afraid, this couldn't be good.

"Guards, take him to the mansion and make the preparations," the Mayor said. He looked down at Guster. "You may be just the boon we're looking for." He laughed coldly. "Welcome to the City of El Elado," he said dryly. He didn't seem to mean it.

The Mayor retreated to his seat, then motioned for the litter to be raised up. The men in the colorful robes heaved and hoisted him back up on their shoulders. Then in one motion, they turned back toward the city and carried him away.

"Wow. A mayor," said Zeke, his jaw open. "I've never met

a real mayor before."

The red robes parted, and four soldiers marched through their midst. They carried spears with long, red banners trailing from the end of the shafts.

"Flatlanders," barked the one in front. He unhooked a heavy chain with curved manacles on either end from his belt and clapped them onto Guster's wrists. They pinched his skin as they clicked shut.

Guster did not protest as his wrists sunk to his thighs under the weight of the heavy iron links. They were outnumbered.

The guard clapped Zeke and Mariah in irons too. Mariah was too weak to protest, but Zeke flailed about, swinging his arms this way and that, like a tornado, until three guards finally wrestled him down.

"This way," said the lead guard. He motioned to Guster, Zeke, and Mariah. Two of the soldiers marched around behind them, boxing them in.

"And you." He pointed his spear at Gaucho. "You are under arrest. We'll let the Culinary deal with you."

They clapped thick-gloved hands on Gaucho's shoulders, chained his wrists to his back, and shoved him toward the city.

Gaucho managed to turn his head back toward Guster and give them a sheepish grin. "Sorry," he mouthed.

"This way," said one of the soldiers behind Guster. He and the other soldier herded Guster, Zeke, and Mariah down the path through the meadow, marching them toward the city behind Gaucho.

The men with bacon strips hanging from their hats fell in behind the guards, following so close they nearly stepped on his heels. They were muttering even faster now, scribbling down notes. One even poked him with his feather quill.

"Ouch," said Guster, more out of surprise than actual pain. "What did you do that for?"

The red-robed man behind him looked surprised. Instead

of responding, though, he turned to his colleague and muttered something excitedly. The man responded, nodding his head and muttering back.

"I think they're teachers," said Zeke, whispering to Guster with his hand blocking one side of his mouth.

Guster nodded. It was possible. Anything was possible way up here. And there caps and gowns did look like something you'd wear to graduation.

A sudden look of dread came over Zeke. "What if they give us homework?" he said. He gulped.

The strawberries grew larger the closer they got to the city wall, until eventually they were the size of baseballs. The path that led up to the city gates grew wider, and the way more steep, until the guards herded them up a staircase of rectangular, dark brown bricks that looked like oversized chocolate bars. The higher they climbed the colder the air grew, until they were at the city's emerald-colored wall. Up close it was easy to tell it was made of solid mint ice cream.

The city wall was at least three stories tall with crenellations set into its top, an impenetrable barrier between the outside world and the city within.

A pair of soldiers marched toward its center from either side and stopped above a massive gate. Two enormous light brown doors opened as they approached, swinging inward. It looked like they were made of polished stone, with chunks of smaller rock—wait, no, Guster could smell it. It wasn't rock.

"Peanut brittle," he said.

The soldier behind him grunted. "Harder than granite," he said. "Nothing can break those gates. Nothing gets in or out of those gates without our saying so."

And with that, the four guards pushed Guster, Zeke and Mariah through the gates into The Delicious City.

Chapter 13 — The Streets of El Elado

Inside the peanut brittle gate, the city was like a painting, or a bag of gumballs. Everything burst onto Guster's eyes with so much color and life.

And the smell—it was remarkable. Mint and chocolate and marshmallow, all swirling gently round and round on the breeze. Everywhere Guster turned his face, it was met with new and delightful aromas.

There were people everywhere—many of them dressed in colorful tights with billowing pantaloons and bright orange, green, or blue sashes. Others dressed in old leather boots that rose up past their knees or simple coarse brown tunics, pushing wheelbarrows full of colorful ice cream in every direction. There were soldiers with billowy pants and shiny chest pieces just like Gaucho. There were children throwing balls in the streets. There were men and women talking excitedly in doorways and pointing at Guster, Zeke, and Mariah as they entered.

The street under Guster's feet was made of a translucent golden substance, hard and smooth, like a sheet of nearly opaque glass. The sun bent as it passed through it, giving it an almost golden glow. He stomped the heel of his boot. The street was hard as ice.

One of the guards grunted. "Haven't you never walked down a butterscotch street before?"

Guster shook his head. So that was it. Butterscotch. He always got little yellow disk candies that were wrapped up in plastic cellophane every Halloween. Those were very hard, and Dad had always cautioned him that if he wasn't careful he'd break his teeth when he bit down on one. But hard enough to pave a street? Did that mean that this entire street was—it seemed too impossible—edible? He resisted the urge to get down on his hands and knees and lick the pavement.

"What are these made of?" asked Zeke as they passed the closest building. It was a sphere, like most of the buildings in the city, roughly carved or put together with what looked like hardened green mud. There were windows carved around the sides and a doorway in the center.

"Bricks, of course," said the guard.

Zeke peered at him, like he was waiting for the guard to tell the whole story. The guard didn't say another word, but what they had seen from far away was obvious now that they were close. The buildings of the city were indeed igloos made of ice cream bricks.

It was impossible. Guster had never seen—or even dreamed of—so much ice cream in his life. And now it was all in one place. How could they have made so much of it? And in so many flavors?

They rounded a corner where a mint, domed building stood right next to a chocolate one. A procession of people marched by, clogging the street. There were so many of them they had to walk elbow to elbow to keep from being squeezed out onto the side streets. They were all shouting and cheering, waving pieces of black and red licorice in the air. They must have been celebrating something, but Guster couldn't tell what.

"Halt!" cried the guard in front. He stopped, planting his

spear into the ground and craning his neck over the people in an attempt to see to the other side. There was no room for him to pass, not without charging into the crowd and knocking everyone over like bowling pins.

"Wait here," he said. "I'm going to see what's going on." He turned upstream into the procession, elbowing his way into the crowd.

The other three guards formed a ring around Guster, Zeke, and Mariah, trying their best to block them from melting into the crowd. It would have been next to impossible anyway with their arms chained at the wrists.

"How strange," said Mariah weakly. She was scanning the crowd. "None of them seem to have parents."

Guster followed her gaze. There were kids younger than Guster everywhere, wandering through the parade. They roamed in packs, with no particular adult watching over them. Had Mom been there, she would have made them go home right away.

"Just my kind of place," said Zeke.

A big man in a brown tattered tunic bumped into one of the guards, knocking him off balance. The crowd pressed in around them, pushing them away from the remaining three guards.

Zeke's face broke into a grin, like a pinball machine lighting up. "I'm going to try it," he said, darting away toward a light, minty-green domed building next to a brown chocolate one.

"You!" shouted the guard closest Guster. "By order of His Majesty the Mayor you are ordered to halt!" He took off after Zeke, shoving his way past the big man who'd knocked the first guard off balance.

Zeke was quicker, even with his wrists chained, dodging and darting between people until he broke through an opening onto the street.

Guster saw his chance. While the third guard leaned over to help the first one up, Guster slipped behind the first one, then pointed at the guard.

"Flatlander!" he cried.

The trick worked. Two men and a woman both turned, their heads whipping around with looks of horror, then confusion, at the guard. "Not me!" said the guard, turning toward them and holding up his hands.

That gave Guster just enough time to dart between two villagers in purple robes, double back, and break out into the empty street where Zeke had already dug his hands into the minty green building on the other side.

Zeke scooped out two handfuls of light green ice cream and shoved them in his mouth. "It's better than I dreamed!" he shouted. His eyes grew wide. "It's mint and delicious, and I want to eat the whole town!"

Guster wasted no time. A city made of actual ice cream. He carved a scoop out with his chained hands. It was cold to the touch, like a snowball when you hold it too long. It felt smooth and creamy, like butter. He wrapped his mouth around his coated fingers.

It tasted so minty and delightful; it smelled a bit like toothpaste squeezed from a fresh tube.

A thrill rose inside him, a feeling of excitement that he had not felt in over a year. Oh how wonderful it was! As cold as it was, somehow, it warmed him with the delight of summers past.

Zeke jammed his other hand into the building and scooped off another handful. He shoved that into his mouth, the emerald ice cream melting down his chin and smearing all over his cheeks. "I can't believe it's so good!"

He glanced right, then darted across the street. "Rocky road!" he cried, dashing for a brown house with nuts and marshmallow embedded in its sides.

Guster ran after him.

"Hooligans!" shouted a voice behind him. One of the

guards thrust the wooden butt of his spear between Guster and the house, knocking Guster back before he could reach it.

The second guard tackled Zeke, wrestling him to the ground.

"Mmmffmm!" cried Zeke, his mouth full, his face and chest smeared with brown and green ice cream.

"Eating someone's house?" the guard bellowed as he pinned Zeke to the ground with his knee. "Such savagery!"

The other guard pulled Guster to his feet, and the third guard brought Mariah up to meet them. "We ought to toss all three of you back out onto the glacier to freeze tonight!" he shouted. "How dare you eat someone's house!"

The crowd had frozen in place as they watched.

The guard next to Guster cracked his knuckles and gave a low growl. "His Mayorship might not mind if we give you some brutal justice right here and now, considering what you've done." He closed in, his fist raised.

"His Mayorship is not the only authority here," said a clear, gentle voice.

The crowd went silent.

Guster turned. On the street, surrounded by procession of people with licorice strings in their hands, was a young woman in an enormous bell-shaped pink dress. Her hips were ringed in draping yellow sashes, she had a fluffy whipped cream collar that sprouted up around her neck, and she wore a large cherry-shaped jewel on her head. Her sleeves were the deep red color of strawberry sauce.

She was marvelous and exquisite, and she reminded Guster of the winner of a pageant he had seen once on TV. He knew at once, without anyone telling him, that the parade and the crowd had gathered to celebrate *her*.

The guard froze. He looked over his shoulder and dropped his fist to his side. The other three hesitated, as if not quite sure what to do next.

"But they're Flatlanders," said the lead guard. "And they

were eating this house."

"Mayor Bollito may disagree with me on this point, but what good is a city built so sweetly that it cannot be eaten?" she asked sternly. "I think it more prudent that we treat visitors with hospitality. Have you ever met a Flatlander before?"

The guard shook his head.

"I did not think so. Who has? Surely they have never before tasted things so wonderful as in our Delicious City." She half glanced over at Guster and Zeke and, for a moment, it even looked like she'd flashed a wink at them. "There is no harm done here that cannot be repaired." She clapped her hands once. "Confectioners!" she called.

The guards backed away from Guster, Zeke, and Mariah. Two men in black fur coats with floppy hats and tan tights scurried out of the crowd. They carried trowels in one hand and ice cream scoops in the other. Behind them followed a boy pushing a wheelbarrow full of buckets, each one filled with a different color of ice cream.

The two men stopped at the wall Zeke had eaten, sorted through their buckets until they found a matching flavor, then scooped out a large ball of rocky road and smeared it into the grooves in the wall until it was smooth. Within moments, there wasn't a trace of either Guster or Zeke's feast.

"There," said the majestic young woman. "Now you can be off, and tell your lordship the Mayor that I will take these new arrivals as my guests." She shooed the guards away. "Whatever grievance he has with them can be taken before the Culinary."

"B . . . but," said the lead guard.

The young woman glowered, tilting her light eyes down at the guards until her brows obscured any kindness in her face. "Now," she said firmly.

All four guards picked up their spears and scrambled down the nearest street, the crowd parting to let them pass. The crowd closed around them, swallowing them up until they were gone from sight.

Guster, Zeke, and Mariah were left standing there, captives one minute, then free again the next. The Confectioners unlocked Guster's chains. They fell from his wrists.

The young woman bowed, her bell-shaped dress swinging as she leaned forward. "I am Princesa Elenora Domingo of the City of El Elado," she said. "You can call me Princess Sunday. You are welcome here. I extend to you my protection and my hospitality."

Zeke scratched his head. "I thought the Mayor was in charge."

The Princess laughed. "So does he, but there are those of us who beg to differ. Our city's leadership is—how shall we say this? Complicated as of late."

She had given them a much more pleasant welcome than the Mayor, that was certain.

Mariah slumped down onto the butterscotch street, her knees bent up to her chest. She was panting and shivering.

Guster rushed to her side. "My sister, she isn't well." He put an arm around her shoulder. "I think the altitude has affected her worse than the rest of us."

Princess Sunday knelt down—not an easy feat in such a voluminous dress—and touched Mariah lightly on the chin. "Of course, my dear. You are not accustomed to life near the clouds." There was genuine concern in her voice.

She stood and clapped again. "Confectioners! Bring me a cup of Marshmallow Cheer."

The two Confectioners scrambled away into the crowd. Within minutes they were back, one of them holding three large white porcelain mugs.

Princess Sunday took Mariah by the hand and lifted her to her feet. "Here," she said, taking one of the mugs from her confectioners and placing it in Mariah's hands. "Drink this slowly. It will give you strength."

Mariah held it to her lips and sipped. "It's good."

Her skin began to bloom from pale white to warm pink. It happened so quickly it seemed like the sun had suddenly come out from behind a cloud and shone on her cheeks.

"Need . . ." Zeke said. He reached for the mug in the Confectioner's hand nearest him. "Uhhh. Uhh. Need strength. Feeling weak." He took two rickety steps forward, like his legs would give way beneath him at any moment.

The Confectioner pressed the mug into Zeke's hands and he drank—not with careful sips like Mariah, but in one big gulp like only Zeke, or a hippo, could do. "It's good," said Zeke, lowering the mug. A sticky white marshmallow mustache clung to his upper lip.

The second Confectioner handed a third mug to Guster. Guster held it to his nose and breathed in the heavy marshmallow aroma. The mug was more than half full. The drink looked like a thick liquid marshmallow.

"Go on," said Princess Sunday. "Drink it before it cools and gets hard. It helps with the altitude."

Guster pressed the cup to his mouth. The Marshmallow Cheer was warm and sticky, and as soon as it touched his lips he could feel them tingle. It tasted subtle and reluctantly sweet, like it was calling softly from behind a curtain, whispering its worth. It reminded Guster of the gooey center of a marshmallow just after you pulled it out of the campfire, then stripped off the smoky shell and stuffed what's left between your teeth.

As he swallowed, warmth rose up from his belly into his lungs. His chest loosened and his head cleared, and, within moments, a headache that he hadn't realized was there had suddenly gone, like he'd just switched off a loudspeaker that had been pounding out bass right next to his ear.

Suddenly, he could breathe again.

"I'm glad you like it," said Princess Sunday, smiling. "We'll have a cup every morning, just to be sure you're well as a waffle cone."

She clapped her hands again. Three tall men in red and white striped pants strode out from the crowd. They were so rail thin their legs looked like long, skinny candy canes. They wore shiny, red cherry medals over their hearts, and what looked like oversized ice cream scoops hung from their belts. Each of them pushed a padded green leather armchair on wheels.

"My Cherry Brigade will take you to my castle," Princess Sunday said. "That is, if you'd like to be our guests there."

Zeke nodded furiously.

"We would," said Guster. It did seem like a much better idea than getting locked up with the Mayor.

Mariah nodded her approval too, and was almost halfway to the chair on wheels.

"I'm delighted," said Princess Sunday. "They can give you a ride."

She motioned to the three chairs, and Zeke and Guster climbed up into one each. The padding was soft and comfortable, and it reminded Guster that he had not had a decent place to sit since he'd left the farmhouse. How long had it been? A week? It seemed like years after all they'd been through.

"Thank you," Mariah said to Princess Sunday. Mariah curled up in her chair. The Marshmallow Cheer had brightened her considerably.

One of the Cherry Brigade took hold of two wooden handles that extended from the back of Guster's chair and pushed Guster up the butterscotch street. Mariah and Zeke's chairs kept pace with his, and they all three watched in wonder as they rolled uphill through the city.

Chapter 14 — Princess Sunday's Castle

They passed a house built from pistachio bricks on their left and two more praline houses on their right, then crossed a small, arched waffle cone bridge that spanned the dark brown river.

"Is that made of chocolate?" Zeke asked.

"Of course," said the guard pushing him. "It's the Chocolate River. It flows all the way through the city."

An aqueduct carrying a rich red strawberry sauce crisscrossed over the Chocolate River but never touched it.

"Where does it all come from?" Mariah asked. She'd seemed to gain strength by the minute, and eagerly peered over the edge of her chair now, studying every new structure as they passed. The Marshmallow Cheer was taking effect.

"All what come from?" asked the guard. He looked puzzled, as if she'd just asked him why sun wouldn't shine at night.

"The ice cream," she said. "I've never seen so much of it in my life. You can't ship it in, at least not the same way we came in to El Elado. And there's so much of it, surely such an enormous operation would have been discovered by someone."

The guard pushing her chair laughed as if she were crazy. "HA! Next you'll be asking if we have the snow delivered to the mountaintops!" He shook his head. "Flatlanders. I guess the stories I've heard are true. You really are crazy."

The guard pushing Zeke shot the other guard a look. "Don't be so judgmental," he said. "You've heard stories of those shiny flying birds made out of spoons from the The Extravío Vigilar. You'd probably have questions about those too." He smiled at Mariah. "Sometimes we forget how special El Elado truly is. This is the only place in the whole world—so says the Princess, and I believe her—where a city like this could be built. It's as if history and geography met in this one moment, and that's when El Elado sprang from the ground." The guard sighed. "I am so lucky to have been born here."

"So, then, where does it come from?" asked Mariah. Mariah had always loved questions. She loved answers even more. "I mean the ice cream, of course. You can't bring it from anywhere else, so it must come from somewhere."

The guard pointed up to the largest mountain behind the city. It was a sharp, craggy peak that looked like a jagged tusk jutting up from the ground. It was planted firmly on the far side of the city where the emerald mint walls ended. The mountain was covered with snow and ice so white and pure Guster wondered if it were frozen solid all the way through.

"You see the glaciers over there?" asked the second guard. He pointed to a pair of glaciers high above the city that cut between the mountain range that encircled the Golden Valley. They were like long, gigantic frozen mountains that had carved their way between the peaks and had spilled over into the valley. There was something so forbidding about them, with their columns of ice and mazes of crevasses that made them impassable—the perfect protection to keep the valley undiscovered for centuries.

"Those glaciers change and move every day, like rivers of moving mountains, inching their way past the rock. They're always pressing their way downward, only inches a week into the valley."

"There are strange forces of nature that make such glaciers. Who knows where they come from?" He shrugged. "Somewhere, deep inside that mountain," he pointed again to the largest, jagged peak behind El Elado, "that snow and ice is pressed and churned into something marvelous and sweet and creamy, and it squeezes out of a crack in the ground in a cave at the base of that mountain."

Mariah looked at him like he was crazy. "It comes out of the ground?"

The guard looked at her and nodded. "Of course." Then his face turned puzzled, one eye squinting and wrinkling as he scrunched up his face. "You do have ice cream in the Flatlands, don't you?"

"Well yes, of course, but . . ." Mariah huffed.

"Then it does not come out of mountains?" the guard asked.

"No, it certainly doesn't. It comes from cows and milk and it's . . ." Mariah paused.

The guard seemed confused. Maybe this was like trying to tell someone that the waves on the seashore came from the moon. It really didn't make sense when you said it.

"Most importantly," said Zeke, "when it comes out of the mountain, what flavor is it?"

"Vanilla, of course!" said the guard. "Pure and cold and white, just like the snow it comes from! Ready for flavoring!"

Zeke looked disappointed.

It was so strange, but hadn't Guster and Mariah used to pack snowballs and plop them onto ice cream cones and eat them like they were the real thing back when they lived in Montana? That had been before they'd moved to the farmhouse, and Guster was only three years old. It was one of his earliest memories.

That snow had tasted sweet and pure; it was different from day to day or place to place, all depending on altitude or time of year or how dense the pack was.

But could it be that snow itself could transform in the depths of a mountain and flow out like lava as pure ice cream?

Guster wanted more than anything to see the source, to touch the ice cream that pressed up out of the ground inside the cold and forbidding mountain.

The Cherry Brigade crossed another waffle cone bridge and turned onto a street that left the houses and buildings behind and zigzagged up a steep blueberry ice cream mountain. At the very tip top was an ivory, vanilla castle with seven towers that shimmered in the golden sunlight.

The castle was a remarkable sight, with cherries set into the towers' pinnacles like gems, intricate marshmallow designs inlaid into the walls, and fluffy white dollops of whipped cream sprouting across the gardens like bushes. There were waffle cone tile roofs, and strawberry ice cream masonry lining the corners of the ramparts and buttresses. Altogether, it was a masterfully made Ice Cream Sundae set on top of the mountain.

They crossed a peanut brittle drawbridge that had been lowered across a bubbling marshmallow moat, passed through a keep lined with orange sherbet, and came to a stop inside a courtyard brimming with raspberries, blueberries, and blackberries set into cloudbursts of whipped cream.

The guard set Guster, Mariah, and Zeke down in the courtyard. Guster hopped from his chair. Zeke reached out a hand and scooped some whipped cream and berries from the nearest bush. He mashed them into his mouth, leaving a ring of whipped cream around his lips.

"I see you're hungry, sir," said one of the guards. "Good. We are just in time for lunch." He led them through an open pair of doors into what looked like a banquet hall.

Warm light streamed through rows of red stained glass windows that smelled like spice. If Guster had to guess, he would've said they were cinnamon.

In the center of the room was a table filled with double and triple-decker sandwiches, apples, roast beef, and crackers and cheeses of all kinds. In the center was a large banana split taller than Guster, with a shiny red cherry as big as his fist.

"Go ahead," said the guard. "Eat up."

Zeke was the first to dive in. Guster followed carefully after. It was all very, very good. He had not eaten a really good meal since he'd left home, and this was enough to make him forget, if just for a moment, how much he really missed Mom's cooking.

When they were finished, they rested on soft benches while Zeke dozed. El Elado was such an amazing place, Guster doubted that his dreams could conjure anything more wonderful.

***

Guster awoke hours later. One of the guards was shaking him gently. Zeke and Mariah were standing at the open door, gazing out into the courtyard at an open-top carriage inset with candy that glittered like precious jewels. It was hitched to four yaks.

Princess Sunday was seated inside, a smile on her tiny face. Guster hadn't noticed how young she looked, her face tapering at the chin like the point of a lemon drop, her features as smooth as a polished white peppermint. "Would you like me to show you the city?" she asked.

Guster rose from the bench and followed Zeke and Mariah into the courtyard. "Very much," said Zeke. The three of them climbed into the coach, and the yaks pulled them out of a gate at the back of the castle, across the marshmallow moat, and out onto a narrow path.

"Is everything here made of ice cream?" asked Zeke.

"Almost everything. It's the one thing we're not running out of. The mountain gives it to us, and our Confectioners shape it and mold it into our houses and meeting halls. Of course, the city is covered in it since it flows from the mountain."

"I am glad you are well and fed," said the Princess, "because we have important and dangerous matters to discuss."

Danger? Guster hadn't considered that anything might go wrong, not now that they were in the Princess's care. They'd come to a city like none other, a place that so many had tried to find, but no one had ever come close. This was the final destination. There was nowhere further they would ever need to go.

"What kinds of danger?" said Mariah coldly. Despite all the wonders and delights, she held an air of skepticism, as if she did not quite believe what the princess had shown them.

"The Trial by Taste," said Princess Sunday. "I sent my Guard into the city to listen and learn what they could of the Mayor's intentions. It is a tradition as old as El Elado itself, and there is nothing I can do, even as the ruling royalty here, to stop it."

Guster felt his chest tighten. "What exactly is it?" he asked.

Princess Sunday frowned. "It is a challenge designed to identify your true character, Guster. In the Trial you will taste wondrous things. Perhaps more than your imagination can hold."

That didn't sound so bad. But the Princess wouldn't know what amazing flavors Guster had tasted in the last year. How could she? "Doesn't sound like a problem to me," said Guster.

The Princess looked sad. "That is not all. Some of the tastes will be wonderful. Others horrible. The most powerful ones may alter your sense of what is real."

Guster shuddered. "If it's a trial, then someone must want to find me guilty."

"I suppose that depends on you. The purpose of the Trial by Taste is to see if you are a pure enough food to be sacrificed to the Yummies—to see if you truly are the Exquisite Morsel. If you do prove worthy, that will be the outcome."

Guster frowned. "So if I pass the test, I get eaten? What kind of reward is that?"

Princess Sunday looked down at her shoes. "Not a very good one, I'm afraid. There are complex forces at work in El Elado. We live in a divided city Guster." She swept her arm toward the buildings below.

There was a patchwork of flavors and colors so beautiful it looked like a tapestry. There were green mints with fluffy marshmallow globs, bright fruity blues, yellow sorbets, and dark fudges so brown they were nearly black.

With all that variety, there was an obvious pattern: a dark, chocolate-colored crescent on the outer ring closest to the plains surrounded a small, rainbow-colored oval on the mountain side of the city where their carriage was parked. The Chocolate River carved a border between the two neighborhoods.

"The Mayor controls the majority of El Elado, the chocolate-and-nutty-flavored neighborhood. It's called the Chocolate Crescent," said Princess Sunday. She pointed. "And here, immediately surrounding my castle, is the last circle of fruit flavors—the Fruitful Streets. That is where the citizens loyal to me live."

Zeke pointed to a lighter colored yellow-brown block in the Chocolate Crescent. "So the Mayor controls the cookie dough too?" he asked.

"I'm afraid so, yes," said the Princess.

Zeke looked crestfallen. "We have to get it back," he said, balling his hand up into a fist.

"I wish it were so easy," said Princess Sunday. "The people are free to pass between neighborhoods, but they generally don't. They've grown accustomed to avoiding each other." She sighed. She sounded sad. "When we found you, it was a special day of celebration. That's why we were in the Chocolate

Crescent."

"Wait, so you're telling me that no one here eats choco-chunk strawberry ice cream?" asked Zeke.

The guard driving the carriage snorted.

Princess Sunday shook her head. "I'm afraid that is true. There is such a division between neighborhoods that if the Culinary did not intervene, there would be all-out war."

She turned to Guster. "People are afraid. There are a lot of citizens of El Elado who want you to be the Exquisite Morsel very badly, Guster. They think that if we feed you to the Yummies, that will satisfy them and they won't leave ever again. They'll protect our borders and keep us safe."

Guster's stomach sank. They'd come halfway around the world to run away from a monster and ended up right in its den. What luck. Now Yummy was coming to devour Guster.

"Just how many Yummies are there?" asked Guster.

"Thirteen," said Princess Sunday.

Thirteen? Guster had been fixated on the one that found the farmhouse. This was so much worse.

"How long until the Yummies get here?" asked Mariah.

"A week. Maybe just a few days," said Princess Sunday. "He was prowling before, tracking you meticulously across the world. Now that he has locked onto your scent, he will come straight here. When Yummy knows what he wants, he can run swiftly."

Mariah shook her head. "But it doesn't make sense. We've traveled by train and plane. We've passed through New York City. We've flown over the Atlantic!"

"Yummy found you before. He will find you again. Besides, Caramelo and Pistachero are loyal to the Mayor. They want you to be the Exquisite Morsel, Guster. That's why they brought you here in the first place. No doubt they left all sorts of clues for Yummy to find. They will have made it easy for him to track you. He'll get here. I wish I could say that he wouldn't."

Guster looked away from the princess. She did seem sincere in her concern for Guster, but he just didn't like hearing about how half the city wanted him to die. There was no way to look at that with rose-colored glasses.

The carriage rolled down a path lined with red, yellow, and green gumdrops the size of basketballs. The sugar crystals on their gummy surfaces glinted like glass in the sun. Even the breeze was alive with flavor. Guster turned his face to the sun. Though it was cold, the air was crisp and his jacket warm. Under any other circumstances, he would've called the day pleasant.

"Hold!" cried the driver.

The yaks slowed. Down the slope, a section of the road was missing. It looked like a large chunk of it had broken off and sunk into the ground, like a giant had smashed his fist into the road from above.

"Sinkholes, My Lady," said the driver.

Princess Sunday sighed. She turned in her seat and scanned the road. "Find a way around, please."

"They are growing more frequent," she said. "And more dangerous. The roads are not the worst of it. There are entire buildings in the city that have disappeared into the ground, leaving families homeless—the ones that escape, that is."

"But what causes it?" asked Mariah. "Is it an earthquake?"

Princess Sunday shook her head. "No. The ground shakes and trembles, but the destruction happens in a very small area. If it were an earthquake, it would likely affect the entire city."

"Then what?" asked Guster.

"I am not sure," said Princess Sunday. "There are many citizens of the city who believe that when the Yummies are satisfied, the destruction will end. That's why they want an Exquisite Morsel."

"That sounds like superstition to me," Mariah scoffed.

The Princess frowned. "Look around you," she said, turning

both hands out toward the creamy landscape. "Isn't that what you would have called this place before you saw it?"

Mariah opened her mouth to say something, then must have decided against it. She settled back in her chair.

"The tremors started one year ago, about the same time that the Yummy fled the city and went into the wide world. It's not so unreasonable to believe there is some connection."

"Correlation is not causation," Mariah whispered.

Princess Sunday raised one manicured eyebrow, tilting her head and cherry crown ever so slightly. "It is not. But it leads one to wonder," she said. "And try telling that to the people. They are afraid. They are looking for answers. They listen to the Baconists."

"The who?" asked Guster.

"The Baconists. They wear the red robes, always with a strip of bacon dangling from their hats. They are the self-appointed scholars in El Elado."

"We saw them with the Mayor when we arrived at the city," said Guster. "They smell salty."

"That is them," said Princess Sunday. "They have convinced the people that they are the only source of true intelligence and wisdom in El Elado. I think the Baconists have too many of our people fooled."

The carriage picked its way carefully around the sinkhole, the driver steering the yaks off the hard-packed candy cobblestone and into the creamy, purple mud. He gave the sinkhole's crumbling sides a wide berth, which Guster appreciated, especially after peering down into the deep pit left where the road had once been. The bottom was a long way down.

Princess Sunday clapped her hands once at the driver. "Come, we must get you back to the castle. Guster, you have to rest before tomorrow. The Trial by Taste will be exhausting, and I want you to be prepared for what will follow."

The driver slapped the reigns. The yaks lumbered forward,

then turned back up another narrow street toward the castle.

"What if Guster is found innocent?" asked Mariah.

Princess Sunday looked away. "I wish that were possible. The Trial does not find people innocent. Either Guster is the Exquisite Morsel, and he will be fed to Yummy, or he is not."

"What happens if he is not?" asked Mariah.

Princess Sunday looked into Guster's eyes. "You will be cast out of the city and left on the mountaintop to die."

A lump formed in Guster's throat.

"I may have had power to rescue you from the Mayor's guard, Guster, but I cannot defy the Culinary," said Princess Sunday. "Their decree stands. Tomorrow you will undergo the Trial by Taste, and there is nothing I can do to stop it."

***

Guster could not sleep. He stared up at the marbled blueberry ceiling, trying to muster the courage for tomorrow.

The only problem was that he had no idea what tomorrow would bring. The Princess was mostly silent about what would actually happen during the Trial by Taste, despite his many questions. All Guster could gather is that it would test his character somehow, and that, as Mariah had described it when they got back to the castle, it sounded like a witch trial. There was no way to win.

He sat up in his bed and threw back the thick quilts. The city of his dreams was quickly turning into a nightmare.

It was time to get out.

Guster pulled on his woolen trousers and socks and buttoned up his parka. Princess Sunday had left their packs with them; he could use his for the journey. But where would he go? He could hide. He could try to hike back to civilization, as impossible as that seemed.

He grabbed an extra sweater and three pairs of socks Princess Sunday had given him. He'd have to go into the mountain.

He unzipped his backpack. The red glow of the jelly doughnut spilled out onto the room, casting an eerie crimson sheen across the walls and floor like a submarine's cabin. It was pulsing faster now than ever before—as fast as Guster's heartbeat.

He'd almost forgotten about it with all that had happened since they'd arrived in the city. Where had it come from? Was it a gift or curse?

If only Mom were here. She would know what to do. Guster tucked the jelly doughnut back into his backpack. If worst came to worse, he could still have it for a snack.

He pulled on his boots and tiptoed past a snoring Zeke into the corridor. One of the Cherry Brigade stood watch at the end of the hall, his back to Guster. The guard was there to keep people from getting in rather than to stop Guster from getting out. Guster snuck carefully down the hall in the opposite direction. He turned left then took two rights until he was at the banquet hall that opened onto the castle courtyard.

There were still sandwiches from that night's supper on the long wooden table. He stuffed three of them into his pack and unlatched the door leading into the courtyard.

It was very cold. The frozen strawberry ice cream walls and ground twinkled in the moonlight.

Three guards patrolled the top of the castle walls. Guster waited until their backs were turned, then darted to the nearest shadow. He paused and then ran for a nook in the wall next to the drawbridge.

The drawbridge was shut tight. He'd have to find another way out. He slunk along the wall, his pack pressed up against the cold ice cream bricks.

Just then the drawbridge opened, the chains click-clacking around enormous gears as it lowered slowly. Guster froze.

As the golden light of dawn began to peek over the mountaintops and warm the butterscotch streets and ivory towers, a procession of men armed with spears and burning torches marched across the drawbridge into the courtyard. There were dozens of them with shining armor chest plates and bright red pantaloons.

At their head was a line of men dressed in bacon robes with square caps. And in front of them was a short, pug-faced man with one monocle and a bright blue ribbon hanging from his chest.

They stopped when they reached Guster. "Hello," said the Mayor, peering at Guster with his gloved hands clapped together. "I hope you weren't leaving. We have an appointment, after all." He smiled smugly. "We are here to escort you to your Trial by Taste."

The time had come.

Chapter 15 — Trial by Taste

Guster stood in a grand chocolate amphitheater in the chocolate district. Both his wrists were chained with heavy irons to a platform. It was past noon.

What must have been the entire city was gathered there, sitting on rows of curved chocolate slabs, each one higher than the row in front of it, all of them ringing the platform in the center where Guster stood. Some of the citizens looked hungry, like they were eager to see Guster fail. Others had pity in their eyes.

Princess Sunday and her Cherry Brigade sat to Guster's right on the row closest the platform. Her Confectioners were with her. A sour expression covered her face.

Zeke and Mariah sat on either side of her portable throne. Mariah looked worried.

To Guster's left, the Mayor sat on a raised platform. His black top hat was polished with oil so that it shone. He was surrounded by the Baconists, and below the platform, a dozen of his Guard kept careful watch, their spears raised. More guards lined the exits to the amphitheater.

Whatever the result of the trial, there was no way for Guster to escape its verdict.

In between Princess Sunday's throne and the Mayor's box sat a row of thirty or more men and women, all in extraordinary, colorful costumes with ruffled white collars that looked like whipped cream had squirt up out of their necks. They wore small caps with feathers stuck in them. Many of the men wore bulging yellow pantaloons that made them look like they had bananas for thighs. The women were clad in bell-shaped red or black dresses woven from fine strands of licorice. Each of the people in that row had something pinned over their heart, either a shiny strawberry medal or a square of chocolate turned on its side so that it looked like a diamond. Some of the strawberries or chocolate squares were studded with marshmallows.

The largest of the men rose to his feet. He wore a bright green costume with banana-yellow pantaloons. "As the Chancellor of The Culinary, the rightful legislature of El Elado, and the mediator in all things, I hereby grant you permission to begin."

The Culinary. Princess Sunday had said that their word was law.

The Chancellor waved his hand in a circular flourish, and a Baconist with nostrils as wide as dimes rose to his feet.

The Baconist sniffed. He hefted an enormous leather-bound book onto the podium. It landed with a thud that seemed to shake the entire audience. He opened it, then read in a lofty, droning voice, "By decree of the established laws of the Delicious City of El Elado, the Flatlander Guster Stephen Johnsonville, being suspected of being the embodiment of the Exquisite Morsel shall—according to the peer-reviewed research and the collected, irrefutable wisdom of the Baconists contained in this volume, and by tradition and by vote of the Culinary and his Majesty the Mayor of El Elado—now undergo the Trial by Taste."

The Baconist closed the book. "Confectioners, you may present the goblets."

Drums echoed at regular, slow beats in the amphitheater.

Three men in floppy hats and short, furry capes scrambled forward, their legs turning furiously. Each had a shallow, wide-brimmed metal goblet in his hands.

They placed the three goblets on a low table in front of Guster, one bronze, one silver, and the last gold. From where he was chained, Guster could not see their contents. They then set the table with three spoons, one next to each goblet.

"The Suspected will now consume the flavor in the bronze cup and describe how it tastes," said the Baconist.

The drums stopped.

Was that it? Guster would tell them what he tasted, and this Baconist referee would tell him if he was correct? There was something far too simple about that.

One of the Confectioners handed Guster the spoon next to the bronze goblet and lifted the goblet toward Guster's chin.

The goblet held a single scoop of pure white vanilla ice cream so delicate it looked like it had fallen from the clouds.

The chains were loose enough that Guster could lift his arm. He set his spoon into the ice cream.

Every eye in the amphitheater was focused on him. It was so quiet, he could hear the mountains creak with age.

He pressed the spoonful of vanilla ice cream to his lips. It was so pure and simple, sweet and sure. It was like taking a bite from a snowball. He felt it seep into his neck, his shoulders, his chest, and then his bones.

It made him . . . what was that feeling? . . . happy. He unzipped his warm puffy parka with his free hand and turned his face toward the sun. It had grown warmer now. It must have peeked out from behind a cloud, the way it shone so warm and strong on his cheeks.

The Confectioner nearest him spoke. "Go on. Tell us how it tastes."

Guster opened his eyes. Now what would he say? How could this be a trial? It tasted wonderful. "Clean. It tastes warm and clean and . . . sure. It tastes sure," said Guster. He slid his coat off his shoulders and let it dangle by the sleeves from the iron chains.

The audience let out a mild gasp, then a low hum and chatter. The Baconists scratched notes furiously onto their scrolls with feather quills. What had he said?

The ice cream was good. What else mattered? How could that prove anything?

And yet, the faces in the crowd were waiting for something. . He felt a bead of sweat slide down his forehead. His neck felt hot.

"Interesting," said a Baconist next to the Mayor.

Interesting? Guster would have to be careful what he said about the next taste.

"Next goblet!" announced the Baconist.

Princess Sunday leaned forward in her seat. She bit her lip. She looked as nervous as Guster felt.

"The Suspected will now consume the flavor in the silver cup and describe how it tastes."

The Confectioner handed Guster the spoon next to the silver goblet and held the goblet out to Guster so he could see. Inside was a scoop of sparkling peppermint ice cream.

Which jurisdiction did peppermint fall under? Perhaps he wasn't meant to know. Maybe that was part of his test.

Guster took a bite. It was cold to his lips, and as soon as he tasted it, he shivered. The sun darkened just a little, and the air grew chill.

It was good—the best peppermint ice cream Guster had ever tasted. Whoever had made it had been . . . sincere. Yes, that was it. Sincere and perhaps a little afraid. Was he doing it again? Was that really someone's emotions he was tasting? It was just a hunch, but he thought he could taste their true intent, and they were . . . concerned.

He opened his mouth to speak. He would tell them it had a

dull nutty flavor with a sharp, sweet aftertaste. "It's . . ."

Something stirred at the top corner of the amphitheater. Guster turned. Up on the top row, an enormous shadow shifted, stalking methodically behind the people seated there. It was hard to make out its features from so far away. It looked like it had no head, just a solid mass of fur and arms, lumbering over toward the aisle that descended between the rows.

Guster dropped his spoon. The light caught the shadow, and it faded from black to gray as it slowly descended, its long, stout arms jerking back and forth as it stalked.

Yummy.

"No!" cried Guster. He pulled on the iron chains with both arms, struggling to free himself, the metal biting into his wrists. Why weren't they running? Didn't they see it?

"Mariah! Zeke!" shouted Guster, his breath bursting from his lungs. "Run!"

Mariah and Zeke turned in their seats and looked up the steps. But they did not run.

More shadows emerged from the back of the amphitheater. One from the left corner. Two more from the right. A fifth from the center. There were more. Of course there were more. The Princess had said there were thirteen in all.

The Yummies stalked downward between the people, more like rolling billows of smoke than tangible flesh and fur. The monsters' mouths opened all at once in gaping, hollow voids.

Guster yanked again on the chains. "Let me go! They're coming!" he cried, pleading to the Confectioner.

The Confectioner cocked his head sideways. He looked puzzled.

"There!" said Guster, pointing to the monster that was already at the bottom of the steps.

The Confectioner turned to look. His head scanned back and forth across the crowd, right where the monsters stalked. He shrugged, then looked back at Guster. "Where?"

Then, as the first of the Yummies reached the bottom step, he began to fade. He stalked forward, slowing down as he came closer to Guster, until, finally it reached out one gigantic clawed paw, turned to mist, and was gone.

Guster shook his head. "Did you see . . . ?" The Confectioner's blank face already told him he hadn't.

The crowd was silent for half a moment, then all at once burst into a roar of conversation. People in the crowd were yelling and gesturing to each other, pointing at Guster and then up at the top steps where Yummy had been. One of the men in the third row stood. "I told you it was him! He's the Exquisite Morsel!" The woman next to him shook her head and pulled the man back into his seat.

The Baconists were standing, some of them shaking each other with excitement. The others were scratching notes furiously on their scrolls. The Mayor glanced over at Princess Sunday, who was sobbing. A slow, malicious smile spread across his face. Whatever it was that the Mayor was hoping for, Guster had done it. He'd fallen into their trap.

The head Baconist with the pointed nose held up both arms for silence. The crowd calmed almost at once. They were eager for more.

"The description of the taste by the Suspected has been duly noted," said the head Baconist. Guster hadn't even told them what he thought. This test was less about the flavors and more about what he saw. Felicity had been convinced that Guster could taste a chef's intentions and emotions in the food that they'd prepared. Was that what this was about?

Then who had made the peppermint ice cream? Were they trying to scare him?

He looked to Princess Sunday. She looked at Guster with pleading eyes. "I'm sorry," she mouthed at him. The ice cream must have been hers.

Fear. Worry. Concern. That's what he had tasted before the

vision of monsters came. Princess Sunday was worried that the Yummies were going to eat Guster up.

"Next goblet!" cried the Master Baconist. "The Suspected will now consume the flavor in the golden cup and describe how it tastes."

The third Confectioner held the golden goblet up for Guster to see. Inside was a light-yellow butterscotch flavor. Guster took the final spoon.

He had to think. He'd played into their hands twice already. Now he *had* to find a way to prove his innocence. He hadn't left home to save his family and traveled all the way to a lost city high in the Himalayas just to die when Yummy finally came to eat him up.

He took the spoon and dipped it into the butterscotch. It was strange how none of the flavors were either fruity or chocolate. They couldn't be linked to the Princess or the Mayor. It was as if all three scoops were intentionally neutral. Why? Were they worried he would know who'd made them? Did everyone else there know who had made each of the scoops?

He pressed the butterscotch to his lips. Mmmm. It was buttery and rich. This one tiny spoonful held far more butter taste than entire bowlfuls of most ice creams. It was strong and good and . . . false. He swallowed.

The audience's expressions changed. They went from jeers to smiles. Their faces softened. They looked on Guster with fondness, much like Mom would have before tucking him in at night.

A short man in a white chef's hat stood up in the second row. Long, white hairs stuck wildly out from under his hat, and he wore a navy, blue bathrobe and slippers. He shuffled into the aisle and lifted a large, red three-tiered cake lined with silver beads. He was very old and looked very familiar.

Renoir. The chef Guster had met in the abandoned Patisserie in New Orleans so long ago. Renoir had given Guster his first taste of the gourmet world. He had been the one to change Guster's life.

What a fond memory. Such happy times. Renoir brought the cake to the bottom step and held it up to Guster.

Hadn't he been killed by the Gastronimatii?

Guster shook his head. No. This was a vision. This was what someone wanted him to see.

Now he understood. Falsehood. Flattery. That's what he'd tasted before the vision began. That was the intent of whoever had made this flavor. They wanted Guster to see something he loved. They wanted to see how susceptible he was to the ice cream's influence. They wanted him to incriminate himself.

They hadn't counted on him seeing deeper. If the peppermint flavor was made by Princess Sunday, then this butterscotch had to be Mayor Bollito's ice cream.

The vision of Renoir faded into mist.

So they wanted to know what he saw, did they? He could give them something to talk about.

He stood up tall, his back straight, and pointed his spoon like a sword at the Mayor. "I see a devil in our midst, with a black heart and clouds of gloom gathering over his head!" he shouted.

The crowd gasped. The Culinary burst into conversation, some pointing their fingers toward the Mayor, others whispering behind their hands and shaking their heads.

The man in the crowd who had yelled at Guster leapt to his feet. "I knew it!" he cried. "Mayor Bollito will ruin this city before he's through!"

The woman next to him yanked him down again. She looked afraid.

There were people rising to their feet, yelling. The Baconists were shaking their heads. Some of them were throwing up their hands and arguing with each other. "Boooo!" cried someone in the back row. Others cheered.

The Mayor rose to his feet and stood atop a stool, so he could be seen. His face was creased with anger. "Guards!" he shouted above the crowd. "The accused is a disruptor of the peace and a danger to our Delicious City! I demand he be executed! Guards!"

"You can't!" shouted Princess Sunday. She rushed to the edge of her box.

Next to her, Mariah looked afraid.

Guster's bluff had worked far better than he could've guessed. He had wounded the Mayor's pride.

Two of the Mayor's guards unlocked Guster's chains from where they were bolted into the ground. Another line of armed guards surrounded Princess Sunday's box, their spears pointed toward her Cherry Brigade. The ring of Mayor's guards surrounding the stage of the amphitheater closed in on Guster.

"You should've chosen your words more carefully," said the guard closest to Guster. He smashed the butt of his spear into Guster's back, knocking Guster forward toward the Mayor's box.

Guster stumbled. This was bad. This isn't what he wanted. He'd been trying to prove his innocence. And then, of course, turn the tables on the Mayor. But execution? Could the Mayor really do that? Guster's knees went weak. He felt like he was going to throw up.

The two guards seized Guster by the arms and yanked him to his feet, standing him up right under the Mayor's nose.

The Mayor peered down over his rumpled cravat at Guster. His face was growing redder by the second. "You'll wish you'd held your tongue boy!" he growled. "Whatever anyone may tell you, I am the supreme authority here, and there is no one in this city that can stop me from punishing you to the full extent of the law!"

He drew a long, curved, silver sword from a scabbard at his side. He lowered the blade toward Guster.

Suddenly, a loud whopping noise beat the air. A swirling tornado blew through the stadium. Someone screamed. The guards loosened their grip slightly, and Guster twisted, looking skyward.

Three heavily-armored, dull-green helicopters descended from the sky. They hovered twenty feet above the amphitheater floor. A dozen ropes uncoiled, dropping out of the side of the helicopters, and all at once, a dozen mercenaries in white-and-gray snow camouflage rappelled out of the helicopters, zipping downward like falling stones. They hit the ground hard, and in less than a second, they had unclipped their harnesses and drawn their rifles.

Then another figure, this one dressed in a baby-blue apron, zipped out of the chopper, her arms flailing awkwardly, the bun atop her head bobbing as she landed. She unclipped her harness and put her gloved hands on her chubby hips. Her face was stern, and her eyes looked like they could bore through someone's skull.

"You have until the count of ten to unhand my son, or there will be consequences like you never imagined!" said Mom with the fury of a lioness.

Chapter 16 — The Mom, The Mayor, and The Mercenary

For one full second, nobody moved. Whether from fear, awe, or both, the guards were frozen in place, their jaws hanging open.

"Flatlanders!" the Mayor. He pointed his silver sword. "Eradicate them!"

The guards swung their spear points toward the mercenaries and charged.

Felicity Casa's men reacted quickly. *Pop-pop-pop!* They fired, grouping themselves into a tight formation around Mom, then fanning outward toward the Mayor's guard.

Something whizzed by Guster's cheek. A tiny dart lodged in the neck of the guard nearest Guster.

The guard fell, his eyes rolling back into his head. Tranquilizer darts. Felicity's mercenaries had used them before.

The second guard looked up toward the helicopters. He looked scared. Guster took a chance and wrenched his arm free, ducking and running toward the nearest mercenary.

"No you don't," cried the guard, swinging his spear outward.

The shaft caught Guster on the side of his shin, knocking him off his feet. He fell onto the cold stone bricks, hitting the ground hard.

His chest and arms hurt from the blow, and he couldn't see straight. It looked like one of the mercenaries, a thick-necked, broad-shouldered grunt with mirrored aviator glasses, was marching toward him. The Lieutenant. He'd come to save them. But how? It didn't make sense. How did they find El Elado?

"Get down, Johnsonville!" the Lieutenant shouted. He raised his rifle and fired. *Pop!* A dart whizzed over Guster's head, catching the guard behind him in the arm.

The guard swayed, then fell over flat on his back.

Guster rushed past the Lieutenant, putting the line of mercenaries between him and the Mayor's guards. "Thanks," said Guster.

"Just here to protect you, sir," said the Lieutenant, his tranquilizer gun still popping off darts into the line of advancing guards.

Guster didn't stop there. He scrambled through the soldiers until he found what he was looking for—Mom.

Mom was running toward Guster too. He leapt over the table where the ice cream goblets had stood and threw his arms—chains and all—around Mom's middle in a big hug. She kissed him on top of the head. Normally, he would've been embarrassed. Right now, he didn't care. He was just glad she was there.

"You're grounded until you're 87," she said.

Guster nodded, his face pressed into Mom's apron. Her clothes smelled like banana nut muffins. "I know," he said.

"Your father and I had no idea where you were! We thought you were dead! Or kidnapped! Or getting tattoos!" Her voice was shrill.

Guster's belly felt heavy with guilt. He'd run away from home. He hadn't meant to cause her such pain. But he had to do it. Could she see that? He'd left home to keep them safe, but now—now they were all in danger once again.

No matter how hard Guster had tried to evade the monster and keep his family away from it, he had ended up throwing himself right back into its clutches.

"Move!" shouted the Lieutenant. The Sergeant and Private were right behind him, backing toward the edge of the amphitheater farthest from the Mayor's grandstand. They were still firing into the line of guards.

A handful of Felicity's mercenaries were pinned to the ground under the guards' knees. A half dozen of the Mayor's guards lay prone on the ground.

"We need to get you to safety," the Lieutenant said.

Guster wasn't sure where that would be. The Mayor had such a stranglehold on his part of the city. Their best bet was Princess Sunday's jurisdiction.

"We need to cross the Chocolate River," said Guster.

The Lieutenant nodded.

"Lead the way," said the Sergeant.

"Not without the rest of my babies," said Mom. Zeke and Mariah were running through the battle, dodging spears and guards.

They punched through a line of the Mayor's guards and circled around to the amphitheater exit where Guster and Mom were hunched low behind the Sergeant and Lieutenant.

Mom pulled Zeke and Mariah into one big hug. "You mean you're not mad?" asked Zeke.

"Oh, I'm livid," said Mom. "You can count on never seeing another sunrise again as soon as I get you back home and locked up in your rooms for the rest of your life."

Zeke swallowed hard. Mariah looked indifferent. She knew just as well as Guster did when Mom was making threats she couldn't keep.

"This way," said the Lieutenant. He led them into an arched passageway in the outer wall of the amphitheater and through the darkness at a fast jog.

"If we cross the river we'll be in the Fruitful Streets, where the Mayor has less control," Guster said. "It's our best chance."

"Good. Ms. Casa is in the choppers," the Lieutenant said. "We'll rendezvous with them once we find a suitable landing area, and we'll make a hasty exit, every last one of us."

"I like the sound of that," said Mariah.

"Do you have a cooler?" Zeke asked. "We should pack some ice cream to go."

They emerged from the amphitheater into the butterscotch streets. There were people everywhere, running from the amphitheater, screaming and stumbling as they escaped the battle inside.

"What a wonderful place," said Mom. She'd stopped in her tracks, spinning to look at the domed houses and storefronts, the chocolate-brick chimneys, the peanut brittle sidewalks, and the translucent, glowing butterscotch streets. "I do wonder if I might get the recipe for that one," she said, pointing at a petite chocolate peanut butter cottage with polished orange and yellow-shelled candy door.

"Can I suggest that now is not the time Ma'am," said the Lieutenant. "Ms. Casa is waiting at the chopper, and we're evading the enemy."

Mom nodded slowly. "Yes. Yes, of course." She stumbled forward, her eyes still fixed on the cottage.

The Sergeant pulled her up the street by the arm. They all ran, Guster pumping his legs, chains dangling from his wrists, Zeke and Mariah right behind him. The three of them quickly outpaced Mom. After a few more yards, the mercenaries too were huffing and bent over, trying to catch their breath.

Guster stopped. "The altitude—they're not used to it. Just like we were when we came."

"We have to keep them moving," said Mariah. She grabbed the Sergeant by the hand. Now it was her turn to pull him up the street.

Zeke took hold of Mom.

Guster led them into a narrow alleyway off the main street. They had to try to throw the Mayor's guard off their tail. They took two left turns, then a right, darting onto streets that led generally in the direction of Princess Sunday's castle.

"What . . . is this . . . place?" the Lieutenant asked between pants. He rested against a mint-green, chocolate chip doorway.

"You mean you don't know?" asked Guster.

The Lieutenant shook his head. "Never seen anything like it."

"Then how did you find us?" asked Mariah.

"Homing beacon. I slipped it into your backpack when I spotted you in New York City. Ms. Casa sent us out far and wide to likely places you might run to. I was lucky enough to find you there in the city."

So Felicity had been searching for them ever since they left the farmhouse. It made sense. She'd wanted Guster to help her find more tasty treasures. She probably hadn't bet that he would find an entire city made of ice cream.

"What homing beacon?" asked Guster.

The Sergeant smiled. "Glowing? Red? About the size of a jelly doughnut?" he asked.

"*You* put that doughnut in my backpack!" said Guster to the Lieutenant. So that's how it got in there. The Lieutenant must have slipped it in when he bumped into them on the street. Guster felt a stab of embarrassment. If they hadn't run from the Lieutenant into Bubalatti's clutches, they wouldn't be in this mess.

"That jelly doughnut is a Felicity Casa special recipe. Well, combined with our tech, of course. She mixed in some of your Mom's ingredients so that you wouldn't throw it away. She wanted it to feel familiar to you," said the Lieutenant.

"Lucky he didn't eat it," said Zeke.

"That is lucky," the Lieutenant said, "but I think he would've stopped when he got to the metal, circuits, and wire bits. We never would've been able to find this place without it. Even if we'd known where to look, our GPS started going haywire before we even got close. There's something about the magnetic fields in these mountains that throws it off. We had to hone in on the signal, or we probably would've crashed into the cliffs."

"Which must be how the city stays undetected," said Mariah, holding her chin.

They ran back out onto the street. "This way," said Guster, leading them left up the sloped sidewalk past two hazelnut houses. This was a good sign. The chocolate flavors were thinning out. They must be getting close to the river.

They ran up the streets as fast as the mercenaries could go, huffing the whole way. Mom seemed to have the worst of it. She was breathing hard, and her legs looked like they were moving in slow motion.

Guster grabbed her hand. "I'm proud of you, son," she said, panting. "I'm just so relieved that we found you."

But wasn't she going to ground him for life? Mom was hard to understand sometimes.

"Your father will be very glad to see you when we get to the choppers," she said.

"Dad's here?" asked Guster. A knot in his stomach hardened. Could Dad really handle this kind of danger? Last year he'd been safe on a business trip.

"And Henry Junior too," said Mom. "Dad's with him. Your father refused to stay home. He insisted on coming to take care of us."

And who is going to take care of him? wondered Guster.

"Over there!" cried a loud voice from across the street. A trio of the Mayor's guards rounded the corner, spears under their arms.

"This way," said Guster, pulling Mom through two wide-open double doors into a massive, red velvet brick building. The words "First El Elado Masonry—All Natural Brickwork" were printed on a sign over the doorway. Mariah, Zeke, and the mercenaries ducked inside.

The interior was cavernous. Two rows of enormous cast-iron tubs twice as tall as Zeke lined either wall. There were stone blocks carved from many flavors of ice cream stacked in piles, each giving off a its own aroma: marbled black fudge, sea salted caramel, and cookie dough.

"This must be where they make the bricks for the city," said Mariah.

Two men in floppy confectioner's hats poured sacks full of dark-brown chocolate rocks into one of the iron tubs while a third stirred the tub's contents with a seven-foot long paddle. A yak pushed a wooden turnstile that turned another set of paddles inside the mixture.

They ran down the center aisle, zigzagging between the stacks of bricks. The Confectioners dropped their sacks and paddles.

"What are you doing here?" shouted the tallest one. "We only make bricks for you if you got the money!"

Guster glanced over his shoulder. The Mayor's guards were right on their tails. The factory was large enough they should be able to lose them, then find a way out the back.

The Sergeant heaved himself against a pile of cookies and cream ice cream blocks. The Lieutenant added his weight, and the blocks teetered, then toppled over, smashing into the ground and blocking the path behind them.

"My masterpieces!" cried the tallest confectioner. "Those were for the new Town Hall!"

"Sorry," Guster said sheepishly, shrugging up at them.

They turned between two of the iron tubs, then passed through a narrow doorway into a dark hallway. It opened up into a room dimly lit by a row of small, glowing orange fires. Above the fires, seven iron kettles hung from the ceiling, their contents bubbling and gurgling from the heat. The back wall was made of brick after brick of red velvet ice cream without a window or door in sight. There was no way out.

"Dead end!" said the Lieutenant. He pressed both gloved hands up against the brick walls. "Frozen. Solid."

Zeke stood on his tiptoes and peered into the bubbling cauldron. He breathed in deeply through his nose. "Mmmmm. Fudge." He dipped his finger into the mixture.

"Hot! Hot!" he cried, jumping backward, yanking his finger out and wagging it through the air.

"We've got to try another exit," said Mom, turning back toward the hallway. "Or maybe not," she said, whirling back around.

The three guards stood at the far end of the hallway, blocking the light from the larger factory room. The Lieutenant raised his tranquilizer gun and fired. *Pop-pop! Ping!*

The guards raised a pair of long metal shields, deflecting the Lieutenant's darts so that they bounced harmlessly to the ground. One of the guards raised his arm.

"Get down!" shouted the Lieutenant. He dropped to the floor. Guster threw himself against the wall as there was a crack and a flash of sparks and smoke. A bullet zipped by and lodged into the far wall, spraying ice cream chips in all directions.

"Lay down some cover fire," said Mom.

The Sergeant dropped to one knee next to the door jam and fired off several darts. Mom pulled on a pair of padded oven mitts from the front pocket of her apron. She took hold of the cauldron and lifted it off the hook where it hung from the ceiling. She bent under its weight, then staggered and dumped it against the far wall. It spilled over, pouring hot fudge all over the red velvet bricks.

The fudge hissed and steamed, eating away at the bricks

until the ice cream softened into a dark creamy mixture.

Ping! Ping! The Sergeant kept firing.

"One more," Mom said and lifted another hot fudge cauldron off its hook. She carried it over to the wall and poured it into the soupy hole. The fudge steamed and gurgled, softening the ice cream bricks even further.

"Lieutenant," she said, pointing to the wall.

The Lieutenant gave the wall a swift kick. It broke, light streaming in through a small hole from the outside.

The Sergeant fired another stream of darts at the guards, who were advancing down the hallway, their shields raised, the darts pinging as they bounced off the metal.

"They're coming!" the Sergeant said.

The Lieutenant heaved himself against the wall. He broke through and fell out on the other side. The sky outside was bright blue, and there was a wide, dirty street leading down to the Chocolate River.

"Let's go!" cried Guster. He grabbed Mariah and Zeke by the hands and pulled them toward the opening.

They ducked through. The Lieutenant was already on his feet, pulling Mom through the door.

The Sergeant backed through, still firing, then dropped a clip from his rifle. "I'm all out," he said.

The Lieutenant frowned. "All the more reason we need to get across that river."

They ran down the street, past two blocks of chocolate marshmallow buildings until they reached the Chocolate River.

"We can't wade across," said Guster. "It's too deep." He couldn't swim with chains on his wrists.

"There's a bridge," said Mom, pointing upstream. Another block up the street a narrow, arched waffle cone footbridge spanned the river. On the far side was a strawberry wall with an open gate. Beyond that were cherry and pineapple ice cream buildings: the Fruitful Streets. Above those was Princess

Sunday's Castle.

All they had to do was get to the other side. Then they would find allies in the Fruitful Streets who could help.

They ran. Guster glanced over his shoulder to see the Mayor's guards charging down the hill after them. Mom crossed the bridge first, with Mariah and Zeke right behind her. The Lieutenant and Sergeant brought up the rear.

Guster ducked through the gate and stopped cold. Mom gasped.

On the other side of the strawberry wall was an open town square studded with gumdrops and bright-red cherry sours. At the head of the square stood the Mayor, his shiny silver spoon in hand. On his left was the Chancellor of the Culinary. To his right was Princess Sunday. She was staring at the ground. Between them and the wall, a semicircle of more than a dozen iron cannons lined the square, all of them pointed straight at Guster. They were trapped.

"I'm sorry," said Princess Sunday. Tears streamed down her cheeks. "But it had to be done."

Chapter 17 — In the Mayor's Mansion

Betrayed. Princess Sunday had betrayed them.

"I will fire this if necessary," said the Mayor. He held a torch mere inches away from the fuse on the cannon nearest him. Behind him stood the rest of his guard, all standing with spears raised. Princess Sunday's soldiers were nowhere to be seen.

The Lieutenant dropped his rifle and put up his hands.

"But . . ." muttered the Sergeant under his breath.

"Now is not the time," said the Lieutenant. "We have the Johnsonvilles to protect. Put down your rifle."

The Sergeant obeyed.

Mom gathered Zeke and Mariah close. "Guster," she said under her breath, "Don't do anything rash." She knew that Guster wanted to run or beat his hands against the Mayor's chest or scream out to Princess Sunday and ask her how she could do this.

The Chancellor, still wearing his bright-green shirt with banana-yellow pantaloons, nodded his head, and four of the Mayor's guards stepped past the cannons. They dangled heavy iron chains in each hand. The guards took hold of the Lieutenant and the Sergeant first, clapping the manacles around their wrists then shoving them across the square toward the Mayor.

They handcuffed Mom and Mariah next. Guster waited for them to grab hold of the chains clamped to his wrists, but they did not. Instead, the guards pushed him and Zeke toward the Mayor.

The Chancellor stared straight at Mom. "You! Do you deny that you are this boy's mother?"

"Of course I am, young man," she said, looking him square in the face. "I went through a lot of pain to bring him into this world, and I can't think of any reason to say otherwise."

There was a murmur and shuffle amongst the guards around them. "I told you," Guster heard one of them say.

The Chancellor's face grew so red it looked like he'd pop. "It's just as Mayor Bollito said! We have a nice dungeon for the likes of you!" He motioned with his head.

Two guards took hold of the chains on Mom's and Mariah's wrists. Mom looked over her shoulder at Guster, her face full of pain. She'd just found them, and now they were taking her away.

"But you were supposed to be on our side," said Guster to Princess Sunday. "You can't let them take her."

She bowed her head. She wouldn't meet Guster's eyes.

The Mayor's guards shoved Guster and Zeke into a carriage. They didn't even let them say goodbye.

"Boys! Dad and I will get you out!" Mom said as the carriage pulled away.

They were driven down through the butterscotch streets toward a large and stately marble fudge manor. The grounds surrounding the Mansion stretched for acres, streams from the Chocolate River winding and branching like fingers across the lawn. The Mansion itself stood on the edge of the plateau overlooking the strawberry plains. Four massive pillars, as thick as redwood trees held up the roof in front, each one a swirl of dark-brown fudge and light-brown chocolate, with flecks of vanilla. The pillars reminded Guster of the marble work he'd seen at some of the state capitols in his history book.

The Mayor's guard stopped the carriage in front of a set of wide steps leading to a grand set of double doors.

The Guard led Guster and Zeke into a vaulted entry hall lined with columns where two grand staircases curved upward to the second floor.

Their greatest chance of escape had been Mom and the mercenaries. And now even their rescuers had been taken captive.

"Zeke, I just want to get out of this place," said Guster.

"But I thought you loved it here," said Zeke.

"I did, but that was before everyone in town decided they wanted me dead."

Zeke frowned. Then he punched the palm of one hand with the other. "We'll find a way, P. I know we will."

The Guards marched Guster and Zeke up the right staircase and into a short hallway. It led to an arched door with a brass ring handle hanging in the center. They opened it. Inside was a study lined floor to ceiling with books. There was a clockwork model of the solar system ticking away methodically in one corner, a telescope pointed out a window toward the strawberry plain, and a collection of antique bronze and silver ice cream scoops mounted on the wall. Most curious of all was a stone bust sitting on the desk with its face pointed away from them.

"Welcome to my library," said the Mayor, bouncing up the steps behind them. He slipped past them with the speed of a puppy, then turned and smiled a disingenuous smile. "Come, beguile your sorrow. There is no need for us to quarrel any longer. The terms of your sentence have been set and fixed by the Culinary. My hands are tied!" He threw up his gloved hands. "Oh, yes, I tried to execute you an hour ago, but let the past be the past! The Culinary said that wasn't appropriate, and who am I—just a little old mayor—to tell them what to do?"

It took all of Guster's resolve not to scream at him. If the guards weren't there, he might have.

"No, no. I won't kill you now." He smiled coldly. "I'm a patient man. I can simply wait a few days until the Yummies come back to eat you. It's all the same to me."

So that was his game now. He'd please the Culinary and get what he wanted anyway. Guster had to find a way out of this.

The Mayor sat down behind his desk and folded his hands. "Now that you are guests, I'd like you to enjoy all that my Mansion has to offer. This library, for example. Did you know that the Baconists have been hard at work here, studying and making sense of the universe since we adopted them as children and protectors of the city so many centuries ago? El Elado boasts a long and storied history, and you couldn't preserve it without scholars on your payroll," said the Mayor, his chest swelling.

Guster was really, really starting to despise this man.

A pair of doors on the left side of the library opened. Three Baconists puttered through them. Two of them held piles of books and scrolls under each arm. The third proffered a tray of sizzling hot bacon. It was the Baconist with the nostrils as wide as dimes who'd read from the big leather book at the trial.

He lifted it toward Zeke and Guster. The bacon smelled salty and meaty, even better than the kind Mom fried up from the butcher's back home.

"Help yourself," said the Baconist with the wide nostrils. He sniffed.

"Don't mind if I do." He blew on a piece then stuffed it into his mouth.

The Baconist held the tray toward Guster.

"No thanks," said Guster. He didn't want them to think he could be bought so easily.

"I think as long as you are guests here," the Mayor said, "it makes sense for us to treat you with hospitality." He cocked his head to one side, turning his monocle in his eye. "We can give you the thing you lack most, the most generous gift we can offer to Flatlanders like you: knowledge."

Guster felt his chest boil inside. Everything about the Mayor was just so aggravating.

The Mayor gestured toward two plush leather chairs. "Have a seat," he said.

Zeke plopped himself down into the chair closest him. Guster sat more slowly.

"You are new here to our city. You haven't had a chance to learn what we have." The Mayor waved a hand. "Salero! Show him," he barked.

The Baconist put down the tray and pushed back his red woven sleeves. He unrolled a scroll with a map on it.

The map was clearly handmade, and the continents looked out of place, like someone had squashed the whole picture. Even the Americas were nothing more than a large island.

Guster stifled a laugh. "There's something wrong with your map," said Zeke, pointing. "Did a three-year-old draw that?"

Salero sighed. There was pity on his face. "You poor boys. You have lived such naïve, sheltered lives," he said, his voice droning through his ample nostrils. "But that was then. I am here to help you now."

"It all started with a voyage," said Salero, hanging the map on the wall. "Five centuries ago, a ship left from the old country and sailed on a journey that took its crew across the globe to places never explored by human eyes." He traced a route with a wooden pointer around the large island in the Pacific Ocean where America should have been.

"Somewhere around this New World, a ship full of men bound for their homes in their mother country Spain veered from its intended course and traversed halfway around the globe. The men aboard were brave explorers, fixed on discovering new places and things."

Salero traced his pointer over the oceans. "Were they lost? Possible. They must have wandered for years on the high seas. But an explorer is never satisfied, and the brave captain of their ship, Palooza del Montana, was finally led by something—or someone—and suddenly changed his ship's course and brought his crew here."

Salero stabbed his pointer into the map on the coast of what looked like India, then traced a line toward the heart of the Himalayas.

"Whether Palooza del Montana tasted hints of sweet cream down on the coasts, or whether he heard rumors of the wondrous Yummy and was searching for a glimpse of the beast, we do not know. Whatever his motive, he left his ship and crew on the coast and pressed onward over one impossible, forbidden pass after another, until a Yummy found him and finally showed him the way to the Golden Valley. Once he had tasted the ice cream here, straight from the source, he knew they could never go back. The outside world, even their homes held nothing so exquisite as the treasure he'd found here."

Salero took the same heavy, leather-bound volume he'd used in the trial from off a shelf. Its pages were yellow and brittle with age.

He hefted it onto the table where it dropped like a stone, the wooden desk quivering under its weight. Salero opened it.

"This is the *Book of Knowledge of The Delicious City of El Elado*. Some may know it by its other name, *The Forbidden City of Flavor and Pain*. Regardless, in it are the names of the men and women who have lived here and ruled here, all the way back to Palooza del Montana."

Salero flipped a dozen pages in the giant book then propped it up. In it was a sketch of the valley, with a more detailed drawing of the city. There were fewer buildings in the sketch, and there was no castle up on the hill. It must have been what the city looked like long ago.

"But once Palooza had tasted it, he knew the men and women aboard his ship, despite all they had seen and tasted in their travels, would not believe him until they had tasted it for themselves.

"So he returned to them and told them what he had found."

"It wasn't long before the ship's crew left their vessel behind for good and climbed the mountains. This was it! The thing they had not known they were searching for! A perfect cradle of nature in which their master chefs could create the most heavenly dessert treasures that the world had ever known!

"They built homes. They fashioned bricks. They made a village. They founded The City of El Elado.

"And so you see, no one, once they find the City of El Elado, ever need leave it."

"But there are legends of this place. They must have gotten out somehow," said Guster. "The whole world thinks it's a lost city of gold."

"The world knows nothing of the Delicious City!" said Salero. He bent low, pushing his face toward Guster, so Guster could smell the salt on his hot breath. "The explorers aboard that ship had seen things in their journey that no one had ever seen. They brought things here that were more marvelous than anything the world had tasted. That is why they stayed. They wanted a place where they could build a society dedicated to such delicious ideals. They wanted to protect themselves from the outside world! Now no one leaves!"

Guster drew his face back. This man, this Baconist, he sounded so oddly familiar. He held the same ideals as the Gastronimatii. Purity. Preservation. Elitism. And all clad in red robes—how could any of them be trusted?

Salero cleared his throat. "It was the beast that showed Palooza the way over the mountains, and if it were not so, no one could have found this place."

"Then how did so many people get here?" asked Guster.

"With time, the city grew," said Salero. "The valley was empty then, only a treacherous flow of pure vanilla ice cream, creaking and grinding across the valley, an unstoppable glacier bent on eroding a path through the mountains."

Salero flipped another page. There was a sketch of several Yummies tracing lines around the city, like planets trace their orbits around the sun.

"Why are you showing us this?" asked Guster. He wanted to know, but he did not like Salero. And he did not like that he had been forced into the Mayor's custody.

"Yummy is a guardian, but then he was also a guide," Salero said. He flipped the page and turned the heavy book toward Guster and Zeke. There was a drawing inside, a very rough sketch of a beast whose neckless head was mounted so that it was one large lump across his shoulders.

"Yummy is the true ruler of this city, Flatlander," Salero said. "He brought us here, and he will show us who will stay. If it takes only one Exquisite Morsel to satiate him, then we will not hold back."

Guster squirmed in his chair.

"And it's not just me who knows it. The people below want Yummy to stay and protect us."

"Of course," said Zeke under his breath. "The Yeti has long been a deterrent to mountaineers in the Himalayan region. The legends are numerous." He patted Guster's arm. "Not that I think that justifies them eating you, of course."

Really? That was all Zeke could muster for a show of brotherly support?

"You need to know your place in this city's history before you become part of it forever," said Salero. He sneered.

The Mayor grunted. "This has been a very educational meeting, but we must show the two guests to their quarters."

Salero backed up, giving the Mayor a wide berth. "Of

course," he said, clapping his giant book shut. "We'll have more lessons later."

Two guards hoisted Guster and Zeke up by the arms and marched them after the Mayor out a door and into a hallway. Guster ducked his head as they descended a narrow spiral staircase that looked like it was made of cookies and cream.

The staircase dropped another two floors. The air was colder and the hallway darker than up above. The Mayor unlocked a door at the end of a hallway. It swung open with a nudge, and the Guards shoved Guster and Zeke inside.

"Your quarters," said the Mayor. "I hope you will find them comfortable. You needn't worry too much. It will only be a matter of days." His lips curled, bearing two pointy canines, then he slammed the door shut tight.

Chapter 18 — The Scoop

The room in the Mayor's Mansion did not look like a prison. Not entirely. There were two soft marshmallow couches, a table in the center made of chocolate bricks, and a tapestry hanging on the far wall that depicted a ship on the shoreline at the foot of a mountain.

There were no windows and no doors except for the one they came through. The walls and floor were made of dark-brown ice cream. There was no way out.

"We're trapped, Zeke," said Guster. "Mom shows up, and everything seems like finally something is going to go our way, and now here we are, shut in a dungeon."

"Yeah, but we're probably safer here than we would be with Mom," said Zeke. "Did you see the way her eyes were burning?"

Guster nodded. He had to admit, there was no fury like their mother scorned. Now at least they might get some sympathy, being locked up in the Mayor's Mansion. Wasn't Mom the one who was supposed to be shut up in prison? And Zeke and Guster treated to fine accommodations? Whatever loophole the Culinary had imposed to keep Guster alive, it had clearly stopped there. Any way they looked at it, they were trapped, and Yummy was coming.

Guster flopped down on the marshmallow couch. He let out a sigh so long it rattled his lips.

"At least they locked us up here!" said Zeke, sizing up the room around him.

"Why do you say that?"

Zeke licked his lips. "Because it's made of chocolate Moose Tracks!" He pressed his cheek up against the wall.

"I don't think that the conquistadors know what Moose Tracks ice cream is, Zeke," said Guster. Moose Tracks was not something Guster expected that a lost band of conquistadors would have known about five hundred years ago. Still, hadn't a select few made it to the outside world to find flavors over the centuries? That explained why they had cookie dough and mint chocolate chip.

"I don't care," said Zeke. "It's got chocolate brownie bits bigger than meatballs. I need a spoon."

Guster shivered and buttoned up his coat. Everything in this city was cold—it had to be to keep the walls from melting. None of the people seemed to notice. Maybe they were just used to it.

"Give me your belt buckle," said Zeke. Guster was wearing the same oval belt buckle he always wore. It was small enough to fit in his palm.

"Why?" asked Guster.

Zeke rolled his eyes and pointed to a particularly rich chocolate vein running diagonally down the wall. "This," he said, "obviously. I'm going to try to dig some out." He held out his hand, waving his fingers toward him with a gesture that said "gimme."

Guster unhitched his belt. It was better than Zeke using his fingernails.

Zeke dug the metal buckle into the wall, scraping ice cream brick shavings into his hand. It took him several scrapes just to scratch out a quarter inch. "It's very solid construction," he said, his eyes still on the wall. He smushed the ice cream shavings into his mouth.

"Oh! But so good," he said, closing his eyes and working the ice cream back and forth in his mouth like a burrow chewing its feed. "Finally, we can be alone with all this ice cream in peace. Mmmmmmm. Bro, you have got to try this."

The doorknob rattled as someone turned a key in the lock. Zeke looked like he'd been hit by lightning. He stiffened up, leaning his head against the wall so that it covered the gouge where he'd scraped the ice cream free.

The door swung open. Caramelo and Pistachero stood there, each carrying a tray with a small bowl of soup on it.

"The Mayor says we can't starve you, especially since your big day is coming," Caramelo said. "In fact, he says we ought to fatten you up." He sneered. "So we got some yak stew for you. You'll find it delicious and fatty too. We wouldn't want to sour the Exquisite Morsel, now would we?"

Guster frowned. "Then why did they send *you* here? I'm starting to feel queasy already."

Caramelo snorted and set the tray down. "Enjoy. It won't be long until one of these meals is your last."

He and Pistachero backed out the door. The lock clicked.

Zeke sighed. He slid down the wall, revealing the gouge in the bricks. "That was close." He shrugged. "Let's see what's for dinner."

"No spoons?" asked Zeke, lifting the top bowl and looking underneath it. "Dinner without silverware? Savages! That's what Mom would say."

That's exactly what she would say.

Funny, she had been taken to Princess Sunday's castle to be imprisoned, but he and Zeke were the ones in a tiny locked cell with no way out.

"They don't want us digging into the walls," said Guster.

"That must be why the stew's cold. They saw what we did to that wall in the factory."

Zeke nodded. "Or what we did to that house. They get very grumpy when we do that."

"Let's try the bowls," he said. Zeke slurped down the stew with one long gulp, then set the thick wooden bowl's edge into his gouge on the wall and dug into it. He managed to shave off a very thin layer of ice cream, but nothing more. It worked worse than the belt buckle had. "Rats," he said. For now, there would be no dessert.

Guster tried some stew. The meaty chunks were spiced and simmered with a skill that Guster had rarely encountered. The chefs and the Confectioners in the Delicious City were experts. That *is* what had founded their culture in the first place. Guster could respect that.

***

Guster didn't even notice that he'd fallen asleep. His belly had been full, and he had been so very tired.

He only awoke because the room was quaking furiously. He bolted upright on the marshmallow couch.

"What's happening?" cried Zeke. He was standing, bracing himself against the corner of the room, his eyes wide with fright.

"It's another tremor," said Guster.

The Princess was right; they were growing stronger. And then it was over. Guster counted off in his head. It must have lasted only five, maybe six seconds. He settled back onto the couch.

They could hear cries and commotion through the walls.

Guster remembered the sinkhole not far from the princess's castle. Mom and Mariah were up there. He hoped they were okay.

"Zeke, we've got to get out of here," said Guster, his voice thick with panic. If the sinkholes didn't swallow him up, Yummy certainly would.

Zeke nodded. "Yeah. We do," he said.

They both settled back into their couches, but sleep did not come for a long time. Then, just as Guster was about to drift off, a panel at the bottom of the wooden door swung open and something slid through.

"Caramelo?" Guster asked.

No one answered.

Guster sat up.

On the floor was a flat sheet cake about two feet long and four inches thick. It was covered in white frosting with red borders. On the top, in big, red frosting letters was scrawled "Look below and look behind." It was signed "A.G."

"Zeke, wake up," said Guster. He shook him.

"What?" said Zeke, rubbing his eyes. He saw the cake and smiled. "Midnight snack."

"I don't think this is from the Mayor," said Guster.

"Even better," Zeke said. "I never liked that guy anyway." He stuck his fingers into the top and clawed out a handful. He shoved it into his mouth.

"Zeke, wait!" said Guster. "We don't even know who A.G. is."

"It's probably from Felicity," Zeke mumbled as he chewed. He dug his fingers back in for more. He paused. "Hey, what's this?" he asked. He pulled a long metal object from inside the cake and held it up.

It was an ice cream scoop at least as long as Guster's forearm, with a sturdy handle and an oversized, metal half-sphere at the end.

"No way," said Zeke. He looked at the Moose Tracks wall. "Finally." He rushed to the wall and attacked it, digging out a large rut of ice cream. It gave easily under the scoop's edges.

"Zeke, we don't even know where that came from," said

Guster.

"Does it matter?" asked Zeke, shoving his face full of ice cream. "I've finally gotten the mouthfuls I deserve."

But who would drop such a tool off in the middle of the night? And who could get past the Mayor's guards to do so? Guster couldn't think of anyone with the initials A.G.

Look below and behind. Guster turned to the hanging tapestry of the ship on the wall. Behind that, there was nothing but more ice cream. And beyond that . . .

"Zeke, we're busting out of here," said Guster.

Zeke stopped scooping. "Now you're talking! Jailbreak! Okay. Here's the plan. We get Mom. We find Felicity's boys, then we bust them out of prison and sneak out in the middle of the night and get to the choppers and blast over those mountains as the city explodes behinds us in an enormous fireball!"

Guster didn't see what a fireball had to do with anything. "What about Mariah?" he asked.

Zeke scratched his chin. "Oh yeah. Her too. She can come if she wants." Suddenly Zeke plopped down on the couch, defeated. "But how do we get out of this cell?" he asked.

Guster looked at the gouge Zeke had dug in the wall. It wasn't the best idea he'd ever had. But it was better than nothing. "We eat our way out," he said.

Zeke's face lit up. "Yeah," he said.

They worked all night, carving out a hole behind the tapestry. At first it was hard work, but the deeper they dug, the softer the ice cream got. They used the first few scoops to cover up the gouge Zeke had made in the wall. They didn't want the guards discovering what they'd done.

Then they kept digging, for an hour or more, taking turns with the scoop while the other one rested.

They couldn't risk leaving a pile of ice cream, so Zeke ate every last bite.

"Just doing my part," he said, swallowing another mouthful

of ice cream.

By the time they were through, they'd carved out a hole deep enough for Guster to crawl inside.

Guster and Zeke were both taking a breather when they heard the key rattle in the lock. Guster was quick. He grabbed the cake and shoved it into the hole and dropped the tapestry, just as the door opened.

Two guards stood on either side of the corridor with Salero between them, his reddish-brown robes hanging like strips of bacon from his gaunt frame. "Time for your morning tutelage," he said, his nostrils flaring.

Had he seen the hole? Guster was afraid to turn around and look.

"Of course, sir," said Guster. He felt hot on his neck. He moved toward Salero, when he spotted the ice cream scoop on the ground behind where Zeke stood. Guster moved to the door, attempting to block the view into the cell. "It'll be nice to stretch our legs—and minds, of course—for a while."

Salero peered over the end of his large beak nose. "Quite." He turned on his heels.

Zeke was right behind Guster, both of them slipping into the hallway and taking off at a brisk pace. The guards pulled the door shut and locked it, then raced after Guster and Zeke before they could get too far unattended.

Salero climbed the spiral stairs upward and led them back into the Mayor's office, where the maps, charts, books, and two plush red armchairs sat.

The two guards took up their posts on either door, spears pointed straight toward the ceiling. Salero motioned for Zeke and Guster to take a seat.

Mariah was sitting on the desk, leafing through the heavy, leather *Book of Knowledge of The Delicious City of El Elado*.

"Mariah, what are you doing here?" said Guster.

Mariah looked up from her reading. Her eyes lit up. "Oh.

They said I could come and hear their lessons. Do you know what is in this book?" she asked.

Guster shook his head. "A little."

"Salero's been teaching me," she said. She placed both hands flat on the pages. "It's quite amazing, really."

Mariah always did love books and learning. Whatever her teachers told her at school was law. But Salero?

Zeke groaned. "I'm on summer vacation," he said. "And this is what I get? More school. This really is not my favorite city if this is how you treat summertime."

Salero's one eyebrow bent upward. "You are here because you must know the history of El Elado."

"Before Yummy returns to eat me?" asked Guster. They were taking an awful lot of care for someone they wanted dead.

Salero's lips went tight. "Consider us fattening you up for the slaughter with knowledge. Besides, I think you'll find this fascinating." He turned the pages of the enormous book and rotated it around for them to see. On the open page were four numbered sentences, all written in a language Guster couldn't understand.

"These are the idols of the mind," said Salero. "Deceptions that cloud our thinking. You are subject to these deceptions, and it is the duty of a scholar to purge them from your head so that you can be clear in your thinking. Your sister seems to be clear of thought."

Mariah smiled proudly.

Salero turned to another page. "A century after the city was founded, it wallowed in ignorance. There was no one to guide the minds of the people, and they were chained to their foolish superstitions. Then, on one of the many ingredient expeditions to the flatlands, the Confectioners brought back a scholar to live among them. He turned on the light for this city. He was a student of an age of enlightenment, and his tutor was none other than Francis Bacon."

"That scholar founded the Baconists," said Guster. He remembered hearing about Francis Bacon in school, though he couldn't say why he was important. All that he remembered was that the man had worn one of those stiff white collars that looked like a tutu around his neck and that he was really smart.

Salero nodded. "Astute. Perhaps we'll be able to save your mind yet," he said. He scratched something down on a piece of paper with his quill. "And since then, the Baconists have grown as the citizens of El Elado discover their love for reason and learning. We have expunged the fogs in their minds."

Zeke fidgeted in his chair. "So I don't get it. Why should we care?"

Guster almost laughed, but the serious, grim expression on Salero's deeply-lined face made Guster think he'd better not.

"I will show you," said Salero. He unrolled another scroll. This one had an aerial view of the city with a rough sketch of Yummy drawn on it.

Guster peered closer at it. There were lines radiating around the center with thirteen monsters surrounding the city, facing outward like guards.

"You see, we have studied these beasts. They are more than just protectors of the city. They are the foundation on which the city is built. They are builders."

He unrolled another scroll. There was a close up picture of a Yummy with notes scrawled next to various parts of the Yummy's body in a language Guster couldn't read. There was a paragraph near the creature's head and mouth, a sentence written under his feet, and another paragraph scrawled next to his enormous, clawed hands. Guster had never seen them up close before—they were large and powerful scoops, like a grizzly bear's hands.

"Do you see his claws?" asked Salero. "At first glance, one would not realize that Yummy makes his burrows in the ice and snow. He digs tunnels deep and far, much like the marmots in the mountains below us. But unlike the marmots, Yummy is a builder. He doesn't just dig holes. He fills the ones that nature leaves behind."

Salero pulled a slender stick of charcoal from the folds in his robes and began to draw on another blank parchment. He drew a crude skyline of El Elado on top of its plateau. Then he drew a network of tunnels beneath it. "The city is built on the ever-flowing glacier of ice cream that springs forth from the mountain. The ground beneath us is shifting, slowly creeping downhill, cracking and rolling in slow motion."

Zeke stirred in his seat. He looked doubtful.

"This is why the city is collapsing beneath us. Ever since the city began, Yummy has burrowed deep, shifting and digging up the ice cream glacier, shoring up the support and keeping the city safe. He is a protector in more ways than one."

"Have you ever seen these burrows?" asked Guster. The idea struck him as odd, if not impossible.

Salero shook his head. "We don't need to. There is evidence enough. Our numbers and the frequency of the quakes all point to this same result. Did you not feel the sinking last night?"

Zeke sat straight up in his chair, his eyebrows crammed together. "That sounds crazy," he said.

Salero turned, his eyes staring like daggers down his beak of a nose. "It is science!" he said, his voice firm and defensive. He swept his arms out over the shelves of books. "Are you going to deny the whole collected work of generations of scholars?"

Guster shook his head. Salero was so sure of himself. "But didn't the quakes just start one year ago?" Guster asked.

Salero laughed, spitting. "Ha! Ask any Baconist. We are the protectors of reason and knowledge. Do you really think that a small boy like you actually can have all the facts?"

"Guster, be reasonable," said Mariah.

Guster didn't feel like he had very many facts. He'd only gotten a B in science last year. But could Yummy have dug and built foundations for the city? And now that he was gone, it all was going to fall apart? Yummy had only been gone for one year. That hardly seemed like enough evidence for the Baconists to build a theory on. It just sounded so . . . outlandishly ridiculous.

Then again, they were living in a city made of ice cream. Anything seemed possible. And the Baconists were all supposed to be so very smart. The idea was daunting.

Zeke started to laugh. "I'm sorry," he said, his eyes welling up with tears, "but what you're saying sounds really, really stupid."

Guster's stomach twisted. Salero wasn't going to like that.

Salero's face went grim. "I see you deny science," he said, shaking his head. "Then I cannot stop the doom of this cataclysm falling down upon your head."

He snapped his fingers. "Guards, take them back to their chambers," he said, "and get them out of my sight."

The guards posted on either door yanked Guster and Zeke from their chairs, marched them back to their cell, and locked them inside.

Chapter 19 — Mom's Cell

Guster pulled back the tapestry. Salero frustrated him so. He was so sure of himself. He was acting as if Guster couldn't—or shouldn't—be allowed to think for himself.

"We have to get out of here," Guster said, crawling into the tunnel. "I'll scoop. You eat."

Guster dug. It was slow at first, but soon he found a rhythm. Within the hour, he'd dug the tunnel another four feet into the wall.

Zeke shoveled leftover Moose Tracks from the tunnel into his mouth. "Mmmm," he mumbled between bites, "so good. Best idea we've ever had Guster. Mmm. A man's gotta do what a man's gotta do."

Guster ate what he could too, but it didn't take long for the ice cream to feel like it was pressing up against his stomach lining, like a lump trying to break free.

After eating all he could, Guster sat back on the marshmallow couch and wiped his mouth. "I'm not sure how much further I can go right now. I'm getting full."

"No problem!" said Zeke, folding the bottom corner of the tapestry up to the top and tucking it in, leaving the wall bare and exposed for further excavation. He scooped out another scoop. "I got this!" He attacked the wall, eating three more scoops before he too started to slow down. He sat down on the couch, pressing ice cream morsels to his lips much slower than before.

"That's odd," he said, staring down at his fingertips. They were green. "Where did that come from?"

Guster looked at the hole. At the very deepest point, the ice cream was minty green instead of dark-brown chocolate like the rest of the tunnel.

"Let me have a taste," said Guster. He still had room enough for a spoonful or two. He was curious. The fact that there was a hidden flavor underneath intrigued him and, truthfully, just felt a little bit strange.

He reached his arm into the hole and scooped out a small green morsel of mint chocolate chip ice cream. It was emerald green and spotted with chocolate chips so deep brown they were almost black.

He tasted it. It was marvelously minty, like fresh, crisp mint leaves straight from the garden. And then there was something more—was it a tinge of strawberry? Barely perceptible. But real.

Guster took another bite. Yes.

Strawberry mixed into mint chocolate chip did not make much sense as a flavor combination. It was not a decision any of the city's Confectioners would deliberately make.

Perhaps there was layer after layer of ice cream, like the layers of rock a paleontologist digs into, each one older than the last.

"Zeke, we have to dig this way," said Guster. He pointed down and to the left.

Zeke looked puzzled, his eyebrows slanting up to one side. "Uh. Okay. How come?"

"There's a hint of strawberry in the mint. That's one of the Princess's flavors," he said. It was only a hunch really. If somehow they could tunnel back toward the Fruitful Streets of the city, they might find a way out.

"It's our best bet," he said.

"Okay, but I'm going to need a minute." Zeke held his hands on his swollen belly. "I'm getting full."

Guster untucked the corner of tapestry and let it hang, covering the hole in the wall. They both took a break, lounging on the couch, the sugar rushing to their heads. For the first time since they'd arrived in the city, Guster felt like things might actually turn out alright.

"Maybe we'll leave the Mayor a note," said Zeke. "It'll say, 'Don't expect our votes. Good luck with reelection.'" He laughed at his own joke.

Guster didn't think it was funny but couldn't help laughing too. He liked the idea of them not being here when the Mayor came to fetch them.

***

Guster slept soundly that night. It was the first time he'd done so since arriving at the city. Perhaps it was because he was so exhausted, or perhaps because the ice cream had a soothing, pacifying effect.

As full as they were, they'd both eaten a bowl of stew the night before. They didn't want the guards to get suspicious. Besides, after all that sugar, it was nice to have something with vegetables and meat in it.

The door rattled and swung open again at first light. Guster blinked his eyes open and turned over on his marshmallow couch.

"Señors, get up. The Culinary has allowed you one hour to visit the castle." It was Gaucho's voice. He was standing in the door.

"Gaucho!" said Guster, propping himself up to a sitting position. "How did you . . .?"

Gaucho glanced backward at the two guards standing over him with their spears. "Never mind that now. It is the politics of the Culinary. They have allowed it as a compromise to your imprisonment. We must hurry while we can," he said.

Guster stood and shook Zeke awake. "What's for breakfast?" Zeke moaned, his eyes still closed.

"We're going to see Mom," Guster said.

Zeke shot to his feet, then yawned. "Gaucho. Hello."

"There isn't much time," said Gaucho. "There was considerable debate and many favors that Princess had to grant in order to allow this. Your father is there. And this Felicity Casa. They found the Princess shortly after you were captured. We must go to them now." He turned toward the door.

Guster and Zeke marched after him. For a moment, Guster worried that the two guards might search their cell. He was relieved when they closed the door behind them and took up the rear, spears in hand and marching just a little too close to Guster's heels.

Gaucho led them up the spiral staircase and through the Mayor's Mansion to Princess Sunday's coach waiting on the front drive. They got in, and the two guards sat next to them, grim and watchful expressions on their faces. Now would be a good time to escape, with only two guards at their sides. It would be easier than tunneling out. Especially since they were already going to the Princess's castle.

A column of a dozen armed guards mounted on horses fell in behind their coach, two of the guards riding up and flanking either side. Guster's heart sank. The Mayor or the Baconists were always two steps ahead of them.

The procession moved slowly through the streets of El Elado. As they passed the scoop houses and shops, the people filtered out of their doors and stood at the edge of the golden butterscotch streets. They wore grim, sour expressions on their faces, and each one of them—man, woman and child—stared at Guster. Some of their eyes were filled with loathing, others with pity, most with anger.

For a moment, Guster felt a pang of guilt.

"They are afraid, Señor," said Gaucho. He was looking at Guster.

"Of what?" asked Guster.

"The thing that they have always been afraid of. Only now, they've seen you at the Trial, and it is getting worse."

The coach turned the corner. There was a massive sinkhole where the street should have been; buildings and houses had collapsed and fallen into the crevasse where the quake had torn the street apart. Guster stared into the hole. The city had fallen into it: wheelbarrows, ice cream scoops, chairs, and furniture, even a little girl's doll. How many people had been hurt? How many had . . .

"It is not your fault," said Gaucho. Guster had never seen the jolly little conquistador look so serious.

"But the people blame me, don't they?" asked Guster. He could see it in their eyes.

"They want a scapegoat," Gaucho said. "They need something that they can blame so they can get rid of it. They think that then their problems will be solved."

Would it be that easy? If all he had to do was give himself to the monster, then maybe it was the right thing to do. Not that Guster believed in their superstitions. One meal for Yummy could not really be the answer they were looking for. But that's what they all wanted, wasn't it?

"Did I ever tell you that as Shepherd of the Yummies, I am sixteenth in line for the throne?" said Gaucho. He stood in the carriage and raised his finger in the air. "If I were in charge, Señor, there would be no Exquisite Morsel, and these people would no longer be locked up in this city forever! They could come and go as they pleased!"

"I wish that it were so, Gaucho," said Guster.

The coach turned down a side street and rolled down a narrow alley. Finally, after more than a quarter hour of the coach carefully winding its way through the wreckage in the streets, they reached the castle gates and stopped in the courtyard.

The Mayor's guards fanned out across the grounds.

"Come, your mother will be waiting," said Gaucho.

They dismounted the coach and entered the double doors into the castle's dining hall. Gaucho led them down a narrow stairway to a brightly lit dungeon. He nodded to Princess Sunday's Cherry Brigade that stood watch at the door there. They turned a set of keys in the lock and opened the door into the dungeon.

The dungeon was hardly a dungeon at all. It was as much a prison as Guster's and Zeke's cell in the Mayor's Mansion was a guest room. It was brightly lit with skylights and wide, comfortable cells. Behind the bars, the rooms were well furnished, with hammocks woven from cotton candy, dressers and chests made of chocolate, peanut brittle tables, and big easy chairs made of marshmallow. There were shelves with books, and a little strawberry fountain bubbled in the corner.

Mom was in the first cell. Dad stood next to her. Henry Junior was in his arms. "Guster! Zeke!" she cried, rushing up to the bars as soon as she saw them.

She reached through the bars with both arms, stretching out for a hug. Guster let himself be folded up in her grasp, Mom pressing his face up against the cold metal.

"My boys. My boys!" she sobbed, turning to hug Zeke.

For the moment, Guster didn't mind. He couldn't help but think about how he'd betrayed her by running away in the middle of the night, committing such an unpardonable act of disobedience. As soon as she finished hugging him, she was going to kill him.

Mom straightened her arms, pushing Zeke back so she could look at him. "Your father and I decided we're going to ground you for so long, you'll never be permitted to go to college!" Her eyes were burning, like they'd jump from their sockets if she were to say another word.

Then she kissed Zeke and Guster, each in turn on the top of the head. "What have you been eating this whole time?" she asked.

"I took some raviolis from the fridge," said Guster. Mom beamed. "And then we got here, and this place—it's so wonderful with all the things you can eat."

Mom nodded. "I was so worried about you," she said.

Zeke rubbed his hair where her wet lips had been. "So you brought Dad?" he asked.

"I wasn't going to let her come alone, and it looks like it was a good thing I didn't," Dad said. He looked surprisingly like he was in his element, all bundled up in a puffy green parka, his cold breath puffing out from under his battleship nose like a cloud. He grinned. "No Johnsonvilles are going gallivanting around the globe without their dad this time."

Dad actually seemed to be enjoying himself. Guster and Mom and Mariah and Zeke had all talked about last summer's events so much over the year, while all Dad could do was listen. Now he wouldn't be left out.

Dad put his arm around Mom. Or maybe he was there to protect her. Either way, Guster was glad to see him.

"How come you're here?" Zeke asked Mariah. She had one of Salero's books in her lap, and she smelled salty. Like she'd been eating bacon. "Shouldn't you be back in your lessons with the Mayor's pet smart guy?"

Mariah looked up from her book. "His name is Salero, Zeke, and I'll have you know his knowledge of history and philosophy is quite impressive. He knows what he's talking about."

Zeke huffed. "Whatever. I can't believe you fall for all that stuff."

"Children," Mom said. She glared at both of them.

"Let's just get on the choppers and go," said Zeke. "We can bust out Felicity's men and be gone. They can't catch helicopters."

"It's not that easy, Zeke," said Mom. "Even if Princess Sunday let us go right now, the Mayor's guards have this place surrounded. And this time, Felicity's mercenaries don't even have their rifles."

The door to the dungeon swung open. Princess Sunday stood at the top of the steps.

"There's more to it than that," she said. "The city is crumbling all around us. It's getting worse by the day. The people want an Exquisite Morsel, Guster. They want you to be the answer to their problems. Those who tend the Yummies say that all of the monsters will be back any day now."

Mom looked like her blood would boil. "You don't actually believe that drivel about the Exquisite Morsel, do you?"

Princess Sunday dipped her chin, refusing to meet Mom's eyes.

"How can you let the Mayor do this?" Mom said. "Have you no sympathy? Would your mother do this to you?"

Princess Sunday's face fell, and a cloud seemed to pass over her otherwise bright eyes. "My mother?" Princess Sunday said. She shook her head. "You heard what the Mayor said. Moms are illegal in El Elado. I don't have a mother. Even if I did, I could never call her Mom like your kids do to you. We're taken away to live in the city orphanage when we're born. I never knew the woman who brought me into this world. She passed away, I think, years ago."

She began to cry. "For the most part, we don't even use the word Mom here. It's not something we speak about openly. The closest thing we have to concrete relatives are cousins. The

Baconists made sure of that."

Mom's round eyes suddenly softened. She reached a hand through the bars to touch the Princess's arm. "I . . ." she stammered.

Princess Sunday dried her eyes. "Please don't pity me. It is our way. Long ago, the Baconists convinced the people that their orphanages and institutions were a much safer place for a child to grow up. To say otherwise is heresy in El Elado."

"Safer?" Mom asked. "Being raised by an institution is better than this?" she said, spreading her arms toward Dad and her children.

"Not every family is like yours, Mrs. Johnsonville. You should count yourself lucky. When people start to think of people like you being the exception, not the rule, they look for alternatives. I didn't say I liked it, but I can't speak against it publicly either—not without being accused of heresy."

Guster had never seen anyone so sad. Princess Sunday's cherry crown seemed to weigh on her like it was filled with all the burdens of the city in one place. In that moment, she did not look like a young woman anymore. Instead, she looked older and more worn down by experience than even Mom.

"Then please," Mom said, "You'll free my boys?"

Princess Sunday shook her head. "I wish I could. The Mayor is separating the boys from everyone else. He knows that you won't leave without them." She turned to Guster. "You and Zeke are hostages."

Mom opened her mouth, and then closed it again. She looked like she wanted to shout at Princess Sunday and give her a piece of her mind but, after what she'd just been told, couldn't bring herself to do it.

"Don't worry, Mom," Zeke piped up. "We have a—"

Guster shot out his hand and clapped it over Zeke's mouth before he could say another word. He had a feeling Zeke was going to tell them about the tunnel, and Guster couldn't risk anyone knowing about that. Princess Sunday had already betrayed them once. There was no telling if she would do it again. Better to keep their escape plan a secret.

"What he means to say is, thanks for the special cake you baked us, Mom," said Guster. "It was absolutely what we needed most." He hoped she would catch his meaning. She would probably know what they were doing with its contents.

"Cake?" Mom asked. She looked puzzled. "I didn't bake you a cake."

Guster was confused. If Mom hadn't, then who had? Where had the ice cream scoop come from? Who was A.G.? He looked over at Zeke, whose face was screwed up in thought. They would have to figure that out later.

Dad kneeled down and clasped Guster by the hand. "Whatever they tell you son, whatever it is that happens over there in the Mayor's Mansion, I want you to trust your instincts. I want you to do what you know is right. And at the end of it all, your mom and I will be waiting for you, and we will be proud."

Guster studied Dad's face. Was there something Dad knew that he didn't? It was one of those moments of Dad-wisdom, and he knew Dad wanted him to fit the advice into their circumstances, like a key turning in a lock. Right now he wasn't sure what to make of it.

So he smiled and nodded his head. "I will."

"It's time to go," said Princess Sunday. "We must obey the Culinary's wishes." The Princess's guards herded Guster and Zeke further into the dungeon to the door opposite the one they'd come in.

Guster glanced back. Dad was looking over at him, his eyes drooping sadly at the corners.

"Son, we'll find a way out of this," he said. "Be sure to take care of each other."

The heavy wooden door shut behind Guster. Behind that was another corridor of cells, much like the ones that held

Mom, Dad, Henry Junior, and Mariah. Those cells held Felicity Casa and her mercenaries.

"Guster," said Felicity. She rushed to the bars. She was dressed in a trim, beige parka with white fur lining the hood. Her blonde hair was picture perfect, and a snowflake earring dangled from each ear. "There's something here, Guster. This is what I was trying to tell you. There are more treasures to find. Archedentus was here." Her perfect, painted face was serious, her eyes earnest.

Archedentus? "How do you know?" he asked. This was too far off any of his known travel routes.

Felicity gestured around her. "This city. The roads. The flavors. The confectionary workmanship like none I've ever seen or imagined. Who else could have done this?" she asked.

It was possible. Or it could have been someone like him.

"The ship that brought everyone here, they were conquistadors! It must have been the very same ship that took Archedentus to Machu Picchu and around the world! After tasting all those marvelous flavors, they found this natural phenomenon and settled here and built a city. This was his grand, delicious utopia!"

How could she be so sure? Most of Archedentus's journeys had been in the Western Hemisphere. It was *possible*, however unlikely.

"Guster, there's more," Felicity said. "The Baconists— don't they seem familiar to you?"

Guster nodded. The red robes. They were all too familiar.

"There's an old Gastronimatii legend about the cult coming out of the mountains in the beginning of time. They saw the polluted flavors of the world and were dismayed, so they resolved to protect what was left."

"You think they started here?" said Guster.

Felicity shook her head. "I'm not sure. I think their history is tied up in this place, but it's been so long, they don't even know how."

First Archedentus and now even the Gastronimatii might be connected to the city. The more Guster learned about El Elado, the more inevitable it seemed that Guster would come here.

"When you came to our farm and you made that mother sauce, did you know that Yummy was coming for me?" asked Guster.

Felicity's face fell. "I couldn't have, though it makes sense, knowing what I know now. You're special, Guster, and as soon as you ate that single bite of the One Recipe, it sent shockwaves of taste and smell across the earth, invisible tremors that only a creature such as Yummy could have sensed."

"Taste Resonance Theory," said Guster.

"Exactly. That's why you can't let this opportunity slip through your grasp!" Her face broke into a smile, her porcelain teeth as white as a toilet bowl. "Imagine what this city has to offer the world!"

Wasn't this just like Felicity? Guster had led her here. That jelly doughnut had been her guarantee that he wouldn't get away. Now she was in middle of El Elado, a Celebrity Homemaker's paradise, making grand plans for the world at large, and, once again, Guster was caught at the center of it.

"I can't help you, Felicity," said Guster. "I've got troubles of my own."

She frowned. "No one else can do this but you," she said.

Guster stepped away. "Right now, the only thing that matters is getting my family out of here," he said.

The Lieutenant stood up at the bars in the cell across from Felicity's. The Sergeant sat beside him.

"Good to see you are well, sir," said the Lieutenant. "Whatever you do, don't give in to the Mayor's demands."

Guster nodded. He wasn't really sure what he would do. The Mayor and Salero were so . . . convincing.

Gaucho tugged on Guster's arm. "Come. We must get back

to the Mansion before the guards force us," he said.

Guster nodded, and he and Zeke followed Gaucho through another door.

"We'll get you out of this mess, sir," the Lieutenant hollered after them.

Guster turned to give him a smile, and the door shut behind them.

Chapter 20 — Zeke's Binge

Guster was silent on the carriage ride back to the Mayor's Mansion. He hadn't realized how much he'd hoped that a visit to Mom and Dad would have given them an alternative. Not even Felicity had a plan. Princess Sunday wasn't able to help them either. They were all just as helpless as he and Zeke were.

Their only way out was to dig.

As they turned a corner, a crowd of people flocked down the street toward the city gate. Some of them were cheering as they ran. The crowd was so large, the carriage had to stop until they had passed. "What was that about?" asked Zeke.

Gaucho shrugged. "There is something important happening. Maybe another parade. I do not know," he said.

When they finally arrived back at the Mansion, Salero stood on the steps waiting for them. For a moment, there was an uncomfortable silence. Then he sniffed and said in a low, even voice, "They're here."

"Who's here?" asked Zeke.

But Guster already knew.

Salero smiled faintly. "Yummy has arrived."

Guster did not move from the carriage seat. He could not move.

"Come," said Salero. "I want you to see the guardians of our city in the full light of day." He motioned, and the guards grabbed Guster and Zeke by the arms and pried them from the carriage. They marched them into the mansion, spears at the boys' backs, and up a spiral staircase out onto a balcony that overlooked the streets below.

From here they could see the gates of El Elado. The people lined the streets, cheering and waving miniature, brightly colored blue, yellow, and red flags. They were marching toward the city's outer wall, a mass of bodies moving shoulder to shoulder like a herd of cows. When they got to the wall, they climbed it, the crowd pinching and squeezing onto the narrow stairways that led to the top of the ramparts. They poured onto the walkway on top of the walls, leaning over and peering out into the luscious valley below.

"There, in the distance, on the edge of the valley!" shouted a man. He was pointing toward the ice cave where Guster and Zeke and Mariah had entered the city.

Guster stood, straining on his tiptoes to see. Far on the edge of the valley, a small white dot moved toward the city. Then there was another, fading into view as it drew closer. Then another. And another. There were more than a dozen of them, moving in a loose formation across the valley.

They were too big to be grizzly bears or yaks. The closer they came, the more Guster could make out their huge, muscular arms, the way their shaggy shoulders connected straight into their heads, or the wide, tooth-filled jaws that stretched across their faces.

Soon, they were at the gate, the people cheering and chanting as they came. "Yummy! Yummy! He will save us! Yummy!" they said.

"The Yeti, mighty beast of the Himalayas, is a territorial creature, always returning to its home after the hunt, ever vigilant over the mighty, forbidden peaks of the East," Zeke recited, his voice a whisper of awe.

The flock of beasts lined up outside the gate. The largest one stood at the point, lifted his head up toward the sky, and roared.

The guards on watch at the gate turned two enormous cranks. There was a groan and the scraping of peanut brittle; a crack of sky peeked between the two doors as the gates opened.

A sudden gasp went through the crowd now that there was no barrier between them and the monsters. There was a mad dash, screaming, and shoving as the crowd pushed against each other, as if they had not realized in their excitement at the spectacle that the monster was coming into their city to walk its streets.

People locked themselves inside the nearest building or huddled on the ramparts as the first Yummy lumbered through the gates. Their feet smashed the butterscotch pavement with each step, their arms swinging slowly like two logs. There were thirteen of them in all, just like Princess Sunday had said.

Guster's throat tightened, and he felt fear rise in his chest. They were finally here, and there were so many of them, all with fangs bared and paws that could snap bones to pieces in their grip. He'd tried so hard to escape them. He and Zeke and Mariah had come so far—halfway across the world. But now this. It was the end of the line. There was nowhere else to run.

"Are you . . .?" He forced he words from his throat, but he couldn't finish them. He wanted to know when he would meet his fate.

"Yes. But not yet," said Salero. "There are customs and protocols. Tomorrow. Sunset. That will be the moment when you save the city."

Guster felt sick. Save the city. That's what they always called it. Did they realize what that meant for him?

He wanted to see Mom and Dad again, to tell them he loved them. There was so much to say that he'd never said before but never thought he would have to.

The thirteen monsters stopped at a wall near the mansion grounds. The city streets behind them were vacant, the people having fled indoors even more quickly than they came. Some of them peeked out from their hiding places, watching and waiting.

The largest Yummy bent low, jammed both of his massive paws into the ice cream ground, and clawed a chunk free. Two more joined him, clawing and digging until they'd carved out a hole in the ground.

A smaller Yummy came from behind their ranks and dove head first, his arms clenched at his side, into the hole. He slid down and disappeared from view.

The line of monsters followed, and, for a moment, they looked more like penguins than killing machines, one after another diving into their burrow. The largest turned to look behind them into the streets, sniffed the air, then turned his head upward, as if searching. He swung his massive shoulders and stub for a head toward Guster. His tiny orange eyes darted this way and that, then finally settled on Guster.

The monster held Guster's eyes for a long, long moment. Guster could not look away, no matter how badly he wanted to run indoors or to find safety behind the Mansion's walls.

They were clear and intelligent, more than the eyes of a beast; they were the eyes of a creature that knew what it was going to do.

Guster shuddered, gripping the banister until his knuckles ached under the strain. Yummy was not some wild beast driven by instinct. It was something more sinister. That would make him even harder to escape.

"I think we've seen enough," said Zeke. He stepped between Guster and the beast. His fists were balled, and he glared hard into Salero's face.

In that moment, Guster felt a fraction of gratitude pierce his fear. He was standing up for Guster, no matter how bad Zeke may have wanted to stare at the monster now that he could finally study it safely from a distance. Zeke was his brother, and at least that he had that.

Salero nodded slowly. "You'll see more of him soon," he said, his lips curling into an almost imperceptible smile.

At a jerk of his head, the guards took Guster and Zeke roughly by the arms and marched them back down toward their cell. Guster struggled at the spiral staircase, digging in his heels.

"Move!" said the guard, shoving him down the first step. Guster teetered, scrambling to catch his balance and bracing himself against the wall. The guards were so much stronger. Even if they broke free, how long could they last in the city before they were captured again?

Their only hope was their tunnel. They had to use the element of surprise. Even that was a long shot, but it was the best chance they had.

The Guards shoved Zeke and Guster into the cell so hard they both fell to the floor. The door slammed shut then locked behind them.

"See you tomorrow," said one of the guards, his words muffled through the heavy door. He laughed.

That was it. Only one day left.

As soon as the door was locked behind them, Guster threw back the tapestry and crawled inside.

It wasn't long before Guster had scooped out, and Zeke had eaten, twenty more scoops of ice cream. The hole was long enough now for both of them to fit; they had to widen it so they could reach in further. They were digging down and to the left, following Guster's hunch.

The bricks were all made of mint chocolate chip now. Zeke scooped out another scoop and held it up to his face, wrinkling his nose. He took a bite. "Hmmm. Strawberry," he said. "You were right."

"They must have built over the original wall," said Guster. "The Mayor probably did not want any trace of Princess Sunday's influence left in his part of town." That meant the city must have at one time been united—a full range of flavors.

The two of them fell into a silent routine: Zeke used the ice cream scoop to scoop out and eat as much as he could, then switched places with Guster so he could sample the tunnel's right, left, bottom, and top. The deeper they dug into the strawberry tunnel, the more he could taste the Confectioners' pride in their work. He could taste how much they loved what they had built.

The tunnel grew. They were at least two body lengths into the strawberry now. Zeke's belly was stretched tight like a sheet over a basketball; it bulged so ferociously from his waist, it threatened to break out with every bite he took.

"It's so delicious, it hurts," Zeke moaned. He slid out of the tunnel and flopped down on the couch. "It's your turn," he said, handing over the scoop.

They began piling some of the ice cream behind the marshmallow couches to ease the burden on Zeke's belly. "This is our last chance anyway," said Guster.

Guster climbed into the tunnel, crawling in on his elbows. It was a tight fit, even for him. He wasn't sure how Zeke had managed.

He wriggled his way to the end and had to stretch his arms out in front of him, scoop in hand. He dug the scoop into the ice cream and tasted it. There it was again—the pride of something well made.

He scraped again, ate, and scraped. He tasted another mouthful. *Vanilla.* He had broken through to another layer. A flavor that was pure and good.

So he followed it.

There was something different about this flavor. Less pride.

Less patriotism. More . . . it was hard to name. It was a wild and fierce vanilla, like a pack of wolves or a grizzly bear.

Guster stopped. There weren't very many likely suspects that had touched this flavor. But this one . . . it was the last thing he wanted to taste. The hint of wild ferocity was unmistakable. Yummy. It had to be.

A lump turned in his throat. Was he digging toward their den? That's how it tasted.

He forced himself to take yet another bite, his fingers trembling, his skin numb with cold. He should back out. He should run. He should dig another way.

But there was also something else in the flavor. It was surprising and curious, and most of all, unexpected. Goodness. Friendship. Like a dog to his master. An undying devotion that hid somewhere between the bared fangs and snarls.

Guster pushed himself out of the tunnel.

"What? What's wrong?" asked Zeke.

He eased himself onto the floor and sat there, hugging his knees to his chest. "I don't know. A new flavor," he said.

This was not something he'd expected to taste. It was not something he could even be sure was real. It was like seeing a figure through a haze—just a silhouette, a muffled voice.

"I think Yummy's lair is down there," he said. It scared him to be that close. The focused intensity in that Yummy's eyes flashed across his mind.

"Zeke, I don't want them to eat me," Guster whispered. What if he never saw home again? What if this was the last time he'd see Mom or Dad? Oh how he wanted to feel a warm summer on his cheeks again.

"Then dig another way," said Zeke.

Reluctantly, Guster crawled back into the tunnel. This time he dug upward, keeping himself as far away from the vanilla tunnel as he could.

They dug into the night. Guster lost track of how many

shifts he took inside the tunnel. He rotated with Zeke every hour. They seemed to be tunneling into the plateau on which the city was built.

Somewhere around the third hour Guster hit chocolate marble swirl. It tasted of ambition and jealousy but did not hold the ferocity of Yummy's vanilla. Anything was better than that.

Their cell was filled with ice cream now. There was no way to hide it or even eat all of it. The only chance they had was to be gone before the Guards came with their morning bowl of cold stew. If they hadn't tunneled out by then, it would all be over.

Somewhere around his fourth shift outside the tunnel, he felt Zeke shake him. Guster had fallen asleep leaning against the wall. He was exhausted. "P, we have to do this," said Zeke, urging him back into the hole. Guster climbed in, shaking the sleep from his foggy head.

He began to dig, faster now than before, when he heard sounds, somewhere deep inside the chocolate marble swirl wall.

He stopped to listen. They were muffled voices. This was a good sign.

Guster dug toward them. The scoop broke through into empty air. The hole was only a few finger-widths across, but it was wide enough for light to spill into the tunnel in one, pencil-thin beam. A soft gust of fresh air broke into the tunnel onto Guster's face.

The voices were clearer now. "You know that if Yummy doesn't eat the boy, this will be the end of your tenure as Mayor." It was Salero.

Guster froze.

"You've been far too outspoken on the matter to the Culinary," Salero continued, "and all the people are well aware of where you stand."

"Yes, I have," sighed the Mayor. "But I stand by what I've

said. The Flatlanders are a plague on this city. Yummy must be satisfied."

"And if the boy isn't the Exquisite Morsel?" asked Salero. "Yummy will reject him. The people will never trust you again. Then you'll have a rebellion on your hands."

There was silence. Guster held his breath.

He had to try to get a better vantage point. He shifted himself ever so slowly up toward the tiny hole, moving sloth-like until he could see through it.

There was a foot behind a large desk only a few feet in front of the hole. Guster had broken through at floor level. Of all places, he had tunneled straight into the Mayor's office.

From his angle, he could see as high as the Mayor's desk. Salero was seated opposite the Mayor, but Guster couldn't see his face from the tunnel.

What he could see was the statue of a head on the Mayor's desk. The very same one that Guster had noticed on his first visit there but had never looked in the face. He recognized him instantly. He had seen paintings of him before in Felicity Casa's castle in France. He had even seen that face in a dream when he'd first tasted the Gastronomy of Peace.

Right there, on the Mayor's desk, was a statue of Archedentus.

"If only you were here to tell us what to do," said the Mayor. He laid a hand on the statue's base. He was talking to it. "You founded this city. You're the reason we're here."

Archedentus? So Felicity was right. He had been here. The conquistadors who had founded the city must be the same ones Archedentus sailed with so many centuries ago, which would put the great chef right here, as one of the founding members of El Elado.

But the Gastronimatii—they had started here in this city too, according to Felicity. How could that have happened in the same place?

"If the boy isn't the Exquisite Morsel," said Salero, "then you must find a way to eliminate him yourself."

Chapter 21 — The Fires Below

Guster pressed himself against the wall. It was all so much at once. Archedentus and the Gastronimatii here in the city long ago. Salero and The Mayor plotting against him if Yummy didn't get him first.

He slid himself carefully, silently, backwards down the tunnel and away from the office. He stopped at the bottom of the incline, panting, more from terror than exertion. He was going to have to dig in another direction. They were running out of time.

There was no time to feel sorry for himself. So Guster got to work. He turned onto his belly and gouged a spoonful of ice cream out of the tunnel wall, then touched it to his tongue. Still chocolate marble swirl. No good.

He slid down another few feet, and then did the same thing. The flavor was weaker here, which must have meant it was mixed with, or near to, another layer beneath the Mansion's architecture.

Guster repeated the process, sampling the ice cream every few feet down the wall. It tasted slightly different each time, the chocolate swirl growing more diluted as he went, the slight hint of strawberry growing stronger, until he'd passed the barrier and crossed over to the strawberry layer completely.

With each bite, there were swirls of emotion and flavor, all blending together in a confusing quarrel of jealousy and honor, courage and sympathy. There was no clear or dominant flavor. There was nothing for Guster to hold on to.

Then Guster tasted it. A hint of cinnamon. It tingled on his tongue, and for just a moment, he was no longer cold inside the icy tunnel.

It was the taste of purpose. The taste of freedom.

He followed it, digging with the ice cream scoop as fast as he could until he'd dug a hole large enough to stick his head into. There was something intriguing about this cinnamon ice cream—something exciting and bold—like it had just been made yesterday.

His ice cream scoop broke through into empty air. Startled, Guster pulled back his hand and widened the hole. A faint glow of orange light shone through it from the other side.

He'd found a tunnel.

Heart racing, Guster dug the hole wider, not bothering to eat the ice cream now—he could shove it into the tunnel on the other side. There was ample room; the tunnel was at least tall enough to crouch in and even walk, so long as he bent low.

As soon as the hole was wide enough to fit his shoulders through, he dove through headfirst.

He landed with a thud on soft ice cream. It wasn't icy like it had been in other places. The tunnel here was warm.

Guster propped himself up on his feet. It would take him and Zeke weeks to carve something like this out of the mountain. This could be it. Their way out.

He needed to find out where the orange light was coming from. Bent low, Guster ran as best he could down the tunnel toward the glow, his back scraping against the ice cream ceiling.

In the soft light he could see the walls were cinnamon, the light glinting off scarlet specks of spice, like quartz shining in a granite cave. Guster took a sharp right, then turned the corner and stopped dead.

Below him, the floor dropped away into a cavern, a large orange bonfire blazing in its center, black smoke curling up toward the ceiling and winding its way out of narrow shafts toward the surface. The bonfire was enormous, at least twice as tall as Guster was, red and orange flames dancing and flickering up and over a pile of coals. The heat pinched the skin on his cheeks. He could only imagine how hot the fire's center itself must be.

There were shovels and picks left behind and mounds of coal piled against the walls, but other than that, the room was empty. At least five more tunnels branched off from the cavern in all directions, like the strands of a spider's web.

Guster tried his best to orient himself. He'd been underground in the dark so long it wasn't easy to figure out which tunnel led back to Mom and Dad. He hoped one of them would. At the very least, they would take him far away from here.

He lowered himself carefully into the cavern, finding handholds in the rough-hewn walls. He wanted to make sure he could climb back out again, especially with the ice cream being so soft from the heat.

He set his feet down on the cavern floor, and, keeping as far away from the flames as he could, made his way along the wall toward the first tunnel.

The tunnel was, just like the one he'd come from, lined with a layer of cinnamon ice cream. He reached out with his spoon and scooped up a bite. It was warm around the edges, like it had been taken out of the freezer a few minutes ago. It tasted delicious. He'd always had a special place on his tongue for cinnamon. He closed his eyes and absorbed the flavor, trying his best to understand its deeper layers. He wanted to feel its nature. What was the person who made it like?

Delicious. The flavor was pure, made of the finest ingredients, like every speck of cinnamon had been arranged in a picture on his tongue. Surely whoever had made this ice cream was providing a way out. A perfect, final escape from their imprisonment. A way to freedom.

And then, faintly, under the layers of mild burning, he tasted it—ambition, a drive for power. Cruelty.

It shocked him at first. This was a beautiful, sparkling cavern, a cathedral to taste. How could this be wrong?

He dug deeper into the wall, scraping into the cinnamon, searching. One inch beneath the cinnamon was deep brown chocolate.

Someone stumbled behind him. Guster jumped so high, his head scraped the ceiling.

"You have been busy. I am impressed!" said Zeke, looking around the cavern, his eyes wide with admiration.

Guster clutched his chest. He was breathing fast from fright. "You nearly scared three days' worth of strawberry chunks out of me," he said.

Zeke shrugged. "Sorry," he said. "I just got bored of waiting and thought maybe something happened to you. So I came looking." He peered over Guster's shoulder into the tunnel.

"Is this the way out?" he said.

Guster shook his head. "Maybe," he said. Zeke had come too soon. There were still things Guster needed to figure out.

"Maybe? Are you kidding? This tunnel is perfect. We've got a ticket to blue skies and sunshine. Let's go!"

Zeke pushed past Guster into the tunnel. "Wait," said Guster, grabbing his arm. "There are still things I don't understand about this place. It doesn't feel right."

Zeke stopped. He folded his arms. "Okay, like . . .?" he said, waiting.

Guster shook his head. "I don't know," he said. It frustrated him. The flavors he had tasted in the tunnels up to this point were trying to tell him something, but they all ended up as dead ends. None of them were the right choice.

He knew that Salero, with all his articulate words, did not ring true to him. Salero was a very smart man—he was a Baconist, after all—but did that mean that he was always right? Did all smart people think the way Salero did?

"Salero, The Mayor, and half of El Elado want to feed me to the Yummies. Felicity Casa wants me to go on another treasure hunt, and I just want to go home." Guster could feel tears pushing at his eyelids. "I just wish Mom and Dad were here to tell me what to do."

"Just do the right thing," said Zeke.

"And how do I know what that is?" Guster asked.

Zeke laughed just a little, but from his face, Guster could tell he was sincere. "I dunno. Isn't it usually just obvious?" Zeke said.

There was something so simple and sincere about the way Zeke said it, Guster wondered if Zeke ever asked himself these kinds of questions at all.

The cave rumbled slightly under their feet. The ceiling cracked, and large chunks of chocolate ice cream fell like boulders onto the fire.

"The cave-ins!" said Guster, bracing himself against the wall.

"Let's go!" cried Zeke, pulling Guster farther down the tunnel. "We have to get out before the whole thing falls down on us."

Guster planted his feet. He knew now what he had to do. "Not that way Zeke," he said. He was afraid of what he was about to do, what his decision would mean. He tried to cover it by pretending he had courage.

"We need to go back," he said.

Zeke looked Guster straight in the eyes. Guster was almost sure he would protest, pull and tug at him until Guster went the other way, but he didn't. "Okay," said Zeke. "You're the Evertaster."

For once, that actually gave Guster a barely perceptible boost of confidence. Guster just had to follow his gut and hope he was making the right choice.

He pulled Zeke into the cavern and scrambled up the melting ice cream handholds back into the strawberry tunnel.

Zeke came willingly, and when Guster dove into the narrow tunnel they had dug with the scoop, Zeke was right on his heels.

Guster shimmied his way down the tunnel back toward the cell in the dark, stopping to taste the tunnel here or there, getting his bearings with each bite.

It wasn't long until he found it again. The wild, ferocious taste of Vanilla—the one that led to Yummy's lair.

Chapter 22 — The Belly of the Beast

It was insane. It was crazy. It didn't make any sense. But Guster dug anyway, scooping mouthfuls of Vanilla onto his tongue. He considered each bite. He wasn't just tasting them, he was *absorbing* them.

"Let me help," said Zeke from behind Guster. "You've been tunneling for the last ten feet. It will go faster if we take turns."

Guster shook his head, even though there was no way Zeke could see him in the dark. "I can't. I have to do this," he said. He *had* to test each inch of the tunnel. He was picking his way along carefully, correcting their course with each bite, adjusting the angle of the burrow according to taste.

The flavors in the vanilla were growing more intense. There was the same, ferocious flavor inside as before, but it had grown until Guster could almost feel the biting and gnashing of fangs. Yummy was neither a chef nor a Confectioner, and yet this was unmistakably his flavor.

But it wasn't the wild, fierce taste that piqued Guster's interest. It was the deep, almost invisible aftertaste that drew him down this path. There was that streak of loyalty in the ice cream. There was something so pure in the flavor that

Guster forced himself to sort through the rage and hunger that threatened to overwhelm it.

Guster turned the tunnel downward, so that this head was lower than his feet and he had to brace his knees against the sides to keep from sliding down and smashing his face against the end. There were other flavors creeping in from all sides now: veins of golden salted caramel, chunks of double brownie fudge, swirls of spumoni. Ugh. How he hated spumoni.

Zeke tugged on his foot. "Did you hear that?" he asked.

"What?" Guster said. He kept digging.

Zeke hissed, "There was a noise. Behind us. I think someone found our tunnel."

A lump formed in Guster's throat. The tunnel suddenly didn't feel very safe anymore. "Are you sure?"

"I think so. There was a scraping. And some voices. They were shouting."

The Mayor's guards. Guster strained to listen Was it morning already? They must have found all the heaps of ice cream from the tunnel piled up in Guster and Zeke's cell.

"Hurry," said Zeke. "Are we there?"

There was tension in Zeke's voice. At least Zeke believed that this tunnel ended somewhere. Guster wished he could be so sure. Guster didn't know where it was going or what would happen to them when they reached it.

They couldn't let the Guards catch them. If he was going to confront Yummy, he didn't want Salero or the Mayor to force him to do it. He wasn't going to face Yummy in chains. He needed to do it because it was his choice, because it was what he wanted to do, not what anyone else wanted.

The metal scoop hit something hard. He slowed down, carving into the cream wherever it was soft, feeling his way with the scoop in the dark. It hit something hard again.

"What's taking so long?" asked Zeke. "We haven't moved in like an hour! They're getting closer."

Guster pressed his hand up against the object. It was mostly flat, with a rough, grainy texture. "I dunno. There's something really hard in here that I can't dig out. It's blocking our path. I'm not sure what it is."

"Well, what does it taste like?" asked Zeke.

Guster pressed his face up to the flat surface then stuck out his tongue. The tip touched the rough, grainy object. He licked it.

Sugary. A pastry. Delicious. Waffle cone. "It's a cone," said Guster.

"Then break it!" said Zeke. His shoulders pressed up against Guster's heels. A faint light flashed down the tunnel behind them. "Go!"

Guster stabbed the scoop into the waffle cone. The metal chipped the brittle surface. Guster stabbed again, hacking at it as best he could in the tight quarters, using the scoop like a miniature pickaxe.

On the fifth strike, he punched a hole in the waffle cone surface. "I got through!" he shouted. There was a dim light below. He hacked again, and the brittle cone fell away, leaving a hole big enough for Guster to squeeze through.

"I'm going in," said Guster. He pushed himself downward headfirst, sliding like a seal through the hole.

He tumbled down, smashing onto a smooth waffle cone floor below him. The impact shot pain through his shoulder and left him gasping for air.

"Freedom!" cried Zeke as he fell from the hole behind Guster. Guster tried to roll out of the way, but it was too late. Zeke landed like a sack of rocks on Guster's ribs.

Guster winced. "Get off me!" He shoved Zeke over, squirming out from underneath his big brother.

Zeke and Guster picked themselves up off the ground, and Guster slid the metal ice cream scoop into his belt under his parka. He peered into the room and tried to make sense of his surroundings.

They were in a huge chamber with waffle cone walls and a low ceiling that stretched into the darkness. A passageway to their left led upward. A pale yellowish glow shone from the end—a tiny point of daylight far in the distance. It cast just enough of a glow for them to see half-gnawed, giant strawberries littering the floor, looking like broken skulls in the dim light. Shattered peanut brittle chunks were piled in one corner, and overturned bowls with globs of chocolate sauce spilled from them and pooled on the floor like blood. Broken candy canes as long as a man's thigh bone littered the ground.

"What is this place?" Zeke whispered.

It was the Yummies' lair. He could taste it. "It's where *they* live," said Guster.

And as scared as he was right then, he still hoped they were doing the right thing. He didn't have the words to explain it, and if anyone were there to argue with him, he wouldn't be able to defend his actions. But it was a hunch, and the words and the understanding and the why of it all could come later because, above all, he had to follow the tiny nudging in the back of his conscience that was telling him this was where he needed to be.

"Okay," said Zeke. He swallowed.

Something stirred.

"Did you hear that?" Zeke whispered.

Guster nodded.

There was a scraping sound in the darkness in front of them. Then a snarl, like a small motor revving.

"I think we should go," said Zeke. He took a step up the passageway.

Guster hesitated. There was something here he had to do.

A pair of wide-set orange eyes opened in the shadows. They drew closer. Then another pair of eyes lit up in the cavern. Then another. And another, each reflecting the dim light with an iridescent yellow-orange. There were more snarls.

Guster felt the hair on the back of his neck stand up.

"Let's go," said Zeke. He tugged on Guster's arm.

The first Yummy emerged from the darkness into the pale square of yellow light. It was white like the snow and bent low, its powerful arms dangling from its shoulders, and its claws scraping razor-thin gouges into the crispy waffle cone ground.

Guster could hear the beast's slow, deliberate exhale. Every feature stood out to him: each hair, the shape of its broad mouth, the wrinkles around the skin of its orange eyes. Even the chipped and broken points of its teeth, like knives embedded in its gums, were all apparent to Guster in that moment.

Every nerve in his body begged him to bolt up the passageway and flee.

The Yummy rolled a white scoop of ice cream toward Guster on the ground with the back of his hand. It was an awkward gesture coming from such a gigantic beast, and Guster wasn't sure what to make of it.

The eyes of the monster looked so deep, like they were expecting something from Guster. They were more than the eyes of an animal. They were windows to a real soul.

Guster stooped, his eyes still on Yummy, and picked up the packed ice cream ball. It was surprisingly warm to his touch. He held it for a moment, wondering what it meant.

Zeke grabbed Guster's free hand. "We go. Now," said Zeke, yanking Guster up the passageway.

Guster shook himself, and suddenly something snapped. They were inches away from the monsters. Go. They had to go.

He took off up toward the light, pumping his legs up the steep waffle cone slope until it was gone and nothing but chocolate ice cream lay underneath.

A wall of fresh air and sunlight hit them as they emerged into the clear morning in City of El Elado.

Guster blinked back the sun's rays. They were standing on

a hill, with a raised peanut brittle stage in front of them. It had two columns, just taller than Guster, with a pair of chains and manacles hanging from them. This stage was not just for any performance. It was built to make a sacrifice.

Guster stopped. The people of El Elado were crowded around the raised stage at the foot of the small hill. There was the Culinary, dressed in their ridiculously bright costumes. There was Princess Sunday and her subjects, nervously crowded at the far side of the hill. There was the Mayor, his oily black top hat and blue ribbon on his chest shining in the light of the dawn. The Extravío Vigilar stood watch at his elbows, all of them dressed in their crimson-and-gold striped pantaloons, shiny breastplate armor, and curved steel hats.

Felicity Casa, the Lieutenant, and the Sergeant stood, their wrists tied, surrounded by Princess Sunday's Cherry Brigade. Felicity looked defiant, her jaw angled upward toward the sun. The Lieutenant gritted his teeth.

And then there was Mom, Dad, Mariah, and Henry Junior. All four of them were also surrounded by the Cherry Brigade. Mom was crying. Dad had his arms folded. He looked ten feet tall right then, like a statue casting a long shadow, ready to fight.

The crowd erupted—some of them cheering, others yelling to Guster something he could not understand.

The Mayor barked an order and the guards lowered their spears, pointing the steel heads toward Guster. This is exactly what Salero and the Mayor had wanted all along. Their plots and manipulation of the Culinary. Their influence over the people. Their sacrifice to Yummy was here.

Guster was not going to get chained to those pillars. The Mayor was wrong about that.

"Run!" shouted Mom, pushing her way through the Cherry Brigade.

Guster spun, looking for a gap in the crowd they could slip

through. They needed a way out, but the people were gathered too tightly at the base of the hill.

The Mayor's guards advanced, their ring spears closing in. There was nowhere to go.

Guster still held the scoop of vanilla ice cream in his hand. There was no time for choices. There was no time for a plan. He lifted the cold scoop to his lips.

It tasted pure and sweet, a simple, mild flavor that ran deep, like a mountain lake. Instantly, the first taste of El Elado's ice cream from Bubalatti's shop in New York came back to him, flashing across his mind, but this was sweeter. This was pure and unpolluted by greed or malice. It had an untainted soul.

"Zeke," said Guster. "We can't stay here." He said it slowly. He wasn't afraid anymore. He knew that he had to follow this through to the end.

"You think?" said Zeke.

"I do," said Guster. He grabbed Zeke by the hand and pulled him down into the passageway toward the darkness.

"Where are we going?" said Zeke, his voice cracked, hitting a high-pitched note. There was panic in it.

Guster shook his head. "Away," he said. He wasn't sure where they would end up. He only knew what lay two steps ahead. Beyond that, he couldn't guess. He broke into a run. They'd need time.

The darkness closed around them as they crossed back into the lair lined with waffle cone. The sound of growls met them and the noise grew until they were surrounded in a chorus of snarls. This was a dead end.

The Yummies were waiting at the passageway's end. The largest one stepped into the dim light from the tunnel. Guster did not know what he would do. He had not meant for things to end this way.

Yummy flexed his claws and roared. The cavern shook, bits of waffle cone crumbling from the ceiling and falling to the floor.

"Guster?" said Zeke, his voice trembling.

Guster held up a hand to his brother. "Not now, Zeke. I know you're trying to protect me. You can go. But I have to be here." He was surprised how confident he sounded.

He took a step toward Yummy. He held up the scoop of ice cream in his palm. "I know you aren't what some people say. I've tasted it."

Yummy shot hot breath through his nostrils. Guster could feel it on his face. Two more monsters emerged from the darkness. They were surrounded now.

"I know that you are here to protect, not to kill," said Guster. "I know that you will kill if you have to, but you don't want to, do you?" He felt strong when he said it.

The lead creature sniffed again. Those orange eyes. They held such intelligence. Such ancient wisdom.

"This city can't go on like this forever, can it?" Guster asked. "This is not how you want The Delicious City to be, is it?" His blood beat so loudly past his ears that he was afraid his veins would burst. There was nothing between him and the monster now. No walls or fences. No oceans or train rides. The running stopped here.

Guster held the vanilla scoop up like an offering to Yummy.

The creature lifted one foot and stepped forward again, his heel smashing into the ground so hard it felt like a tiny earthquake. Then, slowly, he lifted his arms and closed his fingers and thumbs around Guster's shoulders.

It was like being smashed in a vice. Yummy lifted him off the ground. Guster's legs and arms hung like a limp towel.

Yummy opened his sickening, wide jaws. Hot breath blasted out of his throat onto Guster's face. The monster's mouth was a cave itself, with a broad, rough purple tongue covered in buds the size of gumdrops. And all of that was surrounded by teeth. Row after row of pointy, jagged teeth.

He'd made a horrible, horrible mistake. He'd followed his instincts, and now Yummy was going to eat him.

Guster thrashed his limbs, trying to break free. He lifted his knees to his chest and kicked wildly at the Yummy, catching nothing but air.

Yummy grabbed Guster's ankles then lifted him high, dangling him in midair for a moment. Then he shoved Guster headfirst into his mouth and snapped his jaws shut tight with a chomp.

Chapter 23 — The Shield of Seasons

Guster's face scraped across Yummy's rough, bumpy tongue. The sticky, fleshy insides of the monster's cheeks pressed in on him, crushing his ribs, so that Guster felt like he was being squeezed through a rubber hose. He couldn't breathe. He couldn't move. One bite and the teeth would crush him or sever his legs. This was it. He was going to die.

How could he have been so foolish?

In that instant, he had a strange thought: *I wonder what I taste like?* He supposed that he deserved it after all the things he'd eaten.

Then the taut insides of Yummy's cheeks relaxed, and the roof of his mouth lifted. Just like that, the pressure softened. Guster slid down, headfirst, until he was pressed up against Yummy's fleshy throat.

Yummy hadn't even taken a bite. Somehow, Guster had escaped those tearing teeth set in those ferocious jaws. Yummy had swallowed Guster whole.

Then the monster moved. Guster bobbed straight up, then back down again, like Yummy had just hit a speedbump at full speed.

Then it began to bob up and down as it bounded forward. Guster managed to curl upward, sliding himself around until he was upright, his knees tucked to his chin.

It hadn't swallowed him yet. What was it waiting for?

Then it began to run. Its mouth opened just a little, so that a dim light spilled through the gap between its teeth and jaws and Guster could see the walls of the cave. Fresh air spilled into the hot, slimy mouth and rushed past Guster in a blast. Then another blast of air, this time from the inside out, roared past Guster's ears and hair as Yummy exhaled.

It was a strange sensation, being shut inside a sticky, wet mouth, the air rushing in and out. But with each step Yummy took, Guster's confidence grew. There were no bites. No chewing. No grinding. Yummy had not swallowed him . . . yet.

Where was Zeke? Had they taken him too?

Yummy turned a sharp left, then began to climb, surging upward in fits and starts. It was too dark to see, but Guster could feel a hard surface scraping against the front of the creature's enormous mouth as it climbed.

Yummy leapt forward.

A soft, orange light shone again through the open jaws. It grew brighter as Yummy ran, until it took shape. They were in a vast mint chocolate chip cavern. In it was another gigantic bonfire, twice as tall as the last one, burning and melting away the ice cream mountain from the inside.

For a moment, Guster forgot his predicament. These fires had been lit and tended by someone. Someone had to be feeding them the wood to keep them going and to make sure they had enough oxygen in the stale caves so they wouldn't fizzle out.

The cave rumbled. A huge mint chocolate chip stalactite broke free and came smashing down onto the ground, shards shattering outward from the point of impact.

Yummy reeled, lurching to the left to avoid the stalactite, then climbed up into a narrow passageway. He began to run

222

again.

Someone was behind these fires. Someone who was willing to work very hard to destroy the City of El Elado. But who?

This meant that it wasn't some curse from Yummy, or some such nonsense, that was melting the city. It wasn't any of Salero's convoluted explanations. Fires, plain and simple, were behind it all, and someone was lighting them.

Why would anyone want to destroy the Delicious City?

Yummy turned again. The tunnel glowed orange as they passed another fire. If the mountain was hollowed out too much, the entire city would collapse. It wouldn't matter if they lived in the Chocolate Crescent or the Fruitful Streets, they'd be killed in the massive avalanche that would follow. El Elado stood on the brink of disaster.

The tunnel grew dim again as Yummy darted back and forth on a tangled path. He ran for several minutes then stopped, panting. Through Yummy's open mouth, Guster could see a soft, blue light glowing overhead.

They were in a beautiful ice cave, light soaking through the glacier so that it shone a faint blue in the darkness. They stood at the edge of a deep chasm that reached down into the blackness, a bottomless pit that may very well have pierced the center of the Earth.

Yummy turned, and this time opened his mouth so wide that Guster could see the cave before him.

In front of Guster was a beautiful, ivory-white fountain bubbling out of the ground in a flower shape, each petal moving and oozing its way up and out of the ground. It flowed down into a massive, moving river that crept its way slowly down the sloped cavern floor, carving its way out into the light.

Guster sniffed. Even over Yummy's hot, stale breath, he could smell it—vanilla ice cream more pure and sweet than any he'd ever imagined.

This was the origin of the snowball that Yummy had

given him. He had been trying to tell him about this place, communicating with Guster the best it knew how: through taste.

This was the source. This was the place that he'd heard Princess Sunday's Cherry Brigade talk about: the source of all the ice cream in El Elado.

How badly Guster wanted to taste it for himself.

He carefully reached a hand out between Yummy's teeth toward the bubbling vanilla fountain.

A low growl rumbled up beneath Guster, shaking his bones. He pulled back his hand just as Yummy's jaws snapped shut. Everything was dark again.

Now that they were here, there was nothing stopping the Yummy from chewing him up and swallowing him once and for all. Was this how everything would end?

Then the monster began to run again. Each footfall rose and fell higher than the last as it climbed upward along the chasm wall.

Guster shuddered to think how precariously close to the edge of the void it ran. One misstep and they would plummet into darkness.

And then Yummy did an incomprehensible thing: it pivoted, throwing itself into midair. There was a sickening feeling of weightlessness, and then it fell.

It dropped like a stone for what felt like several seconds, when suddenly they hit the ground with a smash.

Guster shook from the landing. From what he could tell, Yummy had landed on his feet. But there was no way they had fallen all the way to the bottom. Nothing could survive *that* fall.

The creature opened its mouth and dim light spilled back onto Guster's eyes. They stood on an icy ledge on the side of the chasm. Yummy had leapt *across* the void.

In front of them was the narrow entrance to another

passageway.

But why? If Yummy intended to eat Guster, wouldn't the bubbling vanilla fountain be just as good a place? Wouldn't any of the tunnels before have worked just fine?

Instead of biting down, Yummy slowly opened his jaws, like the double doors to a hangar slowly grinding open, until his bottom lip nearly touched the ground. His tongue extended like a ramp to the ground, his teeth framing a perfect doorway.

Guster hesitated. He stretched himself carefully up to a bent standing position, his head ducked low under the roof of Yummy's mouth. This was unexpected.

Yummy waited. It did not move. Was it letting him go?

Guster did not want those jaws clamping down again while he was under the teeth. He spent a moment gathering his courage, then pushed off the fleshy throat and dove head first out of Yummy's mouth onto the ice. He slid several feet away from the monster, then scrambled to his feet and spun, ready to dodge an attack.

None came. Yummy slowly closed his jaws shut until his mouth was nothing but a thin line hiding those terrible teeth from view. It sniffed.

Guster let out a long, low sigh. He was soaked in sticky, warm saliva, but he could breathe. The air had never tasted crisper or more full. He wiped his jacket as best he could with his hands. He'd just been let go, or so it seemed. But why?

Yummy sniffed, then his yellow-orange eyes darted to the passageway behind Guster. It took a step toward him. Guster stepped back, uncertain.

Yummy sniffed again. Guster chanced a glance behind his shoulder. The passageway bored into the mountain, a narrow gap in the rock and ice. Above it was a dove on a spoon with an olive branch. Guster had seen that symbol before, but he could not remember where.

"You want me to go in there, don't you?" said Guster.

Yummy snorted.

There was little choice, really. They were both standing on a narrow ledge. Yummy blocked his path on one side. The narrow cleft in the rock was the only other way to go.

"Okay," said Guster. He ducked his head low and felt his way into the passage.

Behind him, Yummy purred.

The passageway opened into a small cavern with a high ceiling like a vaulted cathedral. Pale blue light shone down into the room so that everything glowed soft.

On either side of Guster, positioned at regular intervals around the circular room, were small statues carved from ice. There were several of them, each atop its own pillar. Some weren't familiar to Guster: a noodle tied in a knot, a pineapple, and a cheese wedge pointing skyward. Others were very familiar: an egg, a diamond, and a butter churn.

At the far end of the cavern, a wide sheet of vanilla ice cream flowed down the wall from a crack in the stone above, an ice cream falls almost frozen in time.

This place was a sanctuary. A temple to taste.

Guster listened. There was a very soft scraping sound, like snow sliding slowly down a roof, as the ice cream inched along the rock. It gathered at the floor, where it had spread out from the wall in the shape of a fan. It must have taken hundreds of years to cover the distance.

He stooped and stuck one finger in it, then licked it. Still fresh. And cold and good, like the age had only made the flavors stronger.

Guster tread softly across the room. This was a special, sacred place. He pressed both palms into the ice cream flow on the far wall. It was soft and cold to the touch, and even the muddy feel of it on his skin whispered to him that it was sweet.

His palms touched something hard beneath the flow. He scraped it away with both hands. Underneath was a perfect circle with two squinting eyes and an open, smiling mouth carved into off-white stone, much like the face on a Mayan calendar.

In that moment Guster began to understand. This place was good. It was pure.

Yummy had brought him here for a reason. This was why he'd left the farmhouse in the first place. Guster Johnsonville was the most delicious thing in the whole world, but Yummy had not come to devour him. He'd come to deliver him.

And this was what he was meant to see.

Guster scraped away the ice cream with both hands, tasting it as he went. The more he worked, the more he uncovered, until he found that it was more than just a face. It was a circular shield wider than his arm span.

Its surface was sectioned off into four quadrants, each one with its own central carving surrounded by intricate hieroglyphs. One with a blazing sun, another with three falling leaves, another with a web of crystal snowflakes, and the fourth with a sapling budding out from the ground—a quadrant for each season. In the center of the four quadrants was that smiling face, its eyes shut tight and its mouth open, like it was waiting to take a bite of something good.

More tiny pictures and words were carved around the rim of the stone shield, each one in a language Guster could not understand.

So *this* was what Yummy had wanted to show him. Guster took another taste of ice cream. He stepped back and let the pure vanilla flow through him. He needed to understand what this shield was. The ice cream's flavor was his best clue.

He closed his eyes. It was familiar. Sweet, but tempered, like a plain vanilla flavor should be. In it he tasted echoes of the Gastronomy of Peace. And . . . yes. Of its creator.

Archedentus. He'd been here. Guster was almost certain of it. Had he been the one to make this flow of ice cream? Or had he been the one to make the shield, and then hide it here?

Then, like the last cog in a clock snapping into place, Guster understood. Archedentus had sent for him. It was true. He'd been here in this city so long ago. He'd made this city.

Guster ran his hands across the rim of the shield. There were the symbols there: the chicken and the egg. The polar bear and the butter churn. The Mighty Ape's Diamonds. Each one after the other, they traced out a history of Archedentus's journey. They flowed around the edge of the rim to the very top of the shield, where a ship was docked at the base of an incredible mountain. On top of that mountain was a city made of towers of ice cream.

Archedentus's journey had not stopped at the One Recipe. He'd founded a city of pure and delicious tastes here in the hidden roof of the world.

And he'd sent for Guster, across time and taste, without even knowing who he was. Guster had been called, brought here by the only thing that could have found him: Yummy the hunter.

Guster traced the symbols with his fingertip. There was more to be found. The One Recipe was just the beginning.

It dawned on him with the crisp clarity of a summer morning—his search was not yet over. Over mountains and across continents, Guster still had so far to go.

Yummy purred behind him with one short burst.

"That's right, boy," said Guster. "I see it now. Thank you for coming so far to find me."

Guster startled himself. He was talking to the creature—and he'd known in his mind what it had said to him. It hadn't come in words, but in meanings, like the melody of a song that's sad, or a harmony that's full of hope. It had wanted to know if Guster understood.

Yummy grunted twice. *Take it with you*, it seemed to say. It meant the carved stone shield.

"How?" Guster asked. It was embedded in ice cream that was frozen solid. Even if Guster could pry it free, the stone disc must have weighed a thousand pounds. He'd never be able to haul it across the chasm.

Yummy bent low and nudged Guster's shoulder with his nose. It felt like a dog imploring his master, so Guster reached up and patted Yummy behind his tiny ears. It seemed like Yummy was actually asking for praise. He was seeking Guster's approval.

"You've done well, big guy," said Guster. Over all that land and sea, Yummy had found him. He was carrying on Archedentus's work.

Yummy purred softly again. The deep, rhythmic sound comforted Guster. Yummy had suddenly turned into a friend.

Guster put his hand on the shield. "Can you help me move it?" he asked.

We can, Yummy purred.

Footsteps echoed on the ice. Guster whirled around. There, standing in the narrow passageway was a man in the dark hood. He smelled like pickled ginger.

Fear lodged in Guster's throat.

The man in the hood clapped slowly, two bony hands emerging from his cloak. And then he spoke in a quiet, rasping voice. "Once again, you've found the way for me."

What had Guster done? He did not know this man. How could he ever have found the way for him before? The voice seemed familiar, yet Guster could not place it.

"I don't know you," Guster said, mustering his courage.

The raspy voice laughed to itself. "But I think you do," he said. The bony hands pulled back the hood and robe. A blood-red apron hung like a snake from the man's waist. Underneath the hood was a slender, hairless face that ended in a pointed chin. It was scarred where it had once been smooth. The nose was bent where it had once been straight. The man smiled, bearing pointed teeth in the same sadistic smile Guster had seen before.

Palatus. The Chef in Red.

Guster's heart froze. Here? How? It was impossible. "But I thought you were . . ."

"Trampled? Torn to bits by my own Gastronimatii?" Palatus asked. "Come now, you know better than that. If you never found a body, why would you assume? I made my way out behind the portrait and into the castle's secret tunnels, just as you had come in."

He was talking about The Chateau De Dîner—Felicity Casa's Castle in France. Guster had hoped they'd never meet him again. He'd thought it was over.

"Now you've given me another gift, Mr. Johnsonville. The Shield of Seasons." Palatus stepped toward Guster. He whipped a small tart from the folds of his robe and placed it in the snow, then stepped back.

Yummy leapt toward it and gobbled it up.

"No!" said Guster. But the warning was too late.

The monster bellowed, wobbled on its stout knees, and toppled over to the ground, face smashing into the ice.

"It's a simple recipe for such a powerful sedative," said Palatus. "You would do well to avoid it."

Palatus moved toward the shield. "I have suspected the Shield of Season's existence ever since our last encounter. I suspected that zere was so much more to the story. I watched the Mayor's guards sneak their way out into the world, leaving hints and tracks on the soft ground of the gourmet world; they weren't difficult to spot, clumsy as they were.

"And so I came here." Palatus sighed. "I've been here so long. Searching and tunneling, melting zee city from beneath, to find zis!"

"You set those fires!" said Guster.

"Of course I did. I was ready to tear zis city apart if I had to. So for zis, I thank you, Mr. Johnsonville. You've shown me exactly how to find what I was looking for."

"You can't have it," said Guster, defiant. He stepped in front of Palatus, blocking the shield with his body, spreading his arms.

"I think I can," said Palatus. He grabbed hold of Guster's jacket and, with surprising strength, threw Guster to the ground.

Guster picked himself up. He wasn't going to lose so easily. Luckily, the ice cream scoop was still under his belt. He drew it and swung it at Palatus like a club.

Palatus caught it easily. "My, my. Determined, aren't we?" Palatus laughed. "Where do you think zat scoop came from Guster?" He pushed Guster back again.

"It came from A.G.," said Guster. "It's how we escaped."

Palatus raised an eyebrow. "And who do you think baked that cake? The *Arch Gourmand* perhaps?"

Guster's blood boiled. Palatus helped them escape? "But why?" asked Guster.

"So I could follow you here, of course," said Palatus. "I've been hollowing out the mountain underneath the city for months. I don't know if I ever would have found this without you. You've proven useful before, and you have again."

He'd used Guster. And Guster had fallen for it. He lunged at Palatus.

The chef dodged left, sidestepping Guster easily. Guster landed face first in the snow. Palatus was so strong for such a skinny chef. But no matter what, Guster couldn't let him win.

Palatus retrieved a phone from his pocket and aimed its face at the shield. Then, with a few clicks, he took several pictures of the Shield of Seasons, and stowed the phone away.

Was that it? What had Guster expected? Palatus to carry off the half-ton rock himself?

And just like that, Palatus turned to go.

"I'll follow you to every corner of the Earth," said Guster.

"You won't find what's on that shield without me lurking in your shadow."

Palatus hesitated. "Perhaps," he said. "Or perhaps not. The Mayor is against you. He and his guard are assembled. You are the focus of their hate. I don't think they'll let you leave this city alive."

"You've poisoned them against me!" said Guster. It made sense now. Palatus had been whispering in Salero's ear all along.

Palatus chuckled. "It wasn't hard," he said. Then he walked out the narrow passageway toward the crevasse.

Guster scrambled to his feet and rushed to Yummy's side. The monster had slumped over onto his back. His eyes were closed and his mouth barely open. His chest was heaving up and down in slow, rhythmic breaths.

Guster pressed the palms of his hands into the creature's fur. "I'm sorry this happened to you," he said. It wasn't fair. He didn't deserve this.

Yummy moaned deep in his throat.

"I'll get help," said Guster, though he did not know how he could cross the crevasse alone.

He glanced back at the shield. It would have to wait.

Guster made his way out of the narrow passageway to the edge of the crevasse. It was as empty and wide as it had ever been. A single rope dangled far above him. It jerked in midair as it was pulled upward and out of sight.

Palatus must have rappelled down and then ascended that rope in order to descend into the crevasse. Now he had gotten away.

Guster kicked at a clump of ice. It skittered over the edge and into the darkness below. He should have been able to stop Palatus!

He felt the tips of his ears burn with anger and frustration. All this time, Palatus had been in the city! And Guster hadn't even guessed.

Now what was he going to do? With Yummy unconscious, there was no way to get across. He was stuck here.

The crevasse felt deeper and more deadly silent than ever before. He imagined that it might be bottomless, the way he never heard the clump of ice hit bottom.

He was absolutely alone.

Chapter 24 — The Battle of El Elado

Psst!" A voice hissed in the darkness from somewhere across the crevasse.

Guster nearly jumped, he was so startled by the sudden sound in the silence. He scanned the wall of ice, searching for the source of the voice.

"Up here," it said.

He glanced upward, searching in the darkness. Across the chasm, high up on the ledge, a tiny head with short, cropped black hair peered over the crevasse.

Mariah. Guster had never been so glad to see her.

"How did you get way down there?" she asked.

"Yummy," said Guster. "He's hurt. We found something, but we're trapped."

Mariah smiled. "Not if we can help it," she said.

"We?" asked Guster.

Mariah's face disappeared behind the ledge. "Step back!" she called. Her voice echoed between the walls of ice.

Guster hid himself in the passageway. There was a muffled bang, and something shot across the crevasse and slammed into the ice above where Guster had stood a moment before.

He peeked carefully out of the passageway. The Lieutenant was crouched next to where Mariah had been with some kind of grappling hook gun in both hands. A cord stretched across the chasm from the muzzle of the gun to a spike that had embedded itself into the ice near Guster.

"Hold tight. I'm coming down for you, sir," said the Lieutenant.

He clipped a harness onto the rope with a click and eased himself out over the precipice. He was much higher than Guster, and the rope went taught as he settled his weight on it and began to slide.

He crossed the chasm quickly, sailing over the dark void like a sparrow diving through the night.

To Guster, it seemed to take several frightening minutes, the cable creaking where it had pierced the ice the whole time. Finally, the Lieutenant glided feet-first onto the ledge where Guster was standing and nimbly skidded to a halt. He unclipped the harness.

"How did you get way down here?" he asked.

"Long story," said Guster. "I'll show you." He led the Lieutenant into the narrow passageway.

Yummy was still lying with his back on the ice, his eyes shut and his chest heaving. The Lieutenant took a step back. His hands went to the tranquilizer gun on his belt.

"It's okay," said Guster. "They won't hurt us. He's a friend."

The Lieutenant looked confused.

"Trust me," said Guster. It wouldn't be easy to explain. There was too much. "We need to take the shield back with us."

The Lieutenant walked slowly toward it, reaching out his gloved hand as if to touch it. He stopped "We're going to need reinforcements," he said, turning back to Guster.

He shook his head, as if waking from a dream. "But first we need to get you back to Ms. Casa. And your Mom and Dad. They're in trouble," said the Lieutenant.

Guster felt panic rise in his chest. "What's wrong?"

"The Mayor, sir. He's gone mad. He's on the verge of staging a takeover of the city and waging all-out war against the Princess and the Culinary. It won't be long before he finally plays his hand. After you showed up this morning, we barely escaped with our lives."

What did that mean for Mom and Dad and Henry Junior? They were probably caught in the middle of it.

Guster turned back toward the passage. He set one hand on Yummy. "We'll come back for you," he whispered. He meant it.

The Lieutenant removed a second harness from his backpack. He gave it to Guster to put on then clipped it to the cable that spanned the chasm. He took two ascenders and locked them around the rope, then clipped himself to Guster. Finally, he lodged what looked like interlocking gears into a crack in the rock and secured the cable to them. "Extra protection," he said, then, wrapping one arm around Guster, he stepped out over the bottomless crevasse.

Guster felt his stomach fall away beneath him. He tightened his grip fiercely around the Lieutenant's shoulders as the harness caught his weight and he dangled, helpless, from the cable. The Lieutenant slid the ascenders upward then let them catch on the cable, first one, then the other, inching his way upward at an angle. It was tedious work, and Guster's extra weight was certainly making it all the more difficult.

The cable wobbled and bounced as they moved, until finally, the Lieutenant hoisted first himself, and then Guster, over the edge of the cliff and set them on solid ground. Guster rested on his hands and knees, panting and trying to slow his racing heart down to a normal speed. The Lieutenant unclipped the harness.

Mariah crouched beside him. "Guster, we have to go," she said. "Things are bad."

"Why do you care? I thought you were on Salero's side," said Guster. He hadn't meant to be so angry. It was just that Mariah had been so . . . so sure of herself all the time. She'd sided with *them*.

The pain in Mariah's face told Guster he'd said the wrong thing. He was being unfair.

"I was. Until Salero told me he thinks the world is flat," she said. She shook her head. "What an idiot. He's really got his logic all twisted up in a knot, you know. I guess I just didn't want to be on the wrong side this time."

"Wrong side?" asked Guster.

"Look, after everything we went through last summer, people at school said things. They thought I made up those stories. I was sort of shunned. I was on my own a lot, so I learned you have to be careful when you pick your allies."

"So you chose the Baconists as friends?"

Mariah shook her head. "Okay. Yes. I did. Fine. Sorry. They just seemed so smart. But when I saw how eager they were for you to get eaten this morning, well, I knew just how far they would go. Sorry, Guster."

Guster nodded. There would be time for this later.

"Palatus is here," said Guster.

Mariah's eyes widened. "In the city? But I thought he was—"

Guster shook his head. "So did I, but I saw him. I know what's causing the tremors. It's not natural or magical or anything like that. He set the fires underneath the city. He's melting it from the inside out, block by block. The quakes and collapses are coming from him."

Mariah sat back on the ice. She looked shocked, like her whole mind was twisting about this new fact, trying to wrestle it into a place that made sense. "I . . ." she muttered, but never finished. "Stupid Baconists!" She put her head in her hands.

Guster let it go. "What about Mom? And Dad?" he asked.

The cave shook, shards of ice breaking off the walls and falling into the crevasse. After a moment, it stopped.

Mariah drew her lips tight. "We need to go," she said.

The Lieutenant had gathered up the gear behind them and stowed it into his pack. "Awaiting your orders, sir. But I do suggest we move on the double."

"Yes. Of course," said Guster. He still felt overwhelmed and unsure. He'd just seen Palatus. The Chef in Red was here, in the city. And now, even more overwhelming, there were quiet voices in his head, echoes of the pure flavors he'd tasted in those vanilla ice cream floes.

The Lieutenant and Mariah began to run, making their way past the slow, bubbling fountain and up a tunnel in the rock. Guster followed, uncertain where they were going. He could only see flashes of rock and ice cream as the beam from the Lieutenant's headlamp bounced through the translucent ice of the tunnels.

Something scratched and scuffed against the ice in the darkness. Yummy. His companions were still here, no doubt waiting in the shadows for their fallen comrade to return. A soft, deep rumble sounded in the darkness. They were just snarls and growls in his ears, but in his mind they took on *meaning*. *Our city, our city,* the voices echoed in Guster's head.

Again, he was shocked that he could understand. The reverberations from the pure floe of vanilla he'd tasted were echoing through his head. They had made some kind of connection, like he could taste their thoughts or, in the least, their intent. Like it *resonated* through him.

These animals were mourning for their city. They were crying for their home.

They ran, twisting and turning along the passage until a pale light glowed ahead. It was only a narrow, horizontal ribbon stretching across Guster's vision. As they ran, he saw it for what it was: the open air.

"Go!" said Mariah, sprinting as fast as she could toward the light.

The mountain shook again, the fury of the quake taking hold and wrenching the ground beneath their feet. Guster stumbled. Mariah pulled him up.

With an awful scraping sound, a huge slab of ice caved in right in front of them. The Lieutenant skidded to a stop then leapt the slab and kept running. Mariah and Guster scrambled after him, and they dove onto their bellies, scraping their way through the gap that led to the open air.

Part of the cave ceiling collapsed behind them, closing off half the entrance. Then the shuddering stopped.

Mariah slumped down onto the icy ground and sobbed. "We . . . we were almost crushed in there," she said, tears welling up around her eyes. She'd been so brave that Guster hadn't expected her to cry now. She'd been the one to pull him to his feet.

Yummy, thought Guster. He hoped they weren't trapped in there.

"The city!" said the Lieutenant, pointing down the mountain. Below them, at the base of the mountain, the City of El Elado was in ruin. Whole buildings had collapsed, sinking into enormous holes in the street that had swallowed them up. The main tower on Princess Sunday's castle had fallen over, like a tree felled in the forest. It had crushed the outer castle wall beneath it.

"This quake was bad. The worst yet," said Mariah, her voice quivering.

The damage had finally reached critical mass. The collapsing tunnels were setting off a chain reaction underground.

A sudden, horrific thought struck Guster. "Where's Zeke?"

Mariah looked at him, the panic streaking across her face. "I thought you knew," she said.

Guster shook his head. The last he'd seen Zeke was in

Yummy's lair.

"There's an even more pressing concern, sir," said the Lieutenant, peering through binoculars. "Look at your twelve o'clock. The Mayor's guards are setting up a perimeter. My tactical instincts tell me they're preparing for battle."

In the city square below, on the rise where Guster was to have been eaten alive, a mass of soldiers had gathered carrying red banners. There were hundreds of them, row after row, their rounded steel chest plates and spears glinting in the sun.

They were a pride of lions, all sharp points and ferocity, thirsting for blood. And they were marching toward Princess Sunday's Castle.

"Mom and Dad are down there," said Guster. He couldn't see them, but he knew there had been nowhere else for them to run.

Mariah nodded. She stood and craned her neck for a better look. "When you and Zeke ran off, everything fell apart. The city broke into chaos. There was nearly a riot. A lot of people really wanted to see you sacrificed, right then and there.

"The Mayor's guards pursued you, and Princess Sunday's Cherry Brigade took the chance to make their escape. Mom and Dad fled to back to the castle with Felicity. Mom would've come for you herself. She wanted to, but they got cut off. We got separated then found a way to came after you."

"They're no longer prisoners?" asked Guster.

"They never really were," she said. "The Princess would have let us go at any time. We chose to stay. We wanted to get you out. Now she's dropped the façade. Everything's changing."

So Princess Sunday was protecting them.

"Guster, the Mayor's rallied the people against Princess Sunday. There is a lot of support for his Guards. They're going to attack the castle, and the Culinary will be powerless to stand in their way."

Anger built inside Guster, like water welling up behind a dam. "We have to stop them," he said.

The Lieutenant shook his head. "I'm not taking you into that battle, sir. You're not a fighter, and it's my job to keep you safe. You have to stay here."

A steep, winding path led down the mountain from Guster's feet to the city square. The Lieutenant traced it with his eyes and then scanned the forces below. The steel line of Mayor's Extravío Vigilar encircled the castle wall. The noose was tightening.

"You know that we won't stay out of this, Lieutenant," said Guster. "Mom and Dad need us."

The Lieutenant's mouth went grim, but behind his aviator glasses, Guster wondered if his eyes were twinkling.

The Lieutenant could never back down from a battle. He was honor bound to fight for his friends when they needed him. Guster knew this because that's how he felt about Mom and Dad.

"Fine," he said. "But we're going to get you into the castle behind those thick stone walls." He unbuttoned his shirt pocket and pulled out a small metal key attached to a leather lanyard. "Princess Sunday gave me this. It's a key to a secret entrance into her castle. They built it to escape sieges. Now you're going to use it to sneak in." He handed the key to Guster. "No matter what happens I want you to get back into that castle."

Guster nodded. This was no time to argue. He took the key.

The Lieutenant took one last glance backward. "Stay close," he said.

He charged down the mountain path. Guster and Mariah raced after him, bouncing from stone to stone or sliding down the glacier on their backs when the ice was clear.

"Get down," the Lieutenant said when they reached a low chocolate wall that ringed the city. He peered around the corner.

Cannon fire exploded in their ears, shaking the wall so that

241

it crumbled and cracked beside their heads.

The Lieutenant ducked. "They've got the castle surrounded on the north and west sides," he said, drawing in the dirt with a stick. He didn't even seem to notice the blast. "If we make our way through the streets, we should be able to enter the castle from the south side. We'll have to make a wide berth and hope that the confusion in the streets will serve as a distraction." He drew a semicircle on the ground.

He slung his rifle from off his shoulder and stood up. "Stick close," he said. "And stay low."

The Lieutenant ran, half-crouching, from their cover behind the wall to the corner of a mint chocolate chip house across the street. There was rubble everywhere, chunks of strawberry strewn across the road.

Explosions rang out across the city. Villagers ran through the streets, most of them heading away from the castle. The crowd was a wide river of panic and fear tumbling through the streets. Guster, Mariah, and the Lieutenant charged upstream, Guster hiding his face as best he could so as not to attract attention.

Four of the Mayor's guard charged up the street through the crowd, spears in hand.

"In here," said the Lieutenant, pulling Guster and Mariah into a chocolate alleyway. The Lieutenant hoisted Mariah over a wall and then locked his fingers together, forming a step so Guster could climb over too. Guster slid on his belly over the top of the wall and into a yard with a chocolate pond behind a light-brown marble fudge house.

The Lieutenant jumped over the wall easily, landing in a crouch on the other side. He crossed the yard and peered out over the opposite wall.

Guster stood on his tiptoes so he could see.

"They've got the castle surrounded here. We're still not far enough south," the Lieutenant whispered.

Just a few yards in front of them five of the Mayor's guards were loading a cannonball into the back of an iron cannon on wooden-spoked wheels. The soldiers hadn't noticed them yet. Guster ducked down behind the wall.

The Lieutenant motioned with two fingers toward the back door of the house. Guster and Mariah crept toward it, crouching low. The Lieutenant followed them, and, heaving his shoulder quietly against the wooden door, forced his way inside.

It was dark in the house except for a few dim rays of sunlight filtering through the front windows. They found their way to the front door, winding past tables and overturned chairs.

Something whimpered in the corner. Guster turned to see a little boy cowering in his mother's arms in the shadows. His hair was messy and his face smudged with chocolate, his eyes wide with fear. He reminded Guster of Henry Junior. That's probably exactly how his little brother would look in a few years.

The Lieutenant paused with his hand on the front door.

"Shhh," said Guster to the boy. "We're not going to hurt you." He felt a sudden pain and emptiness, like chords were drawing him toward his baby brother somewhere up in the castle. He had to get back to his family. He had to make sure they were okay. "We're going to try to fix all this," he said. He didn't know if they really could.

"Best if they stay indoors and stay low," said the Lieutenant. He opened the front door a crack, peered out, then, after a moment, he motioned to them that it was all clear.

Guster nodded. They slipped out the front door quietly and back into the street.

They crossed the street, dodging in and out of alleyways. They took several more wrong turns and had to backtrack twice before they finally came to the marshmallow moat. On the other side of a pair of shops Guster could hear the Mayor's guards loading one of their cannons.

There was a crack, no wider than Guster's head, where the wall had been hit with a stray cannonball and had begun to cave inward. Enough rubble had fallen into the caramel moat that Guster was able to pick his way carefully across without getting his boots stuck in the gluey-sweet ooze. The Lieutenant and Mariah were right behind him.

Guster sucked in his chest as tight as he could and squeezed himself through the crack in the wall. Mariah slid through more easily. The Lieutenant paused and peered upward, looking for a place to climb over. He was much too broad to fit.

"Go on ahead," he whispered. He handed Guster the key. "I'll find another way through. The entrance is hidden between a pair of sugar cones in the side of the hill behind the castle."

Guster was afraid. He didn't want him and Mariah to be left alone. Having the Lieutenant there was like having a great big rock at their back. The Lieutenant provided protection. He knew how to keep them safe.

The Lieutenant must have seen Guster's worry. "Sir, go straight to your mother. She needs you," he said, his stare almost piercing behind the lenses of his aviator glasses.

Guster was about to argue when another cannonball exploded across the street, shooting icy chunks of shrapnel into the outer castle wall only inches from their heads.

The Lieutenant ducked, throwing up his arms to protect his face. "Go," he said.

Guster and Mariah ran. They raced around the circumference of the hill as fast as they could go, leaping over rubble and scrambling up broken walls as they went. Huge boulders of dark-red strawberry ice cream flew overhead, drawing wide arcs from the inner castle walls through the air until they dropped like meteors onto the street outside, shaking the ground.

The Princess's Cherry Brigade was fighting back. This was a real battle. It was hard for Guster to believe that this was really happening. In the middle of all the destruction, people were going to get hurt. Maybe even killed if they hadn't already. Mom. Dad. Henry Junior. The Yummy in the cave. And where was Zeke? El Elado was falling apart, and it was tearing people down with it. Guster doubled his pace.

A shot rang out, and a rock not two feet from Guster shattered. He pushed off his left foot, darting to the right and glanced back quickly over his shoulder, his heart racing.

Three of the Mayor's guards were charging up the hill behind them, their pointed steel helmets aimed right at Guster like gleaming talons. Two of them held their spears level, like knight's lances, ready to strike at his heart. The third was armed with a musket, still smoking from the bullet it had just fired at Guster. It was a very old musket, and it would take the soldier at least a minute to reload. Guster didn't want to be there when he did.

Guster grabbed Mariah's hand. He pumped his legs, pulling Mariah along behind him. Oh, how he wished Zeke were there. He veered a sharp left, following the curve of the hill and ducking behind a rocky outcropping of frozen blueberry ice cream.

"I don't know if I can outrun them," Mariah puffed, resting her hands on her knees. "We have to find the two cones."

Guster scanned the landscape. There was no time. The base of the hill above them sloped upward, then turned steep and jagged. They couldn't climb any higher without the Mayor's guards catching them right away. Their only option was to keep running. He took Mariah by the hand again and ran, doing his best to keep the rocky outcropping of blueberry between them and the Guards.

There was another explosion of cannon fire. The mountain shook, and the castle wall above them broke, a huge chunk bigger than a house breaking free. Like an iceberg splitting, it teetered and fell, hitting the ground with such an impact that the ground lurched as it struck. It slid downward, smashing to a halt at the bottom of the slope where two golden-brown sugar cones barely peeked out from the base of the hill.

Their one hope–their secret passage–had been cut off.

Chapter 25 — Yummy's Last Stand

"The sugar cones . . ." said Mariah. Panic and worry cracked her words as she spoke.

Guster dragged her down the hill and around the broken wall. At least it would provide some cover. It wouldn't be long before the guard reloaded. It would be sooner still before the other two caught up, spears in hand.

Guster ran, leading Mariah up the slope. The cones were crushed. They'd have to find another way in. Better to put the wreckage between him and the guards.

The castle wall had fallen over a lee at the very bottom of the slope, forming a small hollow just big enough to peer inside. Guster ducked his head into the hollow, hoping for some kind of hiding place.

Through the narrow opening he could make out the bottoms of the broken cones where the light filtered into the shadows under the wall. Between them was a small iron gate. They'd found it, just out of reach.

Guster clawed at the ice cream bricks. They were frozen solid. "It's too small to fit," he said. If only they could get through, there was space enough inside the hollow that they could probably crawl inside the gate once it was open.

"If the light is getting in, maybe we can too," said Mariah, peering into the hole. She glanced back over her shoulder. "We have to get to the top," she said.

"What?" said Guster. Mariah was out of her mind.

"Just trust me," she said. Without waiting for a response, she scrambled toward the far side of the wall. It was at least two dozen feet away.

When she reached the top, a shot rang out, shattering the frozen bricks just inches from Mariah's head. Guster jumped, fear and surprise jolting up his spine. Mariah ducked, disappearing for a moment behind the top edge of the thick wall.

Guster scrambled up the slope and found her, crouched and panting. From where they stood, they couldn't see the guards on the opposite side of the wall. But Guster knew they were coming.

"Ready? Let's go," she said, hoisting herself up onto the wall at its highest point. Then she dove headfirst, sliding down the broken wall on the frozen ice cream bricks.

There was a scuffing and scraping on the rocks below. Two of the guards came out from behind the wall at the bottom end. "There they are!" said one of the guards, pointing toward Guster.

What is she doing? Guster pulled himself onto the wall with both hands and dove after her, sliding downward, the bricks cold and slippery on his back

Mariah twisted onto her back and dropped through an open window frame still intact in the frozen wall. She disappeared, and then a moment later, her head popped out again, just like a gopher's.

"This way," she hissed.

Guster didn't need her to tell him. He was moving too fast to change direction.

Mariah ducked. He stuck out his heels, jamming them

against the rim of bricks right where her head had been, stopping his fall. Then he twisted without looking—there was no time—and tumbled down into the hole.

It was dark and cramped in the space where the lee of the hill and the broken wall formed a tiny pocket of air. The iron gate's bars crisscrossed in a loose grid, with a heavy chunk of metal in the center where a keyhole was set. It was just big enough to crawl inside, if they managed to get it open.

Guster took the metal key from his pocket and shoved it into the hole. He twisted it, and the key stuck for a moment, grinding past centuries of rust and grime in the lock. Then it gave, and the lock clicked. He tugged on the gate. It held fast.

"Hurry," said Mariah. Guster set both heels into the hill and yanked as hard as he could, throwing all his weight backward. The gate did not budge.

"Something's wrong with it! It think it's rusted shut," said Guster. Footsteps pounded across the fallen wall above them.

Mariah shook her head. "Try this," she said, brushing his arms off the gate and pushing it inward. It swung open easily.

Relief and embarrassment churned in Guster's chest. There was little time to feel stupid, though, as Mariah dove into the opening and the dark passageway behind it. Guster followed, kicking the gate closed and locking it again from the inside. He yanked the key free and scrambled across the rough frozen ground of the tunnel.

They had only crawled a few feet when the guards dropped through the window frame. Guster pushed Mariah up the tunnel from behind. She stopped, shoving herself against a low wooden door until it opened. Both she and Guster dove through just as the guards' spears thrust through the gate. The spears' metal points whiffed through the air in the space where Guster's neck had been only moments before.

"Up here," said Mariah, pointing to a narrow spiral staircase.

The guards shouted something Guster couldn't hear, their

metal armor clanging against the iron gate. Guster was not going to wait for them to aim their rifle through the bars.

"I do not want to do that again," said Guster. He dashed up the stairs behind Mariah, his lungs burning. They'd made it inside the castle, but the battle had raged far closer to Mom and Dad than he would have liked. They had to find them.

But once they did, Guster had no idea what to do next. "Now what?" he asked Mariah.

"What do you mean?" she said.

"We've snuck into the castle, nearly getting ourselves killed in the process, and now what? We can't really help Mom and Dad. We're in as much trouble as they are. This is bad."

Mariah shook her head. "I was kind of hoping they'd help *us*."

Guster pushed open another wooden door at the top of the stairs. They were in a room that looked much like the dungeon Mom, Dad, and Felicity had been locked in, but no one was there.

"This way," said Mariah. She pointed to another set of stone steps. "We are still in the hillside. We've got to find our way up to ground level where the main court is."

She and Guster wound their way up and out of the dungeon, through two more hallways—all deserted—and up another set of stairs, always picking the route that led up.

They pushed a door open and emerged into chaos, the deafening boom of cannon fire echoing off the walls. They stood in what was left of a half-broken hallway, its bricks shattered and scattered across the floor. A gaping hole had been blasted through it, giving Guster and Mariah a clear view of the courtyard below.

Princess Sunday's Castle was in near ruin. Its walls were shattered in several places by cannon balls.

In the middle of it all, the Cherry Brigade was making its last stand. Dad was winding a crank on a catapult, with the help of two of the Princess's guards, until the arm that held the giant ice cream boulder slanted backward, ready to fire.

And in the middle of the smoke and flames, Mom stood across the courtyard, tall and straight, like a general in the middle of the chaos. Henry Junior was strapped to her back, squealing in delight. Her baby-blue apron was tattered on one side, torn by some projectile's explosion. She was barking commands to the small platoon of soldiers that readied another catapult for launch.

A moment of relief washed over Guster. At least Mom and Dad were alive—for now. There was still a chance they could make it out of this.

But there was the advancing army. Princess Sunday was nowhere to be found.

Save the Delicious City, said the voice inside Guster's head. It was the same whispered voice he'd heard inside the cold mountain. The Yummies were in his mind. Tasting the ice cream at the source had connected them to Guster.

And this voice was more than a plea. It was a command.

Guster shook his head. How? What could just he do to save an entire city? He was only twelve years old.

Save the City, said the voice again. Guster felt it in his bones. This time the voice was mourning. There was sadness in it, each word laden with weight and sorrow.

Guster took one step into the courtyard.

"Guster Stephen Johnsonville!" shouted Mom. She spotted him from two catapults away. Her hands went straight to her hips. Her eyes glistened with tears. "Get yourself and your sister underground and out of this battle right this instant, or so help me! You know the rule about standing in the line of cannon fire!"

It all felt like a dream.

"You heard your mother!" shouted Dad. A cannonball exploded behind him, smashing the castle wall and leaving a crater in the hard frozen brick. He ducked and then gave the crank one last turn. "Get down below. Take your little brother with you!"

Dad stomped down on a wooden catch, releasing the catapult's arm. It swung upward, snapping forward with all the incredible force pent up inside its coiled chords. A huge strawberry ice cream boulder flew into the air, up and over the castle wall toward the Mayor's army on the other side.

"That goes for you too, Mariah!" said Dad.

Guster's first instinct was to listen, to run down into the safety of the dungeons where he would at least be out of the line of fire. He didn't want to face Mom's wrath.

"But . . ." he stammered. He wanted to help. He didn't know what he would do, and there was such danger. Maybe it was better to go down below.

The pure ice cream surged through him now. It was warm inside his veins. The feeling came again to him, the taste forming itself into words and meaning.

Our city is crumbling, said the voice.

But what could *he* do?

A dainty hand rested lightly on Guster's shoulder. It came from below, reaching upward to touch him feebly. Guster turned.

It was Princess Sunday. "Guster, I think you truly are the Exquisite Morsel," she whispered. She was cradled in the arms of one of her guards. He held her, curled up like a little girl in her daddy's arms. Her hair was disheveled, tangled, and matted like it had been blown backward by an explosion. Her face was caked with dirt and blood, and her cherry crown had fallen from her head.

A second guard stood nearby, impatient, his eyes darting back and forth helplessly, his spear discarded at his feet. He held the crown in both hands and looked like he wanted to reach out and place it back on her head, like he desperately needed to because, if he did, that would somehow make things all right.

"The Mayor has always thought I was the Exquisite Morsel," said Guster.

"I don't think that it means what the Mayor wanted it to mean," she said, breathing in short gasps. "I think that Yummy didn't go to the far reaches of the earth to find you for nothing."

"Princess, you're hurt," he said. His heart ached for her. He wanted to help her. She needed a hospital. Did they even have doctors in El Elado? "Marshmallow Cheer," he said, desperately reaching for hope. "That will cure you."

Princess Sunday shook her head. "It's not the answer to everything," she said sadly. "Though I wish it were.

"Guster, you brave boy from far away, Yummy brought you here for a reason," she whispered, her voice growing faint.

Guster knew that now. Yummy had wanted to bring him here to find the Shield of Seasons. It all seemed so inevitable now, like no matter what, any road he'd taken would have brought him right back here to El Elado.

"There's something Yummy wanted me to find. It's buried deep in the mountain near the source," he said.

Princess Sunday's face brightened with curiosity. Then she coughed weakly and it faded away. "That is a story I think you should save for another time," she said. "There is something here and now far more pressing and immediate. The City of El Elado needs you, Guster."

"Needs me?" he asked.

What did that mean? He had already found the Shield of Seasons. That's what Yummy had wanted him to do. And maybe Archedentus too, in some roundabout way. But what could he do for El Elado? They were looking to him again to do something grand.

"What, then, should I do?" asked Guster.

Princess Sunday buried her face into the guard's chest. "I do not know. Perhaps Yummy knows. Perhaps they are waiting for someone who finally understands them. Who can lead them."

Guster lowered his eyes. Eating the ice cream at the source sealed the connection between them. Yummy was in his head. But what now?

Save us, said the voice.

He needed help. *It is your city*, he said in his mind. He didn't know if they could hear him. Maybe the connection only worked one way.

What can we do? said the voice. *We are wild. We are pure instinct.*

Guster took a deep breath. The words in his head were so hard to define, like trying to form a picture in the mud—it was a line at first, then a shape. He had to mold it into something real.

"Guster!" said Mom. She was stalking toward him. "You get down those stairs right now, or there will be no breakfast or television or even breathing privileges for the rest of the month!"

There was no time. Guster leapt onto the stairway that lead up the castle wall, and with one last glance at Mom—just at her feet, he couldn't meet her eyes—he dashed *up* the stone steps.

"Guster!" she shouted, panic and anger in her voice. There was no time to reason with her. No time to explain. Guster hardly knew himself what he was doing—only that it was what he *must* do.

He stopped at the rampart three flights up. The Mayor's guards ringed the castle below, their gleaming spear points and chest plates charging forward. They were at the Castle Gates now. The last of the Princess's Cherry Brigade had fallen. The Guard swarmed like angry bulls toward the closed drawbridge, where they'd smashed a hole through the peanut brittle. There was an explosion in the courtyard below, bits of stone shrapnel flying everywhere. In moments, the castle would fall; Princess

Sunday, Mom, and Dad would fall with it.

Guster stood, stretching himself tall on the ramparts. He did not care what danger he exposed himself to. *Rise up, Yummy*, he said in his mind, throwing his thoughts outward toward the mountain. He did not know if they could hear him. *Defend our city. We are not your enemy. They surround us. Do not let them break our city. You are our army. Rise up. Come to me.*

There was only silence.

Then Guster felt a song flowering inside him, up from his gut and out through his lips, a taste in harmony. He hummed it—three notes, simple and long. He recognized them, as they settled into the air and turned to vapor. They were the notes Gaucho had sung so many days ago when they'd first escaped from Yummy on the bus.

They were a call. They were Yummy's song.

Then Guster was silent. He felt a hand on his back.

"Guster, what . . .?" whispered Mariah. She was breathing heavy. She had just run up the flights of steps behind him.

The front lines of the Mayor's guard charged through the outer gates, crying victory, their spears pointed forward. In a moment they would be inside the Castle courtyard.

Then the ground shook ever so slightly, and out of the corner of his eye, Guster saw a flash of white fur break from the hill, like something hatching from an egg. Two thick, furry arms clawed out of the hole, then a blunt, broad head. Another flash of fur broke the ground outside the castle wall. Then another two in the center of the battlefield.

Several more cracks popped, a mass of white fur emerging from each. Like a pack of wolves, they gathered, appearing from all corners of the castle and city. Flowing into one massive column—a sea of white fur, curved claws, and glinting fangs—they charged toward the enemy guards at the castle gates.

The Yummies were a wave of fury and raw strength, their power no longer shrouded in mystery or hidden in the shadows of glaciers as they charged.

There were a dozen of them, all finally seen by the light of day. And in one's enormous mouth, riding with his arm extended outward like a Calvary captain's sword, was a sixteen-year-old boy.

"Zeke!" cried Mariah, pointing to the Yummy. They could see Zeke's bright white teeth, set in a smile as wide as a pickup truck's grill.

"He must have been with Yummy this whole time," said Guster. A small weight of worry fell from his shoulders. At least Zeke was safe. That was one less small burden to carry.

The first Yummies reached the Mayor's guard and broke on them like a wave.

A dozen monsters shattered the soldiers' ranks, wedges of white fury splintering the columns of advancing silver armor and red banners. Yummy swatted the Guards aside, batting them like pillows out of the way and across the battlefield, the men tumbling and their spears shattering to pieces. Some of them tried to fight back, but they were no match for the ferocity of the Himalayan monster. In minutes the Mayor's guards were scattered, broken, and running for their lives in full retreat.

Their army was no more.

Mariah put her hand on Guster's arm. He hadn't realized how tightly he was gripping the frozen brick on the edge of the ramparts. He relaxed at her touch.

"I think we've won," she said. Her voice was uncertain, like she was afraid to believe what she'd said.

The monsters gathered at the foot of the drawbridge inside the courtyard, their arms limp at their sides. They breathed heavily, panting after their burst of exertion. The one with Zeke in its mouth knelt down and opened his jaws wide. Zeke crawled out onto the frozen ground. He did not seem to care that he was covered in spit; instead he stood up tall, like he'd just defeated the Mayor's guard all on his own.

The pack of Yummies lifted their stout heads and stared up at Guster as if they were all wondering the same thing. *Finished?* the voice said in Guster's head.

"Finished," said Guster. "You truly are the protectors of El Elado."

A large one with white mottled fur stood in the front and sniffed and purred contentedly. He closed his eyes. *We go now*, he said.

Guster descended the steps and ran to them. He extended his hand, palm sideways to the nearest beast. The creature breathed warm, moist breath onto his skin. Guster had only glimpsed him before in passing, but that did not matter. They were all as one. "Thank you," said Guster. After all his running, from the farmhouse to New York City to the Himalayas, it was over.

From the very beginning, they had been like two streams flowing into the same river. Felicity's Taste Resonance Theory was true. Now the chase was over. Yummy had let himself be tamed.

Guster lowered his hand, and Yummy backed away slowly, then turned his stumpy head. He leapt over a break in the castle wall and ran toward the mountain. The others followed in a stream, a white, furry flock returning to their home.

Suddenly, the courtyard felt lonely, like an empty home after friends have said their last goodbyes.

Guster turned to Mom. "Guster, I'm so—"

She didn't finish her sentence. An arm whipped around her throat, locking her neck in the crook of its elbow. A short, stubby man with the squashed up face of a pug dog stood behind Mom, a flintlock pistol in his hand. The barrel was pointed at Guster.

The Mayor.

"This city is mine," he said. The top half of his top hat had had been blown away, leaving charred and smudged edges where the polish had been so that it looked like the smoking barrel of a cannon. His blue mayor's badge was dangling from his breast pocket by a thread.

Henry Junior screamed.

Guster tensed. But for some reason, this time he wasn't afraid.

He drew himself up tall. He had tamed Yummy. "Your army is scattered. You've lost," said Guster.

The Mayor's eyes grew wide. His nostrils flared as desperation spread across his face. "No. I'm the Mayor Bollito, Ruler of the Delicious City of El Elado. With power invested in me by the right of . . ." he said, spittle spraying out of his mouth. He turned the gun toward Mom.

"I am—" he said, but before he could finish his sentence, Dad leapt from a broken stone, his fist extended, the bow of his battleship nose thrust forward like an iron wedge. His body hung in the air for just a split second, like a basketball player before a slam dunk, and then his knuckles surged forward, smashing into the Mayor's jaw.

The Mayor's face crumpled, his head flying backward as he fell to the frozen strawberry pink cobblestones. He groaned, then rolled over and did not stir.

Dad landed with both feet set wide on either side of the Mayor's limp form. "*That* is the mother of my children," Dad said, glowering down at the Mayor.

Dad was glowing like a winged, bronze statue mounted on the steps of a state capitol building. He took Mom in one arm. "Mabel," he said. "Are you alright?"

Mom nodded. She nuzzled her head under his chin.

Guster had never seen Dad do anything like that before. Had Dad been a commando or a samurai before Guster was born? There was nothing so incredible as Dad in this moment, and Guster promised himself that he would obey whatever Dad said right away for the rest of his life.

"Woah," said Zeke, his jaw dropped to his chest.

Dad kicked the pistol, sending it skittering across the cobblestones far away from the Mayor's grasp.

Guster turned his head, taking in everything around him—the ruined stone, the broken spear points jutting out of the ground like nails, the guards limping and dragging their friends into what was left of the castle. The remaining Mayor's guard were all in chains, having been rounded up by the remnants of the Cherry Brigade.

They had won. They had beaten back the Mayor's all-out assault on the Castle. It all seemed so surreal now that it was over. Guster had never seen such wide-scale destruction up close. He'd expected that he'd be more nervous, but in the middle of the moment, it all seemed surprisingly normal. Maybe he was getting used to this sort of thing.

"The Princess!" said one of her guards. "She . . ." He hung his head. "Hurry."

Chapter 26 — Heir to the Throne

The Johnsonvilles climbed the steps into the tower on the heels of the guards of the Cherry Brigade as quickly as they could. The guards pushed through the half-open wooden door. Beyond was a strawberry room studded with purple gumdrops and an enormous, lavish bed draped in curtains in the center.

Mom and Dad pushed their way inside. Guster paused at the threshold. He didn't want to go in, not after the guard had explained how badly Princess Sunday was wounded in the battle.

Princess Sunday was royalty. She was splendid and marvelous in everything she did. She was permanent. She was forever. Nothing could happen to her. It just couldn't.

Mariah nudged Guster from behind. He crossed through the door frame, his feet heavy as he took his side by Mom and Dad at her bed.

Princess Sunday was propped up on a set of marshmallow pillows, her golden hair spread out like a waterfall.

She looked so peaceful, like she was sleeping. Her face had been cleaned. Her eyes were closed, and she looked so peaceful, like she'd been lying there for years.

"Princess," Guster whispered, "the city is safe now. The

man who was causing the quakes is gone." She wouldn't know who Palatus was. But he had to tell her the city was no longer in danger.

Her eyes fluttered open. Then she closed them again. "Thank you Guster," she whispered.

Her mouth curved up at the edges in a weak smile, like she was keeping a secret from them.

She did not open her eyes again.

Guster squeezed his eyes shut hard, but that didn't stop the tears from coming.

***

The entire city joined the procession that marched slowly through the butterscotch streets behind the coach that carried Princess Sunday to her final resting place.

There were thousands of men, women, and children from both the Chocolate Crescent and the Fruitful Streets, all shoulder to shoulder as one.

The coach entered the castle, where the guards drew up the bridge and left the people outside to mourn. Then, in secret, Guster led them up the winding path toward the hidden cave from which the source of El Elado's pure ice cream flowed.

Outside of its entrance, on a small cliff overlooking the city made of opaque white ice, they laid Princesa Elenora Domingo of the City of El Elado to rest, forever frozen above the precious city that she had ruled with wisdom.

Guster peered down at the crowds outside the castle gates. "They loved her. Even the ones from the Chocolate Crescent," he said to Mom.

"There is a new feeling in this city," she said, huddling into her baby-blue parka. "I think you are a part of that, Guster."

Dad hitched up his pants around his belly button. "Guster,

I'm glad you did what you did back there on the castle walls," he said. "Your mom and I talked about it. You knew something that we didn't. We think you made the right choice."

He'd run away from home; he'd broken so many rules. "Does that mean I can go to camp when we get back?" he asked.

Mom's bun bobbed as she shook her head. "Oh, no. That's going to have to wait until next year. You're still grounded until then." He could tell she meant business, but she still hugged him.

***

In the late afternoon Guster stood atop a broken section of the castle wall. Zeke and Mariah were with him. Two out of three Casa Industries helicopters were parked outside the drawbridge, but the third was gone. Felicity Casa and her mercenaries were nowhere to be found.

Guster needed time to think. There was so much to absorb after everything that happened there.

The haze and smoke from the battle still lingered in the thin mountain air. Through it, Guster could make out a place where the aqueduct had broken, its ice cream masonry shattered by cannon fire and blown outward like a broken artery.

Glistening red strawberry sauce pumped out the side, flowing in spurts, tumbling down in a strawberry waterfall and splashing onto the butterscotch streets. It pooled there and then gurgled its way down the sloped street, branching into crimson, shining fingers that flowed across the hard candy cobblestone and over the bank into the Chocolate River.

Guster was drawn to the river. He peered out of over the castle ramparts. It was such an accidental combination. What if the flavors blended wrong? What if the ratios were off? It was a disaster waiting to happen.

But the strawberry didn't disappear like he thought it would. Instead, it swirled and wound, spiraling into little whirlpools that danced downstream in the chocolate. They formed a perfect tapestry of red and brown.

A little girl, no more than five years old, saw what had happened and turned toward the bank. She bent on one knee, then pulled a tiny ladle from her pocket and dipped it into the river.

People stopped to stare. Shocked at first, then curious, they stopped to watch.

She brought the ladle to her lips and sipped.

The crowd on the river banks grew, staring and whispering to one another as if unsure of what they'd seen.

Then the little girl turned, her face beaming like a tiny sun. "Delicious!" she said in a voice so clear Guster could hear it way up on the castle ramparts. "It's so delicious!"

There was a murmur of excitement. Two more children dipped their spoons into the new river and tasted its chocolate-strawberry swirls. Then the grownups followed, until the entire riverbank on both sides was lined with the men, women and children of El Elado dipping their spoons—once each—into the flow to taste a flavor they had never known.

At last. Strawberry and chocolate together. It was complete. El Elado could hardly be the same.

Zeke and Mariah climbed to the ramparts and stood by Guster.

"Woah," said Zeke, staring over Guster's shoulder at the strawberry-chocolate confluence below. "Just think, now they can have strawberry with chocolate chunks, and fudge blueberry, and cherry chocolate cheesecake. And peanut butter and chocolate!" He put one arm around each of Guster and Mariah's shoulders, and sighed. "Peanut-peach-chocolate-apple-caramel-butterscotch cookie crumble berry. I've got so many plans for this town."

Mariah looked crossways at him. "I'm pretty sure you just made that up, Zeke," she said. She was smirking just a little, and Guster was almost certain she was trying not to show how amused she really was.

But Zeke was right about one thing: El Elado was free now. It had been held back for too long by its barriers. Now those were gone.

Guster could only imagine what new, groundbreaking desserts might come out of the city in the years to come. It was a new day for the Delicious City. A renaissance of taste.

The Chancellor mounted the rampart behind them, his green and yellow robes flowing in the breeze. Gaucho and two of Princess Sunday's guards were with him. The Chancellor held Princess Sunday's scepter in both hands.

"Guster Johnsonville," said the Chancellor, clearing his throat and standing beside Guster. The guards snapped to attention. "As you know, we don't put much stock in sons and daughters here in El Elado. Perhaps that will change soon. But that means we don't have royal bloodlines either. Our royalty is appointed here according to a chain of promotion within the ranks."

The Chancellor straightened his robes. "The Culinary has debated long about this and has come to the conclusion that, seeing as all those whose positions were next in line for the throne have either been imprisoned for crimes against the City or fled, it seems only appropriate in this circumstance to offer you, by the authority invested in us, to be crowned Prince Guster Johnsonville of El Elado, and ruler of the Delicious City." He offered the scepter to Guster with both hands.

Guster could not believe his ears. He turned to look into the Chancellor's eyes. They were sincere.

"Me? The Prince of El Elado?" asked Guster.

"Yes," said the Chancellor. "We need a ruler now. You're new here, but after everything you've done, I can't think of anyone more qualified for the job."

Guster looked over the grand, majestic city. It was the city of his dreams. He could do so much. He could help them rebuild.

Mom and Dad were loading their things into one of the choppers. Henry Junior was back at home with Braxton. Mariah and Zeke couldn't stay here forever.

"This could all be yours," said the Chancellor, sweeping his hand over the city with its ice cream shining golden in the sun.

Ruling El Elado sounded nice. It really did. But Guster had other places to go. There were things to do. "It's an honor sir," he said. "But I'm needed at home."

The Chancellor bowed to Guster. "Very good sir. I won't say that I'm not disappointed for us, but I will say that I understand. It's been an honor to have you in our ranks."

Guster returned the bow.

"You know what that means then, Gaucho del Pantaloon," said the Chancellor.

Gaucho's eyes grew wide with amazement. He pressed his knuckles to his mouth. "Did I ever mention to you that I am the Protector of the Yummies, Guster Johnsonville? Yesterday, I was sixteenth in line for the throne. But as of this minute, I am number one!"

He let out a high-pitched, quiet scream of joy. "Tomorrow, I will be crowned prince of El Elado."

The Chancellor handed the scepter to Gaucho. Gaucho took it.

Suddenly, the little conquistador stood taller, his arms straight at his sides, his mouth drawn into a determined line, Princess Sunday's scepter in his right hand.

The two guards kneeled. "Your Majesty," they said.

. The Culinary had arrested the Mayor. He was in jail. The Baconists had fled the city. Now it was Gaucho del Pantaloon's chance to set things right.

Gaucho had a good heart, and he cared for El Elado with such a deep devotion. With the right friends to help him, he could lead El Elado to a bright and delicious future.

"Then the Delicious City is in good hands," said Guster. He bowed, dipping his head low to Prince Gaucho del Pantaloon. "I wish you well. May wonderful tastes always find you."

"And you, Guster Johnsonville," said Gaucho, bowing back.

The deep thumping of the third helicopter's blades beat the air outside the castle walls. The time had come. Guster, Mariah, and Zeke descended the steps and crossed the drawbridge. Mom and Dad were waiting there for Felicity's helicopter to touch down.

The blades twisted slowly to a stop, and the whirlwind subsided until they could hear each other speak again.

"You went ahead and did it, didn't you?" asked Guster as the side door of the chopper slid open and Felicity stepped out.

"We can't leave an artifact of such culinary significance up here to rot in these mountains," she said. The enormous Shield of Seasons lay on the floor of the chopper, wrapped with thick padding and secured with wide, yellow ratchet straps.

Felicity and her mercenaries had the manpower and the will to move it. They weren't asking for Guster's approval. Even if he'd wanted to, he couldn't have stopped them.

He lifted the padded cover. The shield had softened slightly next to the heat of the choppers engines. It was soft to his touch. "The cold cave kept it frozen," said Guster.

Felicity smiled. "That's right. It's not made of stone at all," she said.

Guster sniffed it. Cookie dough. It was a giant sugar cookie, all rolled out and stamped with inscriptions, then frozen to keep it preserved.

"It's never been baked," said Felicity. She caressed it with one finger. "Leaves me to wonder." She looked at Guster. "You do realize this is just the first clue in a mystery of much larger significance?"

Guster opened his mouth to reply, but no words came. He did not know what the Shield of Seasons was meant for. Only that it was likely something Archedentus wanted him to find, and that the symbols carved there had to have some kind of significance. Beyond that, he realized, he was woefully ignorant. It might as well have been a slab of Egyptian Hieroglyphs.

"Guster, this shield fits into a picture larger than any of us had realized or even suspected. The Gastronomy of Peace was just the catalyst to open up this world. It's what brought you here after all." Felicity said. "What else remains to be found? Can't you see it? There's more for us to do. We need you." Her perfectly mascaraed eyes were intense but pleading.

Guster considered this. "Then the shield stays with us," he said. "I want it in our barn, where Mariah, Mom, and I can decipher it." He was sure about this much: he couldn't let it out of his sight.

Felicity's face turned calm and cool. "Very well," she said. "So it will be."

She turned to the waiting chopper and twirled one finger in the air. "Rev 'em up boys!" she shouted. "Let's get this payload back to Home Sweet Home."

The pilots started the engines, and the rotors churned slowly until they picked up speed. The Lieutenant helped Mom, Dad, Guster, Mariah, and Zeke aboard. Guster gripped the metal handholds on the chopper wall tightly and looked out over the Delicious City as they lifted off the ground and rose into the air.

It was a good place, El Elado. As the chopper flew away, Guster could see the walls, the strawberry fields, and the butterscotch streets shining and glistening like gold in the sun. The City of Gold. The City of Taste. A place where legends were true.

Guster settled back into his seat with Mom on one side and

Dad on the other. Mariah and Zeke sat across from him. There was another place that he longed for now, and it wouldn't be long until they got there—home, with the familiar smells of fields and woods and Mom's kitchen, all just waiting for him to return.

He could almost taste it.

Look for more exciting books from Future House Publishing!

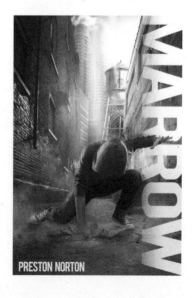

Never miss a Future House release!

Sign up for the Future House Publishing email list:
www.futurehousepublishing.com/beta-readers-club

Connect with Future House Publishing

www.facebook.com/FutureHousePublishing

twitter.com/FutureHousePub

www.youtube.com/FutureHousePublishing

www.instagram.com/FutureHousePublishing

Connect with Adam

Never miss a book release. Sign up for the Adam's email list:
www.evertaster.com

www.facebook.com/AdamGlendonSidwell

twitter.com/Evertaster

Instagram: @adamglendonsidwell

ABOUT THE AUTHOR

In between books, Adam Glendon Sidwell uses the power of computers to make monsters, robots and zombies come to life for blockbuster movies such as *Pirates of the Caribbean, King Kong, Pacific Rim, Transformers* and *Tron*. After spending countless hours in front of a keyboard meticulously adjusting tentacles, calibrating hydraulics, and brushing monkey fur, he is delighted at the prospect of modifying his creations with the flick of a few deftly placed adjectives.

If you liked his book, he'd love to hear about it.
Reviews keep him writing.
Find *Evertaster: The Delicious City* online and
leave him a review.

Want Adam to come to your school?

Adam Glendon Sidwell has visited hundreds of schools across the country sharing his interactive assemblies and encouraging students to read and write. Adam uses visuals from his career as an animator for blockbuster Hollywood films such as *Tron*, *Pirates of the Caribbean*, and *Thor* to teach kids about writing structure, narrative, and theme. Adam's assembly is the perfect educational experience for your school. For more information visit:

www.futurehousepublishing.com/authors/adamglendonsidwell

Contact schools@futurehousepublishing.com to book Adam at your school.